WHO SHE WAS

STORMY SMITH

Cover design by Toni Sarcone of Sarcone Design.
Editing by Monica Black of Word Nerd Editing.
Interior design by Cover Me Darling
Paperback formatting by Athena Interior Book Design

For more information about this book and the author, visit
http://www.stormysmith.com

To every lost soul:
Every day your presence impacts someone's life.
You may never know the extent, but the universe put you
here for a reason and we need you.

PART ONE

CHAPTER
one

Charlie

August

"Are you guys ready for this?"

The overly-excited frat boy in charge yelled into the microphone and the backyard of the Sigma Alpha house hit deafening levels. Inside their dingy kitchen, I shared a wary look with a few of the Kappa pledges.

"As much fun as we're already having tonight, it's about to get real! The fifth annual dating auction is about to start. That means the only thing standing between you and a hot little sorority pledge is your parents' money!"

A petite redhead who barely looked fifteen, let alone eighteen, drew back the curtain of the kitchen window to peek out as he continued and then giggled.

"I can't believe rush week is finally here and tonight is the auction!" She actually clapped her hands together and I forced my eyes not to disappear into the back of my head. "I hope Austin bids on me," she gushed. "He's so hot."

"And you will be yet another notch on his freshman bedpost," I muttered before I could stop myself. The girl behind me in line stifled a chuckle, and I smiled knowing there was someone else who understood how absurd this was.

"Your mom was a Kappa, too?" She asked.

I nodded. The line of sorority pledges filed forward through the kitchen to the back door as the emcee announced the next piece of meat up for bid. I kept my eyes forward and not on the half-filled keg cups and ripped open chip bags.

"Can you believe we have to go through with this just to pledge?" The girl twisted a piece of her hair and I didn't miss the fear that flashed in her eyes. "The worst part was when I told my mom, she was actually excited."

We took another step forward as I shook my head in disbelief. I hadn't bothered to even tell my mother since it wouldn't have mattered. Getting in was all she was worried about and Katie was the only one who ever mattered to her.

Then, I was next. I swallowed down my own anxiety and pressed my sweating palms down my skirt. It was tight and high-waisted, and my heels were higher than I was comfortable with.

Katie would have loved me in it.

I missed my Chucks.

My name came over the crackling sound system and I felt warm fingers encircle my own.

"You'll do great, Charlotte," she encouraged. I hadn't even bothered to ask her name and she'd been astute enough to pluck mine from the bio being read to the crowd. I gave her a tight-lipped smile and returned the gesture even though I wanted to yank my hand from hers and wipe it off again.

I pushed through the torn screen door and pulled the humid August air into my lungs as I straightened my posture and put one foot in front of the other. My smile was so automatic it didn't matter that I didn't feel it anywhere but the shift in my cheeks—not too much teeth to seem fake, just enough for no one to ever think anything was wrong.

The emcee's voice was lost in the cat calls. I heard bids of anywhere from five dollars to twenty as they commented on my rack or how my long hair would come in handy. My fingers tapped out a familiar rhythm onto my hip, one that I refused to acknowledge, but it was the only way I could keep circling the rickety stage.

I had to get into this sorority. It was what she wanted. It wasn't optional.

"Two hundred and fifty dollars." His voice silenced the crowd.

My smile didn't waver as I let out a longer exhale and thanked whoever he was while also praying he wasn't a psycho.

A sweaty, drunk guy helped me off the stage, and I was thankful when my heels sunk slightly into the ground because it was over and all the attention shifted to the next piece of cattle. I followed the turning heads in the direction of my bidder, who was still lost in the crowd.

The crowd shifted as their attention focused back on the next pledge up for bid. The light from the porch found him and he stood facing me, clearly waiting. For a split second, time stopped.

He smirked, catching my pause. The baby-face Trevor had the last time I saw him was gone. Instead, angular features and questioning eyes stared back at me.

I wanted to spin on my heel and run the other direction. Trevor was the slip knot of my life. The carefully intertwined ropes I'd wrapped around the person I used to be—the one he alone had understood and yet still abandoned—could be unraveled with one tug. He could destroy me and everything I'd done to atone for my mistake.

No one knew what I'd done. How it was all my fault. I'd never told anyone so he couldn't know. It was a secret I desperately wanted to share so I no longer had to bear it alone, but knew I couldn't.

"Fancy meeting you here, Charlie," Trevor said as he pushed his thick-rimmed glass up his nose, failing to convince me he was any more comfortable with our impromptu reunion than I was.

I didn't need him anymore. He was the who'd disappeared and left me all alone. It didn't matter that he was the one who knew the rhythm I tapped out to get through the worst of times. Or that in an instant I remembered what real laughter felt like and the feel of ivory under my fingertips. It couldn't matter. Not anymore.

I charged forward, auto-smiled and played the part I'd cast for myself.

"Charlotte," I stated. "My name is Charlotte."

CHAPTER
two

Trevor

30 minutes earlier

"Chug, chug, chug!"

A group of guys surrounded the keg. Two of them held the third upside down as he gripped the shiny silver handle with one hand and held the tapper line with the other.

Sam stared, his head tilting further and further as he watched the guy gulp down beer after beer as his friends cheered him on. I saw a flash of blonde and yanked Sam back toward me, stepping to the side just in time to miss a stumbling girl aiming what was left of her dinner at the shrubbery.

Sam whipped away from the sound of her gagging, pursing his lips. "It's only nine o'clock! Is someone going to help her?"

I nodded and tipped my head in the direction of the three girls rushing toward her, squeals of concern getting to us before they did. Their tight dresses and heavy makeup looked more fit for a club than a backyard kegger, and their heels sank in the grass so they popped up and down, reminding me of the old arcade game Whack-a-Mole. As they passed, I held out the water bottle I'd put in my cargo shorts pocket. A brunette gave me a grateful, unfocused smile as she took it and hurried to hold her friend's hair, instantly telling her no one was watching. In reality, our whole corner of the yard was watching and I even heard a few over/under bets on how long before she'd be passed out.

"You really need to relax, dude. It's just a party." I took a drink of the crappy keg beer they handed me when we entered the backyard. I didn't know which frat house we'd stumbled into, but Greek Street was where the parties were and earlier today my new roommate told me he wanted to check out a college party.

Sam shoved his red hair out of his face and looked around us, skeptical.

"Just a party?" His disbelief and discomfort was evident in his crossed arms and hunched shoulders. On a picnic table nearby, a lanky brunette stretched out with her arms above her head and her tank top bunched around her boobs. She let a guy pour tequila on her stomach, which he proceeded to suck off, capping the experience by kissing her to get to the lime.

"Par-tay," I said, enunciating dramatically. "It's a noun. When used in the context of college students, it typically entails mass quantities of booze—no matter the variety, though watch out for the flammable stuff—loud music, equal parts vomiting and hooking up, and the occasional demeaning act caught by an iPhone."

"I've been to parties," he said with a huff, "but this is a little much." He held his beer like it might have poison in it and I laughed. "You may as well have worn a neon sign flashing 'Freshman'. You've got to chill."

Between the light blue polo his mom probably bought him for Easter, shorts that looked like they had creases ironed into them, and his attempt at long hair, he looked like Samwise Gamgees. A hobbit repping Gap — that's what Sam looked like.

Red crept up his neck and he muttered into his cup, "How do you know so much about college parties anyway?"

"I moved around a lot," I said with a shrug. "I spent a year in Iowa City, which is where one of the country's biggest party schools is." I gave him a wink as I brought the red signature cup to my lips and tried to suppress memories of the talks my dad would give me before he sent me into the fray of drunk Iowa Hawkeye fans. No matter what he said, we both knew I was there to swindle guys into paying me to play songs for their girlfriends. Me, my guitar, and the hope of making enough to stave off the next envelope marked "Final Notice"—every sixteen-year-old's dream.

Not far from us was an intense game of flippy cup, which ended with the final two adversaries spilling more of their beer down their shirts than into their mouths. There were at least two kegs in each corner of the yard, calls for shots were endless, and the sound system was broaching ear-piercing decibels.

The space was wall-to-wall with people and we may have been the most sober ones there. "Sorry I was late getting back," I apologized again. "I didn't expect to get called in last minute to help bar back. Hannah, the bartender and a friend of mine, got slammed out of nowhere by an end-of-the-summer party bus and I live closest."

Sam waved me off, and said, "No big deal, man," but I was sure he'd have been more comfortable being here when things kicked off.

A makeshift stage rose up next to the deck, though calling it a stage was too nice of a description. It looked like someone who failed shop class nailed a bunch of half-rotted pallets together and slapped some plywood across the top to make a runway. So far, it didn't have a purpose, but the night was young.

"Are you seriously considering pledging?" I asked him as his eyes lingered on a group of guys wearing the same T-shirt.

He tipped his cup back and his eyes roamed the crowd as his Adam's apple bobbed, forcing the liquid down.

"Maybe the better question is if you really should be pledging?" I asked, his continual weight shifting and overall nerves a little more concerning than intriguing at this point.

Sam squared his shoulders and stood a little taller, turning to face me. "I am pledging because I am from the middle of freaking nowhere in Minnesota. There were a hundred and fifty people in my graduating class and the only parties I've been to were in the middle of the woods. This is college, and in college, you figure out who you want to be and what you're willing to do to be that person."

I nodded like I understood how all those things correlated and gestured toward the house. Sam immediately set off across the yard. We'd made it only a few feet when the lights blinked out. Strings of tiny white bulbs wrapped around the top of the fence cast a low glow over us all. The whole crowd hesitated for a moment, and in that second, a spotlight popped on and the music turned off.

Sam edged toward me as one of the frat boys stepped out onto the rickety runway, his affiliation clear in the backwards capital E and crisscrossing tails of the lowercase A on his chest.

"We must be in the Sigma Alpha house," I said quietly to Sam, who looked at me like I was insane.

"Of course we are," he whispered. "This is *the house*. Everybody wants in to this house. You get in here and you're basically guaranteed the best four years of your life."

Sam stared intently at the guy on stage, who grinned out at the crowd. He looked like an athlete, trim but stacked. He was probably fast. His hair was cut really short, making me think he was on the baseball team, because those batting helmets were a killer in Iowa heat.

"Are you guys ready for this?" he hollered into the mic.

The crowd roared and Sam and I shared a questioning look.

"As much fun as we're already having tonight, it's about to get real! We've got the fifth annual pet shelter dating auction about to start. That means the only thing standing between you and a hot little sorority pledge is your parents' money!"

A combination of laughter, hooting, hollering, and a few insinuations of exactly what a guy might do with a hot sorority pledge made me slightly worried for the girls.

"All the proceeds from tonight go to local pet shelters, so don't be shy, fellas — and ladies, if that's your thing!" The guy smirked as a few girls cheered from behind me.

"Want to move on?" I asked Sam as I drained my cup. I didn't even like beer, but I was here and it was here and my typical loner tendencies had me wishing I'd pretended I had plans when Sam asked if I wanted to go out. But I wanted — no, needed to make friends about as much as he apparently wanted to pledge. Being chucked from high school to high school as my parents lost and found apartments meant friends were hard to come by and harder to keep.

The emcee started calling out names, random facts about the girls, and the sororities they were pledging. The bidding war was on and I was ready to get out of there.

"I should probably stay," Sam responded, surprising me. "I should probably bid so they know who I am."

I nodded and then pivoted on my heel. "Hey, where are you going?" he called after me. I raised my empty cup as I headed for the keg. If we were staying, I was going to need another drink.

***

I elbowed my way back toward Sam and even over the madness of the auction, found him in an animated discussion with a tall, hot blonde who pointed at her sky-blue, knee-high socks and then poked him playfully in the chest. I was still processing her short denim cutoffs, absolutely stellar legs, and how socks were involved in any part of their conversation when I heard, "There's no red in Manchester."

Sam scoffed at her, looking more comfortable in that moment than he had all night. The blonde looked down her nose at him, and he replied, "And how are all those empty seats in *your city's* stadium?"

She recoiled a moment and right when I thought she might punch him, the girl erupted in laughter and threw an arm around Sam's shoulders. "What's your name? I have a feeling we're destined to be friends," she said. "Anybody who can actually talk soccer is a friend of mine." I was glad they understood the conversation, because I was lost.

I approached as they shared introductions and Sam turned to me. "Darcy, this is my roommate, Trevor. Trevor, are you into soccer?"

We clinked our cups, and I replied, "Nice to meet you, Darcy. I'm not a huge soccer fan, but I've followed the U.S. Women's National Team ever since the World Cup in Germany. That Wombach-Rapino combination is a killer."

She nodded approvingly, as did Sam, before he grinned at her and said, "Darcy and I are bitter rivals and will clearly need a neutral third party if we're going to stay friends."

I opened my mouth to respond when Darcy interrupted. "Hey, my roommate is up!"

I turned and my breath froze in my lungs. Like ice forming on a rainy windshield, the air slowly locked in my chest. I couldn't move. My heart thundered behind my ribs and echoed between my ears. Anger rose like a wildfire, my latent resentment perfect kindling. I hadn't seen Charlie in four years, how in the hell did she end up here?

I couldn't take my eyes off her, nor could I stop the cascade of memories seeing her unleashed. I clenched my fists at my sides, completely shattering the cup in my hand, sending sixteen ounces of beer splattering onto the dirt.

It was the look on her face that broke the spell — the smile she'd plastered on to cover the panic, her eyes moving over every head in the room with focus, her shallow breaths expanding and deflating her chest. She was terrified. She didn't want to be up there and though it went against every ounce of pissed off currently filling my mind, I had to do something. She was my best friend — at least, she used to be.

My heart beat in my ears and I knew it was ridiculous to even think about the fourteen-year-old girl I'd left behind. She was not that girl anymore. The only way Charlie would have been on that stage when I knew her was if there was a guitar or a piano on it. The word repeated in my head...*Why? Why? Why?* I had to know why and this was my chance to make her tell me, or so I told myself as she squared her shoulders and tipped her chin up in defiance of the low bids and catcalls.

"Two hundred and fifty dollars." My voice cut through the noise of the crowd. Both Darcy and Sam erupted into twenty questions and heads turned to see where the sound originated, but I wasn't looking at them. I couldn't take my eyes off the girl who was the direct opposite of the one I used to know. From her long brown hair to her perfectly prim outfit, Charlie looked nothing like the half Goth girl, half band geek I'd known over half my life.

Charlie's tight smile and perfect posture relaxed by a small degree, her relief obvious to me and likely no one else. It was clear she still wanted nothing to do with being the center of attention and I instantly hated the fact that I knew that.

The emcee announced my next two months of spending money won the bid and as I embraced my typical state of broke, I hoped they would buy decent dog food with it.

The small stage she stood on wobbled beneath her sky-high heels as she peered out into the crowd. Between the low light in the yard and the spotlight in her face, there was no way she could see me. As soon as Charlie released the hand of the half-drunk guy who helped her down from the stage, she made her way in my direction.

Her every reaction was familiar to me and I knew the moment it clicked. Her eyes widened slightly and her nostrils flared. Her body stiffened, but she charged forward until she finally stood a short foot from me.

"Fancy meeting you here, Charlie," I said, forcing calm and only allowing a tinge of sarcasm into my tone. I rocked back on my heels, shoved my glasses up my nose, and gave her an easy smile that certainly didn't match my roaring pulse or the trail of sweat trickling down my spine. Questions, statements, and a string of words I'd never be able to take back ran through my head, but I stood there and smiled. Darcy and Sam stayed off to one side, both staring at us but silent.

She inhaled once and then again, her eyes scanning the people around us, noticing their attention had gone back to the auction. Finally, she straightened her shoulders and said, "Charlotte. My name is Charlotte."

"Charlotte? That's what you're going with these days?" Her full name felt like a dirty word coming out of my mouth. It stood for everything she'd hated, yet somehow had clearly become.

"It certainly is, and what I'm doing at all is none of your business," she snapped back at me, one hand balled up and now resting on her hip.

I raised my hands in surrender, but countered with a smirk. "See, that's where you're wrong. You're the one who put yourself up for the highest bidder and I'm the one who just saved you from some asshole who'd want to do more than talk to you, so how about a little more gratitude and less attitude?"

"I don't owe you anything, Trevor," she spat at me.

An assault of emotions I hadn't let myself feel in years ricocheted through my system and I pressed my feet into the dirt to keep from closing the distance between us. Charlie recoiled slightly before crossing her arms and leaning in.

"It appears you owe me no less than three hours of my choosing," I started, my words clipped. She rolled her eyes and I let her, waiting for her gaze to come back to mine before finishing my statement. "I suppose that will give you ample time to explain where in the hell you've been for four years and where you get off acting like it's you who deserves to be pissed about it."

Charlie's mouth fell open and both Darcy and Sam gasped.

Her eyes narrowed and that look of challenge I'd always loved set in her features.

"Before you say something you shouldn't," I cautioned, "just remember why you were up on that stage to begin with." Judgment dripped from my every word and she didn't miss a drop of it. At the start, the emcee explained that not honoring our date meant she could no longer pledge and we both knew this was her mom's sorority. God knows we'd heard enough about it growing up.

Charlie glared at me, her lips flattening into a thin line, and responded, "Fine. You want a date, you've got one. Three hours and not one minute more."

Before I could say anything else, she turned on her heel and disappeared into the crowd. I watched her, torn between going after her, even if all I did was irritate her into yelling at me some more, and leaving the party entirely because I wasn't sure how much longer I could stay knowing we were in the same zip code.

I could still feel her bony shoulders pressing into my chest and hear her sniffle as she told me goodbye for the hundredth time since my dad announced our move. Her fingertips had gripped my back as I kissed the top of her head, and for that brief second, I believed our friendship would last and we would overcome anything together.

It wasn't six months later she completely cut me out of her life—no explanation, no goodbye.

She'd just thrown our friendship away and I'd be damned if I wasn't going to find out why.

CHAPTER
three

In the middle of Beethoven's *Moonlight Sonata*, I slammed my hands down onto the keys, the cacophony of sounds bouncing around the soundproofed practice room an accurate reflection of how I currently felt. I was up, I was down, I was every conflicting emotion I could have been. I shoved back from the baby grand piano, stood up and began to pace the room.

I needed to be practicing and I knew it. Professor Davis took a chance on me and a full ride to Rodgers for musical performance was hard to come by. I needed to focus on my real goals—of getting out of this town and being able to take care of myself, but Charlie—no, *Charlotte*—ate up every available brain cell I had. Rodgers wasn't that big and we'd ran into each other a few times over the last week, and each time, she either completely ignored me or had some snarky comment.

Why do you even care?

I clasped my hands behind my head and stretched backward, giving my back a much needed release as I argued with myself. She was the one who cut me off. We were fourteen, it wasn't like I had a license and could drive the four hours to beat down her door to demand answers back then. I was lucky we even had a landline to call her considering neither of my parents had jobs and phones required deposits after you'd had them shut off so many times for failure to pay. Not that it mattered. Every time I called, her parents told me she wasn't home.

I blew out a long, noisy breath, my lips fluttering. *You're here to work. Don't waste this opportunity.*

I repeated the words over and over to myself, sat back down on the bench and started to play. But with every song, a new memory arose, and before long, I gave up trying to stop the highlight reel of our childhood and how Charlie was tied to every good thing that had ever happened to me.

As my hands and fingers moved of their own accord, I remembered the day she convinced me we should run away. We were seven and her dad was having a bad day. He'd yelled at us for listening to his old records, which was strange since he normally loved when we did, and Charlie stuffed her favorite bear, her iPod and a hoodie into her backpack. She dragged me to my house and told me to pack my bag, that we were out of there. My parents had been fighting for the last few days, so it didn't take much convincing, and we made it as far as the church six blocks from our house before she had to pee. When we opened the heavy door to Sacred Heart, we heard *Fur Elise* for the first time. We spent the next hour hiding in the pews listening to the pianist before the priest found us and guilted us into going home. Of course, we hadn't known the name then, but we found it eventually, and from then on, every time our parents were jerks, she'd look at me and ask, "Should we go find Elise?"

A quick rap on the door interrupted my thoughts and I jumped up to open it, realizing my session time was up. Livvy, another freshman pianist, stood on the other side with sheet music in one hand and a coffee in the other.

"How are things going in there? Need any help?" Her dress was short and her backpack pulled at the material, making it even shorter. Livvy's dark hair, dark eyes and olive skin made her look like some kind of exotic model. She stepped into the room, not waiting for me to move so our bodies grazed each other and I got a good look at exactly how short her dress was as she walked across the room.

The look she threw me over her shoulder was obvious and I took a step forward, intending to see where this was headed, when Charlie invaded my brain again. I didn't have time for drama of the good or bad variety right now. I huffed out an annoyed sigh and pivoted to grab my things. One girl at a time; that was all I could handle. I gave Livvy an apologetic smile and said my goodbyes as she gave me a confused look.

You and me both, I thought to myself.

***

"You're aware stalking is a felony, correct?" Charlie's tone was flat as she tossed the statement over her shoulder. Darcy said nothing, but her eyes danced with laughter as I rolled mine. She walked beside Charlie, but kept glancing back at me.

"Is there a restraining order I'm not aware of, because there are only so many sidewalks and I go to this school just like you," I threw back at her with matching enthusiasm. I was actually headed for my second breakfast, given I'd been up since four cleaning the bar where I worked, and hadn't had enough coffee for this exchange.

"Right," she sneered as she turned to face me, "as if you haven't been following me around campus waiting to cash in on your little date."

I gripped the straps of my backpack a bit tighter and let the stare down continue a little longer before I stepped forward and said, "It could be that, or it could be that I have a full ride scholarship I need to earn, a full load of classes I need to pass, and, oh, yes, a life."

Her head tilted to the side, and for just one second, I thought she might ask me a question. Instead, she crossed her arms and shot back, "You have a life? Since when?"

I shook my head back and forth as I gnawed at the inside of my cheek. I'd seen Charlie around campus as I went here and there and I was almost certain something was up with her. I could see the effort she put into her forced smile and fake laugh. When my Charlie used to laugh, people turned to look at her. It was an uncontrolled sound that came with an infectious smile and spread across a room in an instant. This girl, her laugh was hollow and her mean girl attitude was wearing on me.

"You know, Charlie—"

"*Charlotte*," she interrupted, putting extra emphasis on the last syllable.

"Yeah, so, as I was saying, *Charlie*," I countered, "I wasn't sure I was going to cash in on this *date* because I hadn't decided if you're someone I even want to know anymore, but since you've been so unbelievably polite about it and it's clearly weighing heavily on your mind, let's do it."

Her vapid smile went stiff and her arms tightened around the books she held. Darcy barely suppressed a tight-lipped smile and I stood, forcing a relaxed stance as people walked around our little standoff.

"That's not—" she started, but I cut in, and said, "Oh, don't bother denying it, Charlie. You've obviously missed me if you've noticed me every time we've been within fifty feet of each other, and I wouldn't want to deny you this opportunity. You got up on that stage and earned it, so who am I to hold you back? This Friday at seven. I'll even pick you up like a proper gentleman. Where do you live?"

Her eyes narrowed, but before she could argue, Darcy quickly said, "Tully, third floor, three-twelve." Charlie spun on her, glaring daggers as I gave an appreciative smile. I liked Darcy. She was in my seminar class and I now knew she played soccer, hated idiots, and saw life in a black and white way that made me jealous. She lived in sweats and ponytails and was really only concerned about when her practices were and where her next meal was coming from. Tipping my head in thanks, she shot me a wink.

I intentionally stepped between them, leaning in close to Charlie to whisper, "I forgot how much fun it can be to get you riled up. See you Friday, Charlie," before I walked away, wondering exactly what kind of mess my mouth had just gotten me into.

CHAPTER

four

I retied my tie for the fifth time while Sam watched me from where he lounged on his bed, shaking his head.

"So, explain this to me again. She was your best friend, but she isn't now, and you still don't know why?"

He kept asking about Charlie and I'd brushed off every question, still unable to properly articulate to myself exactly what I was doing.

The tails of my tie weren't even, so I yanked it loose once again and grumbled, starting over.

"It's hard to explain — a long story, really. We moved almost four hours away the summer before our freshman year of high school. For the first few months, we talked constantly. She was my best friend one day and then completely disappeared the next. I'd pretty much written her off, but now she's here, and to be honest, I don't know what the hell I'm doing." It was the truth and the longer I stared at myself in the mirror, the more I questioned pushing this date onto her. It seemed like the perfect answer to her snotty attitude in the moment, but the more I thought about Charlie...well, the more I thought about Charlie, and I didn't want to think about Charlie.

Sam pushed off the bed and came to stand next to me, eying the current mess I'd made with the tie. "Man, you have no idea what you're doing. Just let me do it. This is painful to watch."

Defeated, I turned toward Sam, and he expertly adjusted the tie length then quickly looped and knotted it.

I checked the mirror and shook my head in appreciative awe. "You did that in like ten seconds. What other magic tricks do you know?"

He chuckled and pointed to himself. "Hobbit, not elf. And it was mandatory for church on Sunday. You get used to it when the tie is the only way to show a little personality."

My surprised look only made him full-on laugh. "I know what I look like. Samwise Gamgee, at your service," he said with a mock bow and a smirk. "Who doesn't love Sam, though? I think it totally works in my favor."

"Pretty much everyone has seen Lord of the Rings, so you do have that going for you. You're just lucky I don't look like Legolas," I joked as I shoved my black-rimmed glasses up on my nose and glanced into the mirror at my unruly dark hair. Legolas, I was not. The best I could hope for was Jim on The Office, with the added bonus of glasses that never stayed put.

"You don't seem so sure about this date," Sam said. "Why put all this effort into it?" He waved a hand at my dress pants, button down and tie as I smirked.

"When I go, I go all the way," I replied. "I might be unsure about this date, but I can promise you she wants nothing to do with it. If Charlie wants to battle, I'm going to remind her she's fighting with someone who knows her tricks — or at least used to." I was still wrapping my head around the one-eighty she'd done since we last saw each other.

Sam chuckled and I opted for a topic shift.

"You and Darcy seemed to hit it off," I tossed out as he retreated back to his chair.

"That girl is something. I bet she could kick my ass if she wanted to."

I burst out laughing, but couldn't disagree. "I wouldn't get on her bad side, that's for sure."

"That is the goal. We have econ together so we're studying tomorrow night before our first test. I'm interested to know more about her."

"Interested, huh?"

"Not like that, she's just cool. I've never had a girl for a friend and Darcy seems like the kind of girl everybody wants to be friends with."

I shrugged. "Your call, man, but I think she's interested."

Sam shook his head like I'd lost my mind while I was pulled into a memory of meeting the only girl to have ever been my friend. We were both four years old when my parents moved in next door to hers. My mom made cookies, and as a family, we went over to introduce ourselves. I was shy, but my dad set me down right in front of him, his massive hand on my shoulder, and whispered, "You'll be just fine, son," before Mrs. Logan opened the door. As the parents chatted, Charlie came roaring into the foyer, whipped around her parents, grabbed my hand and yelled, "I'm going to show him my room," as she dragged me behind her. I still remembered her light brown hair in pigtails high on her head and the bright purple shorts she'd worn. The parents laughed and had to physically separate us when it was time to leave. Charlie was the only person in the world who knew my mom and dad hadn't always been disasters. We'd been happy once.

I dug in my tiny closet for the only sport coat I owned. The last time I wore it was only a month ago while I tried to look older and persuade my parents' landlord to give them another rent extension. It took everything I'd saved outside of the money I needed for books to catch them up, which was why I still worked four mornings a week restocking and cleaning some downtown bars. It made the days long and me tired. I kept hoping my parents would grow up and be the adults in our relationship, but at fifty, it wasn't likely.

When I splurged, using my high school graduation money to buy the sport coat, my hope was I'd need it for a concert. I'd just learned my music performance degree required me to perform three memorized piano pieces at the end of the year, followed by a post-show concert where I could play anything I wanted.

One of my songs. I could sing something that actually mattered instead of all these pieces that were supposed to challenge me but never had. The next four years would be a lot easier if I loved playing music as much as I was supposed to.

I stuffed my feet into the least uncomfortable dress shoes I owned and stood up.

"How'd I do?" I asked sarcastically as I turned to face Sam.

He shrugged. "You're no white knight. My money's on the stubborn brunette. She looked like she wanted to rip your heart out and puncture it with the tip of her heel the last time I saw her."

I snorted.

Been there, done that.

***

Sam and I shared a dorm in Millen Hall, but knowing Charlie lived in Tully, I took off a few minutes before seven so I could cut across campus. August in Iowa can be anything from crazy thunderstorms to intense humidity to perfectly amazing, and tonight I was lucky. There was a light breeze making my button down/tie/blazer combination almost bearable.

Nerves started to get the better of me as the elevator ascended. I didn't know this girl Charlotte, but in our limited interactions, I'd seen glimpses of Charlie. Using both of her names made me feel like she had multiple personalities. But right now, each name correlated to an entirely different person.

The elevator doors opened and I let out a long exhale. On the walk over, I'd decided all I wanted to know was whether any part of Charlie was still in there. She was the reason I even made it to Rodgers University. If it weren't for her, I would have never played an instrument at all. I loved writing songs more than playing them, but playing them got me a scholarship to one of the best schools in the Midwest, and that was my ticket to freedom. There was no point in holding onto a grudge. She ended our friendship and we went our separate ways.

I knocked lightly on their door, eyeing the decorations on the outside. Assuming Charlotte wasn't big into glitter, the monstrosity that took over their threshold must have spawned from Darcy. Selfies of the two of them, clearly from the past few weeks, were everywhere. In each one, Darcy's friendly blue eyes and warm smile was matched by Charlie's dull gaze and forced one. I supposed she was at least trying.

The door opened and instead of Charlie, it was Darcy. In every way that Charlie was small and compact, Darcy was long and muscular.

"Basketball, too?" I questioned, cocking my head as the thought fell from my mouth.

She rolled her eyes. "Why does everyone always guess basketball? I never could dribble worth a damn, at least not with my hands. Just soccer. Only soccer."

"Ah." I nodded and waited, expecting her to open the door farther. Instead, she kept herself wedged between it and the wall, blocking my view.

"It was nice of you to drop by, but she isn't coming," Darcy said politely, her eyes conveying the apology she didn't voice.

"Actually, she is," I responded with an easy grin that didn't relay the frustration Darcy's words had lit like a match. All thoughts of letting go of grudges and moving on were gone.

"No—" Darcy started.

"Charlotte Lydia Logan," I yelled past Darcy, "if you aren't out here in the next thirty seconds, I will provide very loud, very specific details about the time you were thirteen and drank so much gin and orange juice you—"

She wrenched the door out of Darcy's hand and flung it open, her palm flat against the surface as she glared at me. In jeans, a T-shirt and no makeup, she almost looked thirteen again. I could see her rummaging through my dad's liquor cabinet, pissed her parents refused to pay for guitar lessons, wanting her to do something "constructive" with her time instead.

"Maybe," she threatened, "I'll provide very loud, very specific details about the time you were so nervous to perform, you puked all over the auditorium bathroom and blamed a fifth grader."

Embarrassment crept up my neck, but I countered with, "The only problem here is you clearly care what all these people think and I do not." I waved my hand at the open dorm doors and heads poking out, listening to our exchange.

"That's crap. You've always cared." Her eyes flicked back and forth down the hall.

I raised an eyebrow. "Looks like I'm not the only person remembering what used to be. People change, Charlie. Or haven't you looked in a mirror lately?"

Her jaw clenched and released and her knuckles went white as her fingertips pressed into the door panel. Nobody had ever been able to irritate us like we could.

Finally, she took a step back and grumbled, "You're not going to leave, I can see the stubborn part of you obviously hasn't changed, so let's just get this over with." Charlie waved a hand into the room and I strode past her and Darcy.

"If you're going to force me to do this, you're going to have to wait." Charlie pointed to a beanbag chair and I didn't hesitate to flop down on it.

"Fine by me, but our reservation is at seven-thirty, so that gives you," I looked down at my watch, "fifteen minutes. Do what you gotta do."

"Shit," she muttered under her breath as she yanked what appeared to be a dress from a hanger in her closet, grabbed a plastic basket overflowing with makeup and closed herself in the bathroom.

As soon as the door shut, Darcy started to giggle, one hand slapped over her mouth and the other giving me a thumbs up. I had to suppress my own chuckle. It was officially Trevor 2, Charlie 0.

CHAPTER

five

Charlie was silent as I pulled out of the parking lot. She sat perfectly straight with her hands folded in her lap and looked out the window as if I weren't even there. My fingers twitched on the steering wheel as I wondered if she was as affected by me as I was by her. Being near her made me ache for the playful banter, inside jokes and closeness we'd shared, and the strong draw surprised me.

I tightened my grip on the steering wheel and decided we needed a neutral starting point if tonight wasn't going to be a complete disaster. I reached out and clicked on the radio as I asked, "Are you still obsessed with nineties music? They've got a decent station here that plays all the good ones." When we were kids, she'd decided she hated the hip hop and teen pop that generally defined 2000s music and we somehow found our way back into the nineties. Her obsession spawned a collection of band T-shirts and influenced most of the music we'd learned to play together.

Smashing Pumpkins' *Tonight, Tonight* filled the car and for a brief second, a pained look crossed Charlie's face before she reached out and smacked the button, sending us back into silence.

"Okay, so no nineties. Duly noted," I said as I attempted to keep my eyes on the road and her at the same time.

"What music do you like?" I asked, trying to fill the void. The downtown restaurant I was able to get reservations at wasn't far, and thankfully, we were already halfway there.

"This is not an actual date and we do not need to play twenty questions," she stated, still not looking away from the window.

"Then exactly how do you propose we spend the next three hours? It's pretty clear we don't know each other anymore and questions are the only way we're going to. Or is whatever I did back then still making you hate me even now?"

Damn it.

I hadn't wanted to say that out loud. I didn't want to go there already.

I pulled into a spot, put my old Honda in park, and turned to face her.

"Charlie," I pled softly, reaching one hand toward her. Before my fingertips could land on her skin, Charlie yanked the door handle and scrambled from the car. I blew out an exhale and got out, making sure to keep my distance as she waited on the sidewalk.

Gesturing toward the restaurant, Charlie's heels clicked on the pavement as we matched pace and walked in that direction. I held the door open for her, which earned me an irritated glower, and let the hostess show us to our table.

"Welcome to Americana, what can I get you guys to drink?" the server asked.

"Water, please," Charlie requested.

"No ice," we said simultaneously. For the first time since I picked her up, Charlie really looked at me. Her eyes searched mine, asking a hundred questions but not giving me a single answer.

She looked as curious and wary as I felt, but it didn't last long before her gaze flicked away and her face went blank.

The server looked at me with a quick conspiratorial smirk that said, "Good luck with that."

"Water for me as well, please. No ice. We'll order in a minute," I said, refocusing on Charlie as I decided what to do next.

Before I could, she said, "You don't need to do this, Trevor. I don't know what you think you're going to accomplish, but it won't work. One dinner, that's all this is. Then you can go back to your life and I can go back to mine," she decreed.

"First, you never call me Trevor, you never have. It's weird, and I'd appreciate it if you stopped," I said as she lifted an eyebrow, her nose wrinkled. "Second, why don't you tell me about this great new life you're living?"

"My life is great," she retorted, flipping her hair over her shoulder, daring me to disagree.

"Is it?" I asked, scratching my jaw. If this was what she wanted, I'd go tit for tat. "Because despite all the glitter-bombed selfies and sorority pledge hoopla, I haven't seen you actually laugh once."

Charlie's cheeks tinged pink and her lips pinched together.

31

"Whether you want to believe it or not — hell, whether I want to know it or not — I know you and find it hard to believe you cashed in your nineties band fetish and combat boots just so you could raid your sister's closet and become your parents' dream child. So, why don't you explain *this* to me," I said, waving a hand at her patterned dress and matching shoes and purse. Her light brown hair was long and loose, another huge contrast from the cropped black hair she'd had in middle school.

"You don't know me anymore, Trev*or*," she said, her voice cold, devoid of emotion, while putting extra emphasis into my full name. "You don't know anything about me. Just leave it alone and go back to wherever you've been for the past four years." The edge to her voice forced me to take a slow breath before responding. If she wanted to go there, we could go there.

"My parents moved and if I remember correctly, it was you who stopped talking to me."

She flinched, the move almost imperceptible, and repeated my statement as a question. "I stopped talking *to you?*" she asked, as if she didn't believe me.

"I must have called you a hundred times!" I tried not to shout the words at her, and Charlie only looked more confused. "I sent emails, I borrowed people's phones to text you. My parents kept moving me around, but I went to the library and even created social media accounts — which you know I hate — to try to find you, but you'd disappeared from there, too. I tried and tried, and I got nothing." I paused, feeling out of breath and depleted from finally saying the words out loud. I yanked my glasses off and pinched the bridge of my nose, needing a moment to get myself together.

"No," she finally said, her tone soft. I looked up at her, hardly able to maintain eye contact as pain I'd shoved down long ago rose like a tidal wave inside me.

"They told me you never called. I deactivated my social media and never got any emails. I left messages with my new number. My parents changed all our numbers. You stopped talking to me. You did this."

A mixture of rage and relief sat in my gut. My mind raced as I tried to reason through what she was saying to me.

"I tried, Charlie. I tried to find you. We kept getting kicked out of apartments. My parents kept moving me around. First it was Omaha, then Iowa City, then Des Moines. I've been in at least four apartments in each city, but I kept trying."

She looked past me, over my shoulder out into the dining room. "It doesn't matter," she finally said, her words clipped and previous attitude back in place. All the emotion I just saw was gone. Her face was blank and her words were empty. "What's done is done, and we aren't those kids anymore. There's no use in going backwards. Let's just eat."

I shoved my glasses back on. "Damn it. Look at me."

Her bright green eyes flicked up and finally stayed on mine. I leaned in, my voice low and as flat as I could make it given the frustrated adrenaline pulsing through my veins. "If you aren't still the girl I knew, then how do I know your right hand won't stop moving because you're fingering Bach, which also means you're holding back whatever you won't let yourself tell me?"

She looked down, saw her fingers tapping out the notes and slammed her hand flat on the table. "Oh, suck it, Trev," she hissed.

I leaned back and laughed, unable to stop myself. "Finally! I knew you were still in there!"

Charlie collapsed back into her chair, the pads of her fingers digging into the black linen covering the table. She exhaled in a huff and her eyes narrowed.

"Of course I'm here, where else would I be?" she demanded. "This is who I am. I don't know what you think you're going to get from me, but you're looking at it. We can eat. You can talk. It won't change anything."

The waitress set down our waters and I couldn't stop my satisfied smile. I had gotten something from her and it changed everything. Our friendship ending was not a case of shitty circumstances; there was more to this story and I was going to find out what it was.

"What?" She yanked the wrapper off her straw and shoved it into the glass.

"We are going to eat. And we are going to talk," I said as my choice became clear. "Because from here on out, you're not getting rid of me, Charlie — not again."

She exhaled slowly, her shoulders dropping. "Fine, whatever. Talk." Then she muttered, "You never would take no for an answer."

"Desperate times call for desperate measures," I replied with a wink. She threw her balled up straw wrapper at me and then flipped her menu up like she could hide behind it. She may have thought I wasn't listening, but I caught her soft response: "Touché."

***

We cut across campus, both looking everywhere but at each other. The moon was full and I took it as a good sign Charlie wasn't running to get away from me. Our dinner conversation was only mildly awkward, but as I got her onto safe topics like movies, books or anything that really had nothing to do with her specifically, she slowly relaxed.

As we walked, a memory crept up on me.

"Do you remember that time you decided we should become pro skateboarders and spent the whole summer making up chores we could do for our parents so they'd give us more allowance?"

She turned to me, incredulous, and said, "Me? Since when was that my idea?"

"Um," I started, swallowing down my laughter, "since you were the one obsessed with Avril Lavigne and that ridiculous skater boy song. That whole summer you swore it was your destiny to play guitar and sing in a band."

She immediately protested, going so far as to reach out like she was going to swat at me before she yanked her hand back to her side and continued. "A, we were ten and anything you think you should grow up to be at ten should never be held against you. And B, not true! You wanted to impress Whitney Saunders and her boyfriend was always in the skate park. You thought you could actually compete with a seventh grader," she scoffed.

"That's not how I remember it," I declared, knowing we were both technically correct.

"Right," she said, her eyebrows rising. "Just like you always remember the time we snuck into the movie theater as being my idea when in reality, you were the one who *just had to* see Iron Man 2 for the third time."

"You had a crush on the ticket taker, don't lie," I accused, pulling back and making an appalled face at her. "What was his name — Willy or Freddy or something insanely lame? All I know is he wore more eyeliner than you did, which is saying something when we were only twelve, and by now has probably found his home among the circus folk."

She burst out laughing, a genuine, from-the-belly explosion that surprised us both. I found myself laughing alongside her and as the sound dissipated, I couldn't wipe the smile off my face.

"What?" Her posture stiffened and she took a small step away from me, creating distance between us I didn't want.

"I asked you earlier if you'd actually laughed since you'd been here and now I know you have." I shoved my hands into my pockets, trying to give her the space she clearly needed.

Charlie crossed her arms over her chest and took quick steps toward her dorm. I took a few running strides to catch back up and fell in step with her.

As we approached Tully, I looked down at my watch. "It's nine fifty-eight, your three hours of punishment will officially end in two minutes."

Charlie was already on the second step, but she stopped and turned to look down at me. Her fingers were tapping a rhythm on her right thigh, and for an instant, I thought I saw a whisper of a smile on her face.

"I wouldn't go so far as to call it punishment," she said as her eyes flicked around, finally connecting with mine. They stayed there for just a moment and the edge of her mouth curved up in the tiniest way before she spun on her heel and headed for the door.

I rubbed at my jaw to try to hide my smile. "I'll see you around, Charlie."

I stood there for a moment longer than necessary and was rewarded by seeing her look back my way before the door closed behind her. I gave a quick wave and her face flushed, knowing she'd been caught.

As I walked back to my dorm, my head a mess of questions, I was absolutely certain of one thing: you don't get many second chances in life and I wasn't wasting this one. I wanted my best friend back.

CHAPTER

six

September

Shoving open the door, I left the Fine Arts Center, thankful to be done with my practice session and debating whether I needed a nap or coffee more, given I was on my third consecutive night of less than five hours of sleep.

I made my way across campus, loving every second of the seventy-degree day. As I got near the student center, I scanned for Charlie. Since our dinner last weekend, we'd run into each other a few times, and while she was still standoffish, she had toned down the mean girl routine a little.

Earlier that week, I saw her sit down outside to have her afternoon snack and decided to chance joining her. We had a tiny bit of conversation, and each day we ended up at that same table, we had a little more. I kept coming and she kept not asking me to leave. I called it progress; Sam called me insane. I was clearly the optimist of the dorm room.

I couldn't help but notice the woman who'd displaced the girl I knew. Curves replaced straight lines, the years peeling away her childish wonder and leaving thick armor in its place. I hated the fact that I didn't know what drove her to a place where she felt she needed protection, even from me.

As I got within a few feet, I greeted her, but Charlie said nothing. She stared in the opposite direction, her face blank.

"What's wrong?" I asked, coming around the table so I could see her face. Charlie's gaze was unfocused, but her eyes betrayed her. I saw the panic almost as acutely as the inner monologue swirling through her mind. I watched her wince once, then again, and wondered what she could possibly say to herself that hurt so much.

I reached out, afraid she still didn't realize I was even there. Her hands were in her lap, so I brushed her tricep with my fingertips, and said again, "Charlie, hey."

She jerked away from me, a short gasp giving away her shock.

"Did something happen? Are you okay?" I retreated back to my side of the table, giving her the requisite amount of space.

"It's nothing. Don't worry about it," she rushed out, leaning down to grab her food out of her backpack.

"Come on, don't give me that. You have the same look you had when you didn't make..." my voice trailed off, the dots connecting. All day today, girls squealed with delight and guys fist-bumped and chest-bumped over their pledge cards. Sam danced his Sigma Alpha card in front of my face for a full thirty seconds before he would let me eat lunch.

"You didn't get into Kappa Phi." Charlie's gaze flicked up to mine. She gave me a tight, sad smile as her shoulders and hands rose up and then fell back down.

"My mother will be so proud to hear I couldn't get in to her alma mater, even after all her donations," she spat, her bitterness clear.

"You don't want to be stuck hanging out with all those ridiculous, bleach-blonde half-wits anyway. Darcy's awesome, and you've always got me and Sam." Truth be told, I knew nothing about sororities or the people who made them up, but I hated how down on herself she was getting for something so unnecessary in the scheme of life.

"Typical Trevor response — damn the man, right? Be happy with what you have? I've got goals. I've got plans and things I have to do," she almost shouted.

"Whoa. Calm down, Cha—"

"I told you to call me Charlotte!"

"And I told you to stop calling me Trevor. So, here we are."

We glared at each other from across the table until she let out a deep sigh.

Finally, she removed her food from the plastic container.

When she picked up her snack, my nose automatically wrinkled and I didn't bother holding back on giving her a hard time. I never would have before, and she needed to see I was still me, even if, buried under all that hostility, she didn't think she was still her.

"Blech, you still eat those things? Since when has lunch meat, cheese and a pickle ever actually been considered a sandwich?" I leaned in, eyeing the combination she'd been eating since we were kids. There was a comfort knowing some parts of her were truly still intact. She took a large bite, her eyes narrowing, as I asked, "Where's the bread? You're going to kill yourself eating like that."

Charlie started coughing, her face turning cherry red. The coughs became deeper and her hands went to her throat.

I leapt over the table and smacked her back. "Spit it out! Come on, spit it out!"

Seconds before I would have thrown her over my shoulder and took off for the nearest building, a chunk of pickle went flying into the grass and she gasped for air.

Without thought, I pulled her to me, one hand around her, low on her back, and the other at the back of her neck, below her long thin ponytail.

"Breathe. Slowly, breathe." Her hair smelled like flowers and the only thing on my mind was the fact that I didn't want to let go.

We stayed there just long enough for her breathing to return to normal. She relaxed into me for a fraction of a second, but then shoved back and scooted across the bench, out of arm's reach.

I saw the panic — the way she leaned away from me, tightening her arms around herself. It happened every time I got within an inch of touching her. It happened last week when I poked her side after making a joke she didn't laugh at, and again as our hands touched when she let me borrow a pen.

"I told you about pickles," I said, acting like nothing happened while willing my own heartbeat to return to normal. "They're the devil, and you should really ban them from your life. Everyone should."

"Right, everyone should because you said so?"

"Wait, what?" I wasn't even sure what we were going to argue about, but given the pinched expression on her face and the fire in her green eyes, it was coming.

"We should all do whatever Trevor says because he knows everything. He sees everything. He can fix everything. Isn't that right?" Her snide tone was only barely out-matched by her condescending look.

"Whoa, where the hell did all that come from?"

"Nowhere," she said sharply. "It didn't come from anywhere. And you really need to stop following me around like a puppy dog begging for scraps of attention. It's getting a little pathetic."

I gnawed at the inside of my cheek and mentally counted to five, but it wasn't helping today. "And you need to stop being unnecessarily bitchy in order to scare me away, because it won't work."

"When are you going to get it? I'm not interested in whatever *this* is." She flung a hand between us.

"That's just fine, because I'm interested enough for the both of us," I said, leaning in. "You keep pushing me away and I'll keep stepping closer. We can do this dance forever, but eventually you're going to understand that no matter who you think you are, I think you're still the girl I knew."

Her chest heaved with shallow breaths and her cheekbones shifted as she grated her teeth together.

Finally, she took a long inhale and then sighed as she rolled her eyes. "Why can't you just let it go?"

"I'm trying here, don't you get it?" I exclaimed, surprising us both. But I'd broken the dam and I couldn't stop the flood. "I see you and you're so different, but you're still you. You're still Charlie. You're still my friend and I miss you. I miss us. And you can snap at me and push me away, but I'm just going to keep coming back because I want to know what happened after I moved away and how this all got messed up to start with. Don't you want to know? Don't you miss me, too?"

I held my breath as blood roared through my veins and waited for a reaction — any kind of reaction — from her.

Her face paled and her hands trembled on the tabletop. Finally, she spun on the bench and started gathering her things, refusing to meet my eyes anymore. "I can't do this. I've got to go. I'll see you later, maybe tomorrow."

"I have a surprise for you," I spat out, still reeling from her absolute lack of response. It was probably pathetic, she was right, but I couldn't let her just walk away. Charlie stopped, but looked none too pleased about the lack of distance between us.

"What could you possibly have that I need?" She shot off.

I couldn't stop the snort of amusement at her expected sarcasm. I told myself this wasn't just self-inflicted torture; this was for the greater good. There was one more thing I could try to get through to Charlie and this was my chance. The idea had been brewing for a few days and her not getting into the sorority gave me the perfect opening.

"Space," I said with a knowing smile. "I want to get you out of here, to take you somewhere I know you'll love. A place that serves the best Mexican in all of Des Moines."

Her eyebrows rose, her interest piqued, as I'd hoped. Charlie loved Mexican. She ate at my house every week for years because we always had Mexican Mondays and my mom knew how to make some amazing Mexican.

Charlie tilted her head and stared, the wheels in her head turning. Another set of squealing girls erupted from behind us and Charlie closed her eyes briefly.

"This is off campus?" she asked as she reopened them, resilience etched in her pinched lips.

"Indeed," I said in a conspiratorial whisper. "Way off and away from all these prying eyes and the sorority pledge bullshit."

She was utterly still and I waited. I knew it was coming and so did she. It was inevitable. There were too many people. Charlie was always either in class or surrounded by her former pledge sisters or the students on her dorm floor. She needed space.

She needed it in third grade when we got lost in the woods behind our houses trying to find the best place to build a fort. And she needed it in middle school when the popular girls took issue with her Hot Topic T-shirts, thick eye-liner and black hair. That was when I started teaching her guitar in the band room over lunch. Little had I known, she was a prodigy in her own right.

"Pick me up at noon Saturday and let's have lunch."

"There's just one thing I need to know first," I said before she turned away. "You said you have big plans and I still don't even know your major."

Charlie shook her head and rolled her eyes before responding, "Political Science. I'm pre-law."

"Of course you are." I suppressed my scowl. "Do you write songs anymore?"

"Not really. That was always your thing," she responded, no longer meeting my eyes.

I wanted to tell her if writing songs was my thing, then playing them should still be hers, but it was clearly too soon.

"I'll see you at noon on Saturday."

Her brows drew together, like she expected more argument from me about the obvious abandonment of her dreams.

"See you, Trev," she finally responded.

I tipped my head and gave her an easy smile, pushing my glasses up. One more try. What we had was worth just one more try.

***

"This seems risky," Sam reiterated for the fourth time, and he wasn't wrong.

"I just need to know if it's still there. That's all. I know what I'm doing," I assured both of us.

"According to their site, it's there," he replied as his fingers flew over the keyboard of his laptop.

I stood in the middle of our small dorm room and quickly popped each of my fingers and thumb. It was a habit, especially after a longer practice session, but it was also comforting.

Sam opened his mouth, but then quickly closed it. "What?" I asked.

"Are you really sure this is a good idea? How do you know she isn't happy and you're barking up the wrong tree?"

"Does she seem overly happy?" I asked, giving him a deadpan stare.

Sam's lips twisted into a grimace and he scratched at his jaw. "Well, no. She seems really unhappy actually."

"Exactly," I replied. "And I get that people change as they grow up, but how do you go from being someone who lived life by their own rules and wasn't afraid of anything to someone who conforms in every way possible and shuts out the world? It just doesn't add up."

"But why you?" he asked. "Do you really believe she didn't intentionally cut you off? Is she worth the price you might have to pay to find out?"

My immediate thought was, *of course she is*, but I took a moment and instead replied with, "I don't think I have a choice." Sam's brow furrowed, his skepticism apparent, and I explained, "Nothing about her is making sense to me. I can get behind her change in look, she's not thirteen anymore, but when you've known someone more than half your life, you know when something is wrong and when they are hiding things. We've always been able to read each other and even though the outside looks different, I can't walk away until I know she's actually okay. Maybe we're friends at the end and maybe we aren't, but I won't give up until I know one way or the other."

Sam nodded and I sat down at my desk, intending to flip through my notebook and reread the last few verses I'd written on my latest song, but my phone rang. I recognized the special tone and had to force the phone from my pocket to my ear. Quickly stepping into our bathroom, I answered.

"Hi, Mom."

"Hey, baby," she drawled.

Shit.

"Mom, are you drunk?" I already knew the answer.

"Oh no, Trevvy. I promised you I wouldn't drink and I haven't," she replied, the slurring words contradicting her lie.

"What do you need?" I didn't want to ask. I kept telling myself I would stop answering and stop asking, but I'd never been strong enough to actually follow through.

"Well, the thing is, your dad ran into a little trouble—"

"At the track? He lost all your money again, didn't he? Didn't he just finish a job?" I was trying so hard not to yell. My head dropped back against the wall and I continued to bounce it against the sheetrock while I tried to stay calm.

"Don't talk like that about your father. It's complicated. He's complicated. His last order fell through and he's very upset."

"I don't have any money, Mom. I'm in college fulltime, or did you forget? I'm taking a full course load and I'm already working more than I should to pay for my meals and so I can have a life. They won't give me any more in student loans."

"You always come up with something. We really need your help. They're going to shut off our power," she whined.

"I thought you were caught up," I started, but then stopped myself. It didn't matter. My mom kept promising to stay sober and she really did try, but only for a few weeks at a time. If she wasn't blowing money on booze, my dad was investing it in the local economy via the casino or his bookie.

I sighed. "I'll see what I can do. When is the payment due?"

"Oh, thank you, baby," she said, her shrill exclamation grating on my nerves. "It's, um…due tomorrow."

"Great. That's just great. Text me the information, I've gotta go." I hung up before she could completely ruin my day and texted my boss to see if he needed help tomorrow morning. I also reconfirmed phase two of my plan was still good to go. Both were a quick yes.

I stood in the bathroom, my forehead against the cheap paneling of the door, and asked myself yet again how I came to be the parent in my household. But I'd been asking myself that question since I was fourteen and I still didn't have the answer.

CHAPTER
seven

We approached the restaurant and Charlie shot me a wary look. I couldn't deny Tasty Tacos looked out of place with its crisp, clean Southwest-style building set in the middle of an area built long before we were alive. A mix of low-income housing and legacy Des Moines businesses dotted Grand Avenue and I could only shrug.

As I pulled into a parking spot, I reassured her. "This is legit, Charlie. Best tacos in town, I swear."

"How do you even know about this place?"

"We moved again my junior year and ended up in Des Moines," I explained as I held the door open for her. "It used to look really rundown since this is the original location, but they just leveled the old place and built a new one."

As we walked through the first set of doors, I pointed to the original owners in the photo. "Their slogan is 'Nada es impossible' because in nineteen sixty-one, the original owners started with basically nothing and now there are five restaurants in town. It's pretty typical for this one to have a line out the door every day at lunch."

I watched her take it all in — from the green booths, to the sombreros hung on the walls, to the lengthy, but simple, menu.

"Do you mind if I order for both of us?" I asked as she stared at the individual white plastic letters placed on the old-style brown menu board. Some were crooked, a few looked ready to fall off.

"There's basically only one thing you can order your first time," I said, popping my eyebrows.

That got a chuckle from the small, Mexican man behind the register. "Fine. But I want nachos, too. Queso Blanco nachos — with everything," she demanded, eager anticipation lighting her eyes.

I ordered two beef and bean tacos for me and a taco and nacho for her. After we filled up our sodas and sat down in a booth to wait, Charlie surprised me by initiating further conversation.

"Why did you move again?" she asked, pushing her hair behind her ear. I was still getting used to her hot and cold personality switches. She was either obnoxious and snide or quiet and withdrawn. Today, she was on the quiet side.

Though I assumed she'd eventually ask where I'd been, it wasn't a topic I really wanted to discuss. But if I wanted Charlie to open up to me, I figured it was in my favor to do the same.

Luckily, our number was called at the same moment I started to speak. Hopping up, I grabbed the tray, added some taco sauce and snagged a handful of napkins.

I doled out the goods and squeezed a huge helping of sauce onto my taco.

"The thing about these tacos is they are magical," I said as Charlie gave me a skeptical look.

"You wait and see. Between the fried, fluffy shell, meat and bean combination, lettuce and freshly-shredded cheese — mmm-mmm-mmm. Toss some of their homemade taco sauce on top, and I'm telling you, *magic*." I started to take a bite as she grabbed the sauce and said, "You also sound like a commercial."

"You may want to test some out before you add it," I said mid-bite. "The sauce is made fresh every day. Some days it'll burn your mouth off and other days it's mild."

Charlie squirted some taco sauce on her finger and then popped it into her mouth. My brain immediately went in the wrong direction. The direction of the gutter — the last direction it should be going when thinking about Charlie.

"Oh, I like this," she said with a groan that didn't help my mindset before topping her taco with a solid helping. "Now, answer the question, Trev."

"Trev?" I questioned, one eyebrow rising. "And I haven't berated you once today for using my full name. Look at how far we've come."

Her mouth was full, so all I got was an eye roll as she wrinkled her nose in an attempt to make fun of me.

"Question. Answer it," she mumbled, one hand in front of her mouth.

"We left Muscatine because my parents lost our house," I said, shifting uncomfortably in my seat.

"You never told me that," she accused. She actually looked upset and a small part of me was glad. I wanted her to care about what happened to me, too.

"I was embarrassed," I admitted. "Remember that time they convinced us we should camp in the backyard during our sleepover? The next morning, I figured out we needed to cook on the fire pit because our gas oven didn't work. A few days later, it was miraculously fixed, which meant my dad actually paid the gas bill."

She gave me a sad half-smile. As little kids, we thought my parents were perfect. They encouraged me to pursue any kind of art, they were lax about rules and they loved Charlie. But you got older and understood it wasn't normal for most of your mail to be stamped "Final Notice".

"They weren't always so bad," she interjected, as if reading my mind. "Your mom helped us make all kinds of awesome stuff. She let us make cookies and she never got mad when we made a huge mess of her kitchen, not like my mom would have. And your dad would take us on the most epic adventures. Do you remember the stories he'd tell? He came up with the coolest reasons why we should investigate the garage or hunt down mythical creatures in the forest." Charlie laughed to herself and I let myself enjoy the memories. It didn't take long for the reality of what my parents became to crash back down on me, though.

"They didn't tell me when mom stayed home to paint it wasn't to let her live her dreams but because she got fired," I continued, trying to stave off the anger that came with these memories and what their selfishness cost me.

"I mean, why would they when I was eight? Either way, when the economy collapsed, a lot of people were laid off and my dad was one of them. He took it as a sign that he should also be able to pursue his passion, so we moved first to Omaha for a year, and then Iowa City when Omaha 'just wasn't good for us anymore'." I used air quotes around that last part because even then, I knew it was an excuse for my parents to run from whatever new mess they'd created.

"They thought it would be easier to sell Mom's paintings and for Dad to start his furniture refinishing business in Iowa City. 'People needed to salvage things, not buy new,' he'd kept saying."

"Your dad always made us the coolest stuff," Charlie commented, and I wondered if she was trying to help me control my emotions. "Remember that old table he melted all those crayons onto and then covered with glass? I never could believe he dragged that thing all the way to our fort."

The image of my dad, with his big beard and hiking boots, lugging a real oak table he'd made just for us, was all I could see. I heard his booming laugh when he finally got it there and it took up most of the little hut we constructed from leaning plywood pieces and palettes.

"Gotta bring some class to this place," I said, mimicking his deep baritone. "That's what he said when he put a four-hundred-dollar table in that shack." It was one good memory buried in hundreds of shitty ones.

Charlie shook her head, laughter spilling out as she tried and failed to contain the taco meat inside her puffy, fried shell. Grease dripped a steady stream, coating the thin paper in her plastic basket, but she didn't seem fazed. She actually looked to be enjoying the mess.

"Do you remember when Katie found our fort and she freaked out and told your parents?" I asked. "I think she was just pissed we didn't invite her to join us," I chuckled. "What's she up to these days anyway? Is she done with school yet?"

Charlie's mouth was full and she chewed slowly. The laughter faded from her features, the tiny indentions of lines around her mouth disappearing. Finally, she answered me, her tone flat.

"Katie and I actually aren't that close anymore. She's studying abroad. She decided to go to, ah…Paris. You know she always loved fashion."

"Sucks you guys aren't tight anymore. I was always a little jealous you had an older sibling," I admitted.

We lapsed into silence as we ate our tacos. I could feel her pulling away from me with each second we weren't speaking and I didn't like it.

"So, what'd you think?" I asked as we started piling up the trash on the tray. "Pretty amazing stuff, am I right?"

"Not bad," Charlie responded with a shrug, for once letting me hold the door for her without any kind of backlash.

"What?" I exclaimed. "Are you insane? Those are the best freaking tacos you're going to find!" I bumped her shoulder with mine as we walked to the car.

"Don't lie to me, *Charlotte*," I scolded, walking backwards in front of her and wagging my finger in her face.

Finally, Charlie laughed and raised her hands. "You win. That was the best taco I've had in a long time."

"I see you're learning," I said, standing tall and looking down on her tiny five-foot-five frame. "It's pointless to argue."

She rolled her eyes. "Let's go, almighty one," she said, as she ducked into the car. The tension from the restaurant had dissipated, and for that, I was grateful.

54

I climbed into the driver's seat and grinned at her as I buckled my seat belt.

"We will go, but not home. Not yet."

***

"No, no, no!" Charlie groaned, smacking the top of the pinball machine. It was the most animated I'd seen her.

I tossed quick glances over my shoulder as I continued crushing Heihachi in Tekken 3.

"Need another quarter?" I yelled over the music and video game sounds coming from every corner of Up-Down.

I jumped when her hand snaked around my waist to grab the tokens I'd lined up across the lip of the machine, losing my advantage in the game.

"Nope," she said, a full grin on display as I almost died — both literally and figuratively. I was smacking buttons and swearing as I bumped her with my hip.

"Move, you wretched woman. If I die, I'm coming for you!" I kept thumping buttons and eventually caught the perfect leg sweep/super punch combination to take Heihachi out.

"Yes!" I yelled when the level ended. I turned to Charlie, who was sipping a Dr Pepper. "Winning!" I pumped one fist in the air.

She shook her head and went back to the bay of pinball machines. It was almost a strut. I couldn't take my eyes off her hips or the way her jeans clung to her butt — a butt she never used to have, and one I should not be noticing. In the darkness of the arcade, she was different. She was relaxed and the last thing I needed to do was ruin a moment when we were finally being just us.

I brought my eyes up right before she turned back to me and asked, "How are we even in here? This is an over twenty-one place, isn't it?"

Up-Down was a grownup paradise. All the old arcade games but with a full bar. It was packed most nights, which I only knew because it was one of the places I took care of in the early mornings.

"I know a guy," I said as I forced my eyes back to Tekken and the start of a new fight.

"You 'know a guy'," she mimicked with full on air quotes I caught in my peripheral.

I had to laugh. "I actually do. Mike is a pretty cool guy. I work for him and he knows I won't break the rules. He lets me come in and game before they open, and I asked him if we could come in today. Just don't tell all your friends!"

"Not to worry, your secret is safe with me," she responded, smacking the pinball controls.

We both continued to play our separate games — her sticking to pinball, Pac-Man and Skee-Ball, while I owned some Mario Kart, Mortal Kombat and Street Fighter.

Once I shut everything back down and washed our glasses, we climbed the stairs from Up-Down to the street level and squinted against the sunlight.

"Come on," I said, grabbing her wrist and pulling her around the corner. I let go quickly, but smiled to myself when she didn't automatically pull away.

We walked up toward Raygun and I was shocked to learn Charlie had never heard of the iconic T-shirt store that managed to make fun of everyone so well, they barely offended anyone.

"You have to see these shirts. I can't do it justice, so you have to read them yourself," I assured as Charlie looked thoroughly skeptical.

"I don't understand how you haven't heard of these shirts. Celebrities buy them. They make fun of every major happening, especially anything that happens in the Midwest. Kiss me I'm Iowish? Des Moines Hell Yes? Everybody knows those."

Charlie shook her head. "I never got back into social media and don't really watch the news. It's all negative crap, and who really needs to know which celebrities are sleeping together? And they call themselves journalists," she huffed.

"Fair enough," I replied, laughing. I'd never been much into social media either, barring my random searches to see if she'd actually pop up. I hadn't even gotten a smartphone until I started working at the bar and could afford the bill myself.

As we approached the first window display for Raygun, I deviated. Sitting just off to the corner on the sidewalk was a small, standup piano. It was covered in bright pink and teal paint, geometric shapes that varied from side to side, and just above the keys, "Play Me" was scrawled in black. Des Moines recently started a public piano project and pianos decorated by local artists of varying shapes and sizes were situated throughout downtown.

I sat down on the bench and looked back at Charlie, who appeared somewhere between scared and intrigued. It was exactly what I'd hoped she'd look like. She ran from music faster than any other topic we broached and I wanted to see if our music might change anything for her. I tipped my head toward the piano and didn't wait for her. I started to play, the chords erupting from the piano. It was a little off key, but that didn't matter. At the appropriate time, I started to sing.

We both knew the words by heart. Oasis was just one of many nineties albums we'd obsessed over and this was her favorite — it was our favorite. I finished the first stanza, the last few lines building like the ache in my chest. This wasn't all about me getting to her. Selfishly, this was also about me. It was about the fact that I'd thought about her every day I'd been gone.

I felt Charlie come up behind me and then watched her circle to the front of the piano. As I continued, she rested her hands on the top and closed her eyes, both hearing and feeling the strains. It was her position any time I sat on the bench instead of her.

I continued to sing as I worried the fire in her heart was actually out. There were moments I caught tiny pieces of her — a look, an old catchphrase — but then she hid from me again. Charlie didn't understand that so much of who I was started with her. She was solid ground amidst the earthquake of my childhood. She remembered days I struggled to believe had even been real.

I paused, closed my eyes and waited. Like the answer to a prayer, her low soprano picked up right where I left off. She was quiet at first, her voice soft, but it built as she went on. Opening my eyes, I watched her; I'd always loved watching her sing. The slight sway of her body and the way she gave herself over entirely to the music was magical. She was art come to life. She was beautiful.

The sun was at her back and Charlie glowed from the inside out. She was truly stunning and in that moment, a switch flipped inside me I never knew was there to begin with.

I wondered how true the lyrics were for her. There were so many unsaid words between us, the stories we each could tell…who knew where we should, or could, even start.

It was my turn again. We'd sung this together a thousand times and the tradeoff was automatic.

My brown eyes locked on Charlie's now open green ones. There were people gathered around us, but it didn't matter. This mattered — the excited flush in her cheeks, the brightness in her eyes and the breeze ruffling her hair while she licked her lips and filled her diaphragm to sing. This was all that mattered.

Would I save her? The words floated toward me. Her exhales were my inhales. Silent questions and answers bounced between us.

Could we save each other? I had to believe it wasn't too late, that we could still get through anything together.

For the last chorus of *Wonderwall*, I joined her. Our voices matched perfectly; they always had. Mine low, where she was high. Our harmony was spot on and I felt the goosebumps rise up my arms and down my back.

The last chord faded and a slow smile crept over my face. The crowd clapped, but Charlie froze. The happiness she'd exuded for the last four minutes was gone. Her eyes filled with tears and her fingers gripped the edge of the piano, her knuckles white. She wouldn't look at me. She opened her mouth and closed it a few times, but said nothing.

I pushed back the bench and stood, but before I could say anything, she ran. Like a bolt of lightning, she broke through the crowd and took off down Grand Avenue.

It took me a full block to catch her as I berated myself for pushing too hard. She was crossing the street when I finally matched my step to hers. She wasn't full on running anymore, but hugged her arms around herself and walked as quickly as her short legs would carry her.

We walked toward the river in silence, finally stopping on the bridge.

"What happened back there?"

She sniffled, her eyes never shifting from the water. It rushed by in a hurry with no true destination, so much like the two of us. How could we possibly know what the future would bring when we were so busy running from our pasts?

Finally, after a few very long minutes, she whispered, "Desperate times." Between the river and passing cars, the words were barely audible.

I turned, put my back against the stone rail and looked up. Giant puffy clouds made their way across the sky as fear slid down my spine. While sometimes used as an inside joke, those words in this context actually meant this was much worse than I ever expected. Charlie clutched the edges of the rail with the same desperation as the piano.

I reached my left hand out and let it rest on her forearm. She flinched, but didn't pull away. Her eyes came to mine. They were filled, but no tears fell. I traced my way up to her hand and pulled her fingers away from the stone one at a time. Interlacing mine with hers, I finally responded, "Desperate measures, right?"

She nodded, the first tear trailing down her cheek as she bit into her bottom lip to stop it from trembling.

I reached out and wiped the tear away, leaving my hand in its place.

"I'm here, Charlie. And I'm not going anywhere. When you're ready, we'll talk about it. Until then, we won't. Okay?" I wouldn't push her like this again.

Closing her eyes, she leaned into my palm, and it took everything I had to stay where I was and not pull her to me.

"You're here now," she murmured. The words were so soft, but they gutted me all the same. It confirmed my worst fear: something terrible happened when I wasn't.

CHAPTER

eight

"You two get the popcorn, we'll get the seats," Sam suggested.

"Done," I agreed. I felt a hand on my butt and swiveled to find Darcy shoving a twenty in my back pocket. She blew me a kiss and took off behind Sam, cackling the entire way at my obvious discomfort.

I shook my head as I dug out the bill and my wallet.

"I think she's certifiable," I said to Charlie as she scoped out the candy selection.

"She certainly is something, but I love her." She chuckled to herself as I leaned in, my face right next to hers.

"You know you want the Sour Patch Kids," I whispered.

"Is that so?"

"You always want the Sour Patch Kids," I affirmed.

"You know, it is possible my tastes have changed since we saw the last Twilight movie," she argued.

I stuck my tongue out at her, which got me another chuckle. Since the piano incident, my only goal was to make Charlie smile. I hadn't brought up what happened and I didn't ask questions. All I focused on was rebuilding our friendship and giving her a place she felt comfortable. The less I pushed, the less she pushed me away...so far, at least. When Darcy and Sam suggested hitting the movies tonight to see The Martian, I was shocked when I only barely had to prod her into it.

"What can I get for you guys?" the high school kid behind the counter asked.

I straightened and stepped forward to order. "Two large popcorns, one large Sprite, one large Dr. Pepper, annnd..." I waited for Charlie to make her selection.

She groaned, and said, "Fine, yes, I want the Sour Patch Kids."

I held in my laugh, but couldn't stop my "told you so" expression, which earned me a pop in the shoulder I was more than willing to take. Charlie's reaction to us singing together that day had shocked me at first and still worried me even now, but it also broke down the barrier she'd been trying to keep in place between us. We'd walked away from the bridge that day and had communicated in some way every day since.

The kid put our popcorn on the counter and Charlie reached out to grab both bins. I snagged her hand mid-air and turned her to face me.

"Don't forget, I meant what I said, Charlie. I'll be here for you whenever you need me from now on," I said, holding her fingers in mine.

She shifted and her eyes darted left then right before coming back to mine. "I may never be ready." Surprisingly, it wasn't indignant, just a statement.

"You may never be, you're right," I agreed. "And maybe we need to handle this like every other passive aggressive millennial out there and communicate via text message to be comfortable talking about what's happening. However it needs to go down, I'm here."

"Why do you have to be so optimistically persistent?"

"Why do you have to be so adorably stubborn?"

Charlie gave me a toothy smile. "Part of my charm, I guess."

"Can your charming self grab about a hundred napkins so Darcy doesn't use poor Sam's fancy new hipster jeans as her napkin like she did last time? I think he was on the phone with his mom for a solid half hour discussing how best to get the grease and butter out. I can't handle a reprise."

We both laughed as we collected our goodies and headed toward our theater.

Just before we stepped inside, Charlie turned back and looked up at me.

"Thank you."

It was the last thing I expected and I couldn't even muster a response before she pulled open the door and disappeared into the darkness.

***

I dumped the dirty mop water into the mop sink, trying my best to keep the alcohol stink from splattering my jeans and glasses. As I refilled the mop bucket with clean water to finally tackle the bathrooms — AKA the worst part — my phone vibrated in my pocket.

"It's five a.m., what the heck?" I said to the empty bar. I scrambled to wipe my hands on the clean towel tucked into my back pocket and dug my phone out to find Charlie's name on the screen.

Charlie: Are you awake?

Trevor: Yep, at work. Why are you awake?

Charlie: Can't sleep.

Trevor: I can't believe Darcy isn't up playing hacky sack with her soccer ball.

Charlie: Her and Sam were up late studying for Econ.

I was pondering an appropriately sarcastic response to make fun of our roommates for becoming the other half of our platonic double dates when a new message brightened the screen.

Charlie: Have you written any new songs lately?

"Yeah and they're all about you. Because that's not weird — or new."

Embarrassed, though there was no one around to see it, I shoved my phone in my pocket and turned the water back on. Steam rose from the mop bucket as I squirted soap and sanitizer in and waited for it to fill. Today I was cleaning the Royal Mile, which was owned by one of Mike's buddies. It was a European pub decked out in all dark wood, dim lighting and beer signage. Darcy and Sam would love this place. It was a haven for soccer fans to sing their loudest, most crude European chants during matches.

"Oh, screw it," I said to myself, quickly twisting the handles back to off and grabbing a stool from the bar. I sat down, got my phone out and told myself again this was going to be good for us.

Trevor: As a matter of fact, I have. But I'll only show you mine if you show me yours.

I waited as the little ellipses told me she was typing.

65

Charlie: Okay.

My hands shook slightly and my chest tightened. Reminding myself vulnerability went both ways, I typed in the words.

Trevor: She's like an Indian summer
A soft, warm breeze across your skin
Then, just as quickly, the leaves start falling
And she's gone again.

She's the rhythm my heart beats to
Her exhales the breath in my lungs
Yet she doesn't understand
The hole she's filled or what she's done.

For a time, I thought I could do it
I could stand against this world on my own
But now she's here and I've realized
Without her I'll never be whole.

My thumb hovered over the send button. There was no going back from this. But…truth was truth, and while I wanted to help Charlie through whatever happened to her, I couldn't deny the build between us.

I quickly hit the button, locked my phone and went back to work. She would either respond or she wouldn't, but I had one hour left, both bathrooms to clean and a fridge to stock.

Ten minutes. Twenty minutes. Finally, at the half hour mark, just as I talked myself into the fact that she thought I was a psychopath, it vibrated.

I almost dropped the case of bottles trying to balance it against the bar with one hip while I pulled my phone from the opposite pocket.

Charlie: He is rain drops against brittle petals

Bringing life back into this broken vase
He is a hundred thousand stars
Carrying wishes I've whispered into space.

He is every promise I broke and every lie I told
And he is the only one who sees I don't fit this mold.

I am fractured, I am splintered and I am bruised.
I am me, I am them and I am no longer the girl he knew.
But she fights and she claws and she refuses to give
Because he came and he laughed and he made her live.

I read and reread her words a dozen times. She was coming back to me and there were so many ways I could respond.

Trevor: We are seriously angsty, aren't we?

Lightweight sarcasm was always a solid approach.

Charlie: We are indeed.

I let the conversation sit while I locked up, but as soon as the keys were in my coat pocket, my phone was out again.

Trevor: You know it doesn't matter, right? You are who you are and whoever you are is the person I want you to be. I've always just wanted you to be happy.

Again, I waited for her response. With my car running, I sat and stared at the screen.

A single heart appeared. And that was all I needed to spend the rest of the day smiling.

CHAPTER
nine

October

I wound my way through the stacks of books and rows of tables until I found her tucked into a corner sitting sideways in an overstuffed chair. Her hair in a ponytail and her legs kicked over the armrest, Charlie was engrossed in the book in her lap. She chewed on the end of her highlighter and scowled at the text, not noticing my approach.

I took a quick right and came around behind her, holding my breath until my face was just to the left of hers before I whispered, "Boo!"

Charlie yelped and jumped out of the chair. Her book and highlighter went flying, notepaper sailed across the dingy maroon carpet and she was too busy trying to breathe to yell at me. Both her hands clutched at her heart as I fell into the empty chair and lost it.

"You...you...*asshole*," she hissed once she could function again. My shoulders shook with my not-so-quiet laughter. I should have been watching though, because she came at me with her textbook like she was swinging a baseball bat. I hopped out of the chair and we did a strange little dance where she kept swinging and I kept evading until I dove for her, knocking the textbook to the floor as I wrapped one hand around both her wrists. From there, I twisted her around until her back was to my front.

Charlie squirmed and shimmied in my arms, wriggling around in a way I kept telling myself not to like. I also told myself I wasn't holding onto her just so she'd keep doing it.

I was lying on both accounts.

Finally, the librarian came around the corner. He glared and told us to get our act together or get out. I let Charlie go, ducking my head and stooping to the ground to start picking up her notes. She mumbled an apology and dropped down beside me, using her ponytail as a curtain between the librarian and us.

"You got us in trouble," she grumbled at me as he huffed in irritation before walking away.

I grabbed a handful of paper and stood. "You never used to mind a little trouble if it was worth it," I teased.

Her cheeks tinged pink as she snagged the pages from my hand and started to shuffle them back in order. "You were supposed to be here a half hour ago," she scolded.

Just at the corner of her mouth was a swipe of yellow highlighter and my guess was she'd tried to chew on the wrong end. Instead of responding to her question, I reached toward her. She stilled but didn't recoil as I closed the short distance between us and gently rubbed over the spot.

She looked confused, so I said, "Highlighter," except it was more of a whispered exhale. I was acutely aware of how light a pink her lips were and how soft her skin felt under the pad of my thumb. I inched closer and her lips parted, drawing in a short breath. My hand cupped her cheek as my eyes traced her face, edges and angles so known to me but an entirely new landscape.

When I looked into Charlie's eyes, there were questions I couldn't answer, but something new as well — intrigue. She looked as confounded by what I'd done as I was, but just as I wasn't stopping myself, she also wasn't trying to stop me.

With a small smile, I stepped backward and broke contact before the moment was ruined in some other way. "I'm sorry I'm late," I apologized. "I ran into Professor Davis in the FAC and we were talking about my music theory assignment."

She nodded, bringing one hand up to her face where mine had just been.

"It's fine. Should we study?" she asked, her tone distracted.

"Yeah, we probably should. Want me to quiz you from your notes?" We'd met in the library every night this week and I knew she had a test tomorrow. At the mention of it, Charlie snapped out of the haze I was desperately trying to hold onto.

"That would be great. All this structure of the Government stuff is baffling."

She had so quickly become someone I needed again, though the scope of that need was still undetermined.

Throwing her backpack over her shoulder, Charlie pointed toward a study room. "We could..." she started, then stopped, pivoting on her heel and heading the opposite way. "We should sit at the tables. Yes, the tables are better."

I followed her, not saying anything but grinning the whole way.

***

"You guys are going to the party, right?" Darcy asked.

Sam and I followed her and Charlie into Mars Café. I needed caffeine so badly. Between work, class, homework, practice and trying to spend time with Charlie, I was exhausted. They wanted me at the piano four hours a day and I was lucky to get in two. I was worried the professors were going to realize that while I had the talent, I lacked the passion for performance.

My mom hadn't called to do anything other than berate me for not coming over for dinner since I paid their electric bill, but I knew it wouldn't last. She'd been sober for fifteen days — or so she said. If she was, I had about five more days before she relapsed, and I was taking full advantage of the quiet.

"I don't know," I said at the same time Sam said, "Of course we're going."

"Sam, while I know you love the Sigmas, I don't know if I have a frat party in me." I pulled off my glasses and rubbed my eyes.

"The whole school is coming to this party. It isn't like we're actually hanging out with the Sigmas," Sam argued. "Besides, not all of them are utter and total douche canoes. For example, look at me." He stretched his arms wide to go with his sarcastic smirk.

My head dropped back and I groaned.

"You guys are like a couple," Charlie said, laughing. I snorted in rebuttal, which only brought on another giggle. I lived to make her laugh lately.

"I'm just trying to get Mr. Old Man over here to do something fun. Because, you know, we're in college and you're supposed to have fun," Sam chided, swiping his hair out of his eyes and pulling on the popped collar of his polo. He'd been trying to dress better, but hadn't quite found his style. Currently he looked like a chubby golfer, which was a significant upgrade from Hollister Hobbit. But who was I to judge when my entire wardrobe consisted of jeans and superhero T-shirts?

"Fun is defined by the person having it, my overbearing friend. I have lots of fun," I said, winking at Charlie before turning to the counter to order a large Americano.

"Riiiight," Darcy cut in. "You and Char have all kinds of fun doing homework in the library."

"Homework, yeah," Sam added, "that's exactly what they're always doing."

That earned him a smack to the back of the head from me and an elbow in the gut from Charlie.

I looked down at Charlie and raised my eyebrow, requesting an opinion on the party. She sighed, then shrugged, her eyes flicking toward them before giving a slight nod.

I interpreted her gesture and added a sigh of my own. "Fine, we'll go,"

We all slid into a booth, Sam and Darcy grinning at each other while Charlie and I shared a wary look.

"Now, the real question is should we do a group costume?" Darcy asked. Immediately, Sam jumped in and the conversation took a turn I couldn't stomach.

"Costumes?" I mock-whispered across the table to Charlie, propping my cheek on my fist. "Why do there have to be costumes?"

"Perhaps because they're required for a Halloween party?" she replied, suppressing a smile. "Besides, I'm sure your old Spiderman costume still exists. It isn't like you've outgrown super heroes." She pointed at my Flash T-Shirt and gave in to the snort of laughter she'd been holding back.

"Are you going to be Mary Jane again?" I asked, leaning in, not hiding my hope for the affirmative.

"I only wanted to be Mary Jane because she was a singer."

"Mmmhmmm, so you say. But if you want to hold my hand again the whole night, I won't stop you."

Charlie escaped into her latte, but I saw the flush in her cheeks. We kept dancing around the change we both felt and the more she warmed up, the more satisfying her reactions to my flirting were.

"I'll tell you what," I offered, "you decide what you want to be, and I'll come up with something that complements it."

"Won't that look like we're there together?" she countered, looking over my shoulder.

"Won't we be there together?" I shifted in my seat until she was forced to look at me.

"But as friends."

"If friends is what you want, then we'll be there as friends."

"I just…I don't want to…" she fumbled over her words until I interjected.

"You don't want to mess things up and neither do I. So, we won't. Friends?" I extended my right hand.

She looked down at it and then back up at me, tilting her head in question. I lifted my eyebrows and smirked.

"Friends," she said, slapping her right palm to mine. We smacked palms twice, flipped our hands, smacked the backs together twice and then fist-bumped.

We both fell back against the booth laughing while Darcy and Sam looked on utterly confused, which was the exact reaction we wanted from other kids growing up. The secret handshake had returned, but she didn't know my fingers were crossed behind my back.

CHAPTER

ten

"Are you sure four more people will actually fit in here?"
I yelled through the crowd toward Sam, who was dressed
up as Samwise Gamgees.

From his layered homeless look on top, complete
with a saucepan tied to his cross-body bag, to the flipper-
like Hobbit feet worn over his shoes, he looked every bit
of Frodo's sidekick. Sam nodded and yelled something
back toward me, but I'd never know what it was.

Charlie was between us as we cut through the
crowd, but she stayed close to me. She looked back, her
features pinched and eyes darting around the room.
Throngs of people were packed into the house, sweat and
booze permeating the air. I wasn't overly comfortable
myself and damn sure wouldn't be leaving Charlie's side
since she'd gone with nineties Gwen Stefani as her
costume. This wasn't the first time I'd seen her in tight
pants tucked into combat boots, a cropped tank over a
sports bra and her hair pulled into tiny knots all over her
head, but it was the first time her sports bra was
necessary, her pants left nothing to the imagination and

her bare stomach seriously tested my ability to keep my hands to myself.

Darcy appeared out of nowhere, her floor-length white gown meant to make her Galadriel the elf. Instead, it reminded me of that girl from Frozen. She yanked us into a corner where there was some room to breathe and shoved a flask toward Charlie. Charlie started to shake her head, but Darcy wouldn't have it, her long blonde hair down around her shoulders swaying back and forth with each twist.

"Come on, Char," she whined. "Can you pretend you don't have a giant stick up your butt just for tonight? Because I know you're fun and it's okay if other people know it, too." Clearly, Darcy had more than a few sips before now, but even mildly insulted, Charlie never could turn down a challenge.

I hid my smile, turning to look over my shoulder so I could come back straight-faced. Charlie's eyes were narrowed, but she was already mid-swallow, just as I knew she'd be. Two gulps and the coughing ensued.

She gripped my bicep, still coughing, as she passed the flask to me. I lifted it in salute and dropped my head back. The smell hit before the taste and the Fireball skimmed my throat down to my stomach.

"A warm hug, right?" Darcy grinned as she popped back another shot and passed it to Sam, who pulled a fifth of the same from his bag.

"Ah! I knew we were friends for a reason!" She wrapped an arm around Sam and smacked a kiss to his cheek. He grinned and they clicked containers in cheers. The song changed and Darcy squealed before almost throwing the flask at Charlie and dragging Sam toward the dance floor.

"Are you sure you're cool?" I asked.

Charlie shrugged. "It isn't like I haven't had alcohol before. I'm pretty sure I don't remember most of sophomore year."

I opened my mouth to ask what she was talking about when she shoved the flask toward me. "Drink. Just drink with me. I want to have fun. I never have fun. And you only barely have fun. Are we anti-fun?"

The tip of the flask was red where it was pressed against her lips — lips I wanted to be pressed against. The baseline was thumping in my head, along with my erratic heartbeat.

"We are *not* anti-fun." I took another drink and we passed the flask back and forth until it was gone.

I dropped it into the pocket of my vintage Gavin-looking cardigan just as an old school Ja Rule song started playing. We looked at each other and burst out laughing.

"Do you remember when I taught you how to dance?" she asked, a mischievous grin on her face as she looked up at me from under her lashes.

"Of course." I was thirteen and knew exactly how to dance, not that I told her that.

"You were so terrible," she laughed, her hand on my arm, lingering longer than usual. "I had to stand in front of you and put your hands on my hips. For all the music you could play, you couldn't find a beat to save your life."

The memories were still vivid. Her short black skirt, Tragic Kingdom T-shirt and the same boots she was wearing now. We'd danced to the same handful of songs for a solid hour. I had to force myself off beat just so she'd pull me closer, berating me the whole time, while I smiled from behind her.

"I appreciate the vote of confidence. Shall we see who has what skill now?" I challenged as I held out my hand.

She eyed me, her chin coming up.

"If you're afraid, that's okay," I teased.

Charlie brushed my hand away and strutted toward the floor just as Ed Sheeran came on. The bassline of *Bloodstream* was distinct. Even through the building buzz and shitty speakers, I knew it right away.

I let her walk away from me, content to simply watch, for now. As much as I wanted to take command of the moment, she was still hesitant and I wanted these changes to be her choice.

Charlie didn't turn back to me. She found a small space and started to move. It was a flow that began with her shoulders and melted down to her hips. Her arms moved out wide, as if she were conducting the piece with her fluid movements, punctuating the drums with her hips while the music beat in her veins. Her head dropped back and it was too much to be so far from her, to not be touching her.

Quick steps brought me within inches. I rested my hands on her hips, my fingertips skimming the fabric, and hers landed on top of them, squeezing before reaching back out and up. Her feet didn't move, but no other part of her stayed still. I skimmed my fingertips up the sides of her abdomen, feeling her ribs as she stretched her arms high overhead. I continued, my hands trailing up her arms until they reached hers. Our fingers intertwined and she pulled me toward her, closing the final few inches between us, locking our hands together.

Her hips were a constant figure eight, increasing as the song picked up and slowing when Ed decreased the tempo. She controlled the exchange, her back pressed against my chest. I moved with her, easily keeping her rhythm and forcing a few of my own adjustments as the song overtook me as well.

My eyes closed and I tasted cinnamon as he sang about the chemicals burning. Charlie pressed herself back against me, her weight still in her toes as she moved. Her head dropped back on my shoulder and she brought our joined hands down to her hips as the song hit the crescendo.

"Tell me when it kicks in," she sang as she danced, the movements punctuated — hard hits of her hips, her torso swaying left then pulling right. My hands gripped her as we leaned into each other. I sang with her, my mouth next to her ear. I sang until the lyric disappeared from my mind and all I could think about was Charlie and how close she was to me.

She stilled briefly, then turned her head to expose her throat. I seized the opportunity, tasting the salt from her sweat and feeling the softness of her skin. Her relaxation — the fact that she not only gave me permission but encouraged me to take this step — was a win. I took the moment for myself just as much as for her, trailing a line of kisses across her shoulder. But then Rihanna started squawking some unintelligible pop song and the spell was broken for both of us.

Charlie turned around and looked at me, her eyes full of something I'd never seen before: desire. That same desire had me seconds from lifting her off the ground and kissing her senseless. I took a small step forward when Sam jumped between us, his attempt to dance looking more like a seizure.

"Don't you love this song?" he yelled, throwing his hands in the air. "I love this song!" We couldn't help but laugh with him.

"That, or you love Fireball," I countered, my eyes on Charlie. Her tongue slowly grazed her lips and I had to look away.

He paused, squinting his bloodshot eyes thoughtfully before a grin broke out. "It also could be that I love Fireball."

"I LOVE FIREBALL!" Darcy whipped into the mix, her white dress already stained with who knows what. She grabbed Charlie's hands and dragged her farther out onto the dance floor. Charlie gave me an apologetic smile over her shoulder as she disappeared into the crowd.

***

I wrapped Gavin's old man cardigan around Charlie's shoulders and shivered a little at the change in temperature from inside.

"Do you think they'll miss us?"

"Nah, those two had enough Fireball for all four of us."

She giggled and took a wobbly step.

"Charlotte, are you drunk?" I teased, my hand at her elbow.

More giggles.

"No," she lied, losing the battle to stop her laughter. "Of course not. But, are you?"

"Maybe."

"You are, aren't you?" she accused, stopping and peering up at me.

"I just might be. You'll never know."

She huffed. "I know we only got drunk twice, but I never could tell with you."

I rested my forearms on her shoulders and leaned down so we were nose to nose. "There are lots of things you couldn't tell."

"I know you wanted to kiss me," she blurted out.

"Is that so?"

"Back there, I knew you wanted to kiss me. I wanted you to, you know. But you never *actually* kissed me, on the lips," she said, tapping two of her fingers to her bright red lips.

I leaned back a little, trying to tame my frantic pulse and ignore every impulse screaming to give her exactly what she wanted.

"I wanted to actually kiss you," I finally said. "But I won't, not yet."

Her bottom lip popped out and she crossed her arms in a full-on sulk. Sulking shouldn't have made me want to kiss her more, but it did.

"Why? That's dumb, Trevor."

"Don't call me Trevor. And it isn't dumb," I convinced myself for the tenth time in as many seconds.

"Wanna know why?" I asked, needing to keep my mouth doing something other than kissing her.

"Not really."

Reaching out with both hands, I put one on each of her cheeks and leaned in until my lips were only millimeters from hers. I felt each warm puff of air she exhaled and both loved and hated myself for what I was about to *say* instead of *do*.

"It isn't dumb because the first time I *really kiss you*, we will both be sober and you'll be the one who asks me to. I won't need Fireball, Ed Sheeran or anything else. *You* will choose *me*, Charlie, and it will be the best moment in either of our lives."

The only sound was her cinnamon-scented exhales.

"Do you believe me?"

She nodded, her eyes never leaving mine.

"Why do you do this?" she asked.

"Do what?"

"Make me feel things and question things and make me wonder why I'm doing all this? Why do you care so much and make me care so much and make me miss you when you're gone?" She squinted up at me, her anger outweighed by exasperation.

"Because our lives have been tied together since we were kids and I've been making decisions with you in mind for as long as I can remember. I miss *you* when you're gone and *you* make *me* feel things. Why do *you* do that?"

"I...I don't mean to. You're just...part of me," she sputtered.

"And you are part of me." I stepped to her side and crooked my elbow.

"For the record, Trev, I'm forgetting this whole not kissing thing ever happened," she said, sighing dramatically as she looped her arm through mine.

"Good luck with that."

CHAPTER

eleven

November

"Florida."

"Hawaii."

"North Carolina."

"Maine."

We lay on the floor of Charlie's dorm room, a bowl of popcorn between us and a movie we weren't watching in the background as we alternated places we'd rather be than going home for Thanksgiving tomorrow. The easy comfort of the conversation was both reassuring and frustrating. Charlie acted more like her old self every day, but gave me no inkling as to why she deviated to start with.

"Maine?" Charlie sat up to throw a piece of popcorn across the divide, missing my mouth completely.

"I like crab cakes," I explained. "And Adirondack chairs. Well, I've never sat in one, but they look cool as shit."

She laughed, which made me laugh.

"You don't talk about your parents," she commented. Out of nowhere topic changes weren't new, but I didn't want to talk about this particular topic. Not with three voicemails sitting on my phone from the last two days and God knows what situation to deal with.

"Neither do you." I rolled onto my side and propped my head in my hand. "Do they still not get you? Is that why I haven't seen your guitar?"

Charlie stared at the ceiling for a good minute. "Yeah."

"Do you miss music?"

She sighed. "Yeah, but I didn't realize how much until…well, you."

"What do you miss most?" I couldn't help myself.

"The way I didn't feel so alone when I was playing. It didn't matter if it was the piano or the guitar, the notes wrapped around me—a buffer between me and whatever was going on in the world."

"We could write together, you know. We were good at it. I still have all our old stuff."

Her eyes widened, then crinkled at the corners. "Of course you do. You don't throw anything away."

"Untrue! I don't throw anything *of value* away." She tipped her head in agreement.

"Charlie?"

"Yeah, Trev?" She kept my gaze, but responded hesitantly.

"Why are you a Poli Sci major?"

Like a light switch, she shut off. Charlie rolled to her back, stilling for a split second before she stood.

"You should probably go," she said as she yanked the blanket from the floor and started tossing the pillows back onto the beds.

"Why?"

"Because, it's late, and you should."

"Not happening."

"I don't want to talk about it. You said I didn't have to talk about it."

"I did," I agreed, finally standing up. "Two months ago, and I haven't brought it up, but neither have you. I didn't forget what 'desperate times' means to us. I didn't forget the nights my parents got stoned with their artist friends and you snuck me into your bedroom so we could write songs and I could forget about the shit show that was my life. And I didn't forget how your mom always guilted you for not being more like Katie and the time I found you in our fort, crying because she shredded your favorite vintage Matchbox Twenty T-shirt.

"Don't you get it, Charlie?" I asked. "I hate seeing you like this, all deer in a headlight, looking at me like I killed your puppy or I'm going to break your heart. I'm not here to hurt you, I'm here to help you. I'm here to do what I've been doing my whole life...what you've been doing your whole life. We save each other. *We* are the desperate measures — together. But you have to trust me."

"I don't need to be saved and you can't break my heart," she said slowly, backing away from me.

"I don't want to be saved," she continued, her head shaking back and forth. "I can't help you. I can't help anyone. I'm going to drive home next week and spend the holiday with two people who will barely speak to me except to ask me what my grades are and remind me I won't reach my full potential until I pass the bar. My mother will hyper-analyze everything I put on and my father will pretend—"

She snapped her mouth closed, taking a quick, deep breath and shaking her head. "It doesn't matter. It doesn't matter what either of them will do. I can't stay here and I don't want to be there. But, off to Pella I will go and miserable I will stay."

"Pella? How long have you lived in Pella?"

She closed her eyes, her lips pressed together and fingers tapping out notes on her thigh. "Since junior year."

"You've been an hour from me for two years. I can't believe that," I mumbled, snatching my glasses off and pushing a hand back through my hair.

"And why is this all on you?" I continued, shoving down the anger and trying to find a calmer middle ground again. "I mean, I'm guessing Katie isn't coming back from Paris just for Thanksgiving, but won't you guys have your aunts and uncles over?"

Her rigid posture remained. "She won't come home for Christmas either. And they don't really come around much anymore. Too long of a drive just for dinner."

"Then just don't go. You don't have to. It's just a day filled with dry turkey and canned cranberry sauce. It's not like your mom can cook. There is nothing to look forward to, so just stay with me." It didn't matter that I had no idea where we would stay.

She looked over my head, her eyes closing again as a sad smile tilted across her face. "I can't. Thank you, but I have to go. I just have to. And I need you to leave it alone."

I studied her while her eyes were closed. Charlotte was back. In front of me, Charlie had just wilted, all the vibrancy and life gone, a desolate shell of buried pain left in her wake.

She finally opened her eyes and we stared at each other.

"Want to come to my practice session?" I blurted out.

"What?"

"I need to practice. They want me on the piano four hours a day and I don't usually have time. But you could come to the FAC and tell me how much I suck. It might help me focus. My technique needs work. It always needs work."

"I don't know..."

"You said you missed music, so just come with me. You can pick the pieces if you want, or just sit in the corner and listen. I won't talk and you won't have to." In that moment, nothing mattered more than getting her into that room and wrapping her in the protection my music could provide.

"I...I guess."

"The piano won't bite. Don't look so terrified."

She sighed. "The piano isn't what I'm worried about."

***

I sat on the front half of the bench, my arms as relaxed as they could be, elbows higher than the keys. The posture was ingrained in me. It was so default, I found myself sitting at cafeteria tables that way.

Charlie sat on a stool in the corner of the small room. She looked at me like she knew me but didn't. Like she expected me to either crack a joke I made in eighth grade or peel my head off and reveal my alien core. It was nice to see we both had to work at seeing each other for the people we were now.

I grabbed my glasses and tossed them to the top of the piano. I didn't need to read sheet music for this, I just needed to let it flow. Practicing daily meant it was everything and nothing at all to sit down and let the music pour out. My fingers flew over the keys as I tried to simultaneously remember and forget everything about Charlie.

Finding her was both a blessing and a curse. It was no secret I'd come to want more than just her friendship, but she also reminded me of everything I fought to get away from. I looked at her and saw a potential future built on choices I hadn't wanted to make, but also my unfortunate past. The moments we were just Charlie and Trev were the ones where none of it mattered and I hoped we'd have more of those, for both our sakes.

Schumann's *Fantasie* in C was a constant musical stream of consciousness rendering me incapable of doing two things at once. Each time my mind strayed to the quiet, complicated girl in the corner, my hands demanded my attention.

It slowed down for a brief space and I glanced up to find her leaning against the wall, lost in the sound. The transitions weren't perfect and my pacing wasn't spot on, but it didn't matter. The music surrounded us, a blanket of security from the madness waiting outside.

"Why doesn't music matter to you anymore?" I cut off the song prematurely and the last notes echoed off the walls before fading.

Like a marionette on a string, Charlie snapped upright.

"It isn't that simple," she said, her irritation blatant in her tone. "We don't all have parents who let us do whatever the hell we want."

"Right," I snorted, not intending to come off so annoyed. "Remember my parents? Those delinquents who could barely function, let alone take care of a kid? They never *let* me do anything, they simply didn't give a shit about anything that didn't benefit them directly. So, try again."

Her wall was back up in an instant. Her face went blank for a second and then the mask slid over it. She sat straighter, her chin up as she looked down at me. She was about to say something we would both regret. It was too much. Her here, in this space, not letting me in *again* and passing judgement on things she knew nothing about.

"Jesus, Charlie," I exclaimed. "All this 'I don't need anybody' bullshit is going nowhere with me and I'm not buying this front you've built up. I've always seen right through you and *you are not okay*. Eventually, you're going to stop with all this and tell me why, because I can't do anything for you until you do."

I barely had time to duck before her stool crashed into the soundproofing foam behind me.

"What the f—"

"ENOUGH," she screamed, her face flushed red and eyes wild, her perfect veneer shattered. "I don't understand how you expect me to just be the girl I was four years ago! She's gone. Don't you see, she's *gone*, and she's not coming back because that girl doesn't matter anymore."

I was afraid to move. Charlie stood, deep breaths heaving her chest as her eyes filled. Her arms were still up, where they'd been when she released the stool.

"She can't matter anymore," she whispered.

Her arms lowered to her sides, inch by inch. She backed up until she hit the foam and then slid down the wall. I started to rise, but she threw a hand out.

I sat back down and stayed there, unmoving and ashamed at my outburst.

"*Free Fallin'*," she said quietly, her head tipped back as she looked up at the ceiling.

"I need the guitar."

She nodded, so I stood and moved to the opposite corner where an acoustic guitar was propped.

I grabbed the guitar and stool and made my way to sit in front of her. Charlie's knees were pulled to her chest, her forehead now pressed to the center. Her arms were wrapped around herself so tightly, I wondered how she could breathe, but I heard small sniffles that told me she was not only breathing but trying not to cry.

It wasn't Tom Petty she wanted, but the slow, acoustic version by John Mayer. My fingers plucked over the strings and I closed my eyes. I couldn't sing to crying Charlie. The problem was, this was also my mom's favorite song. I could easily see her, sitting on the old yellow recliner that now looked dirty orange, grinning as she swayed back and forth. She would sing along, first just mouthing the words, but eventually giving in to the pull and singing out loud. She lost herself, just as I did, just as Charlie did, and as I remembered a time that felt so long ago, I berated myself yet again for ever loving music.

The words kept coming and I tried to focus on Charlie, on what she needed. I hit the crescendo of the song and it was everything and too much all at once. How could I ever explain the music that paid my tuition and gave me my only shot at a future was something I hated?

"Why did you stop?" Charlie asked.

"I didn't realize I had," I admitted, feeling my hand flat against the strings and sound hole.

She peered up at me as tears tracked down her cheeks and empathy shone in her eyes.

Her words were choked, but she forced them out. "You understand, don't you? They did it to you, too?" she asked.

"They did what?" I was afraid of what admitting it out loud would do to the focus and drive I tried so hard to maintain.

"Your parents," she said, a fresh tear popping, her green eyes swimming in red. "They took everything beautiful about music and twisted it into something ugly. They stole your soul."

I had no words. For the first time, I felt tears prick the back of my own eyes. I had doggedly pursued music for so long, it was the only thing I knew to do—the only thing I knew I was good at—but she was right. My parents had twisted what was once passion into a monetary gain, an exploitative act that stole my teen years and generated more anxiety than pleasure. Yet, here I was, because I had no idea what else to do.

"I had to force myself to practice, to be ready for this program, but I want to play *for you*. I want to play *our songs*. They were the last time I felt like I knew who I was."

I watched her mouth move, but I didn't need words. Not breaking eye contact, I set down the guitar and crossed the small space between us, sliding down the wall next to Charlie. I turned my hand over, palm up, and held it out to her.

"Desperate times," I whispered, holding her gaze.

She put her hand over mine, intertwining our fingers.

"Desperate measures," she whispered, laying her head on my shoulder.

CHAPTER
twelve

I stood outside the door and debated leaving. After my confession to Charlie, I could hardly stomach the idea of being anywhere near my parents. My insides heaved and swirled while my mind raged, telling me no good could come from this. It was eleven in the morning and I'd already been up for seven hours after getting called in early to help with the night before Thanksgiving madness. I clearly wasn't the only one who needed help dealing with family.

I'd almost convinced myself to leave when the door wrenched open and my father stood in front of me.

"Trevor, don't just stand out there, son. Come in here and help your mother. You know she has no idea what she's doing," he said. His deep baritone should have been warm and inviting. Instead, it was short and clipped.

"And a happy Thanksgiving to you, too, Dad," I muttered as I entered their shabby apartment.

Instantly, a hand was on my chest, pressing me against the wall.

"Do you think you're something now because you're going to some big university with a bunch of rich kids? They don't have half the talent I do. You don't have half the talent I do," he hissed.

One look and it was clear, he was blitzed.

"No, Dad," I recited, monotone. "Of course I don't think I'm anything, especially compared to you. I just want to get a degree so I can get a job. If they want to give me scholarships to play, that's their stupid choice. Obviously, if you'd stayed with music, you'd have already surpassed where I am."

He snorted, the booze on his breath finally making its way to my nostrils. Whiskey. Should make for a good night.

"You wouldn't know shit if it weren't for us. We made sure you had lessons. We gave you every opportunity. If anyone had ever given me the time and effort *and money* we gave you, I'd have made it to Nashville and you probably wouldn't even be here."

"Thank you," I gritted out. "I know how much you sacrificed for me." The words made me want to reach for the bottle myself. He didn't know shit about sacrifice. But he did drop his hand and lumber back to his beat up orange recliner, dropping into it so heavily, I thought the whole thing would collapse beneath him.

I shook my head and made my way through their tiny, dirty living room to the kitchen. My mom stood at the counter, flour all over her shirt. One hand was on her hip and the other held a recipe she was muttering at.

"Hey, Mom," I said. She jolted and turned to me with a surprised smile.

"Hey, baby." I did a quick assessment and found her eyes clear and bright, but her hands slightly trembling. She was still sober, which was shocking.

I put the rolls I brought on the table and hung my coat over a chair.

"What can I help with?"

She blew out an audible breath. "I am attempting a pie crust, but I'm close to throwing in the towel on this. We might be having cinnamon rolls for dessert."

I had to laugh. It was rare to see my mother this way — the way she'd been when I was really young. She used to try new things constantly, always willing to admit when the dish was a disaster and just ordering pizza. Dad and I were always good sports, but it had been a long time since I'd seen her do much more than lift a glass.

"Why don't you let me take a look?" She handed me the recipe, grateful appreciation evident on her face and the peck I got on my cheek.

"Want something to drink?" I stiffened and Mom quickly added, "I made iced tea and lemonade. I wasn't sure which you preferred these days."

"Tea, please, no ice," I forced out, swallowing down the anxiety that had spread like a firework.

She laughed. "Of course, I didn't suddenly forget your strange aversion to ice."

I skimmed the recipe and eyed the ingredients on the counter. Baking wasn't exactly my forte either, but I noticed a key ingredient issue.

She handed me my tea as I explained, "The butter needs to be really cold. I think your problem is you left it on the counter too long. Let's put it in the freezer and start over."

Mom pursed her lips and blew out, rolling her eyes. "Of course. It had to be something that simple." Her dark hair was a mass of curls going in every direction under her red bandana. She'd managed to get flour in it as well, making the dark brown look almost salt and pepper.

Mom went to the corner and turned on the old radio, tuning into an oldies station. She started to hum along with the music as I put the sticks of butter in the freezer and set a timer for fifteen minutes. We re-measured ingredients and checked on the small ham in the oven.

"How are your classes? Do you like your professors?"

I shrugged. "They aren't bad. I have to practice a lot. They want us in the FAC four hours a day, which is rough. But juries are at the end of spring semester and I have to ace them."

Now, it was her turn to shrug. "I can't imagine it would be a problem for you. I'm so proud of you, Trevor. To get into such a great school and play real music."

"Real music?" my father interrupted. Neither of us saw him enter the room. He leaned against the doorframe, his arms crossed and mouth a tight line.

"Come on, Jonathan. You know what I mean," my mother instantly backpedaled. I watched her shrink away from him and anger ignited inside me.

"I know exactly what you mean, Belinda. He's playing Mozart and Bach and all that other shit I've always hated. Pretentious trash no one with real taste likes. You're saying everything I taught him to play, the real greats like Billy Joel and Elton John, was a waste of time." The memory of the hours we used to spend with him patiently teaching me chords, singing along to my butchered versions of his favorite songs, hurt more than his actual words.

"Actually, they want me playing both," I interjected. "I can't just play one style or I won't grow. So, yesterday, I played *Rocket Man* and *Canon* in D." It was a lie, but my father relaxed against the door as he studied me.

"What have you been working on?" I asked as the timer went off and I retrieved the cold butter.

My father started detailing a refinishing project, fully entering the room and taking up a position to my right. He stood directly in front of my mother, making it clear our conversation no longer mattered. She and I connected gazes over his shoulder and she gave me a sad smile before taking a seat at the table. As much as I hated her drinking, in moments like this, I understood it.

***

My father's snores rumbled from the living room. An incessant, sinus-clogged sound I was sure kept the neighbors awake. I could hear their TV through the kitchen wall, so there was no way they didn't hear him.

My mother continued handing me dishes and we silently washed, dried and put them away.

"It was a great meal, Mom. Thank you," I said for the fourth time. It really had been. We'd sorted out the pie crust, the ham was perfect and the pineapple slices were my favorite. She made mashed potatoes, which weren't bad from a box, and her favorite green bean casserole.

"You're so welcome," she gushed. "It's the least I can do. But you look tired, Trevor. Are you getting enough sleep?"

I was tired. I was working every morning of Thanksgiving break to try to get ahead. Finals were looming and I wouldn't have time to work if I wanted to do well.

Charlie was in Pella and while we texted multiple times a day, it wasn't detailed, and I missed seeing her. It was driving me crazy not knowing how she really was or what was happening.

"I'm fine. I'll sleep over Christmas break," I assured her.

"Well, about that," she started, her eyes fixed on the murky dishwater. I inwardly groaned. I had been waiting for the shoe to drop all day.

"Your father may have made some commitments for you," she said, her words barely above a whisper.

"Commitments? Is that what we're calling it these days?" I struggled to maintain my calm and keep my voice low.

"*Trevor*," she tried to scold me, but it wasn't happening. Not today, not if he was pulling this again.

"I won't do it, Mom. Not only is it illegal, but it could get me kicked out of my program."

Dropping her head, her hands gripped the edges of the sink and her elbows were locked. She was humiliation wrapped in pain, weighed down by an abusive, ego-driven asshole she refused to stop loving. We both remembered who he was before he became Jonathan Adler the gambling alcoholic, but the difference was I accepted he wasn't going to revert.

When she looked up at me, I saw the apology before she spoke — this apology and every other apology she'd whispered in my ear as soon as his back was turned.

"You have to, Trevor. You have to do this. Your dad owes money to a lot of people. For his supplies, for bills, for…" she trailed off.

"His gambling debts," I finished.

I swiped my glasses off and pinched the bridge of my nose. I loosened the grip on my glasses, afraid I'd snap them. I couldn't afford to replace them, especially now.

"How much?" That was always the question.

"We need two thousand dollars before the end of December," she replied, defeated.

My head snapped up. "Two thousand dollars?" I exclaimed.

"Shhh." She immediately crept toward the living room and confirmed my father was still passed out. With the amount of whiskey he added to his coffee, I could have led a marching band through our living room, yet she was still scared.

She came back toward me, the pleas already forming on her lips. I held up a hand.

"Just don't," I snapped. "Don't say anything. Don't you dare defend him or remind me how much you helped me. You were supposed to help me. *You had me.* You remember I'm actually *the child* in this dynamic, right? The one you're supposed to protect and help. It's not supposed to be the other way around."

"It's not—"

"No," I interrupted. "It is that simple. It's as simple as both of you getting jobs and being grownups. I can't make two thousand dollars and pass my finals. Do you understand I make ten dollars an hour?"

"Your father booked you some gigs," she started.

"Oh, gigs? Well, that's fancy." I threw my hands in the air.

"These are actually some nice places," she said meekly.

"Nice? Nicer than the strip clubs in Cedar Rapids? Or the dive bars in Iowa City? Or the bar on the East Side where I ended up with stitches after some idiot decided to throw his glass at me because *Brown-Eyed Girl* was his and his ex's song?"

My mother stared at me. Tears brimmed in her eyes and as much as I wanted to hate her, I knew this wasn't her choice and only partially her fault. My help also helped her. I clenched and unclenched my jaw, swallowing words she didn't deserve.

"How long have you been sober?"

She stood a little taller. "Forty-five days. Not one drop in forty-five days."

"You fall off the wagon once in the next month and I'm gone," I stated. "I won't show up for any of the gigs. I'm doing this for you, not him. And I won't do anything for you if you're drunk. Stay sober and look for a job. *Help me.*"

She nodded enthusiastically. "I will. I promise, Trevor. I will stay sober. And I'll go look for jobs starting on Monday after the holiday madness dies down. You're right, I should help, too. We'll do this together. You and I will fix this together. Like a real family." She came toward me, her arms out. I stiffened, but allowed the hug.

I collected my coat and walked through the living room to the front door. Standing at the foot of my father's recliner, I wondered what happened to the man who used to carry me around on his shoulders and why he'd given up on us.

CHAPTER
thirteen

December

I set the coffee cup on the library table and noticed the tremble in my hands. They ached, but like my arms and back, that was nothing new. The realization that this was my fourth cup today had me reaching for a protein bar.

I dug in my backpack until I found my stash. When I looked up, Charlie was standing on the other side of the table.

It was strange how the breakdown in the practice room brought us closer together instead of pushing us apart. Now, it felt like we were on a more level playing field. Neither of our lives were pretty; we were just trying to make it through and it was easier to do that together.

"Hey, stranger," she said, tucking her hair behind her ear.

"Hey," I replied. "Sorry I've been MIA. Finals are kicking my ass. How are you?" I gestured to the chair opposite me and we both sat down.

"Pretty much the same," she said, eyeing my coffee. "My international relations prof seems hell bent on driving me to drink."

"Take the coffee, Charlie," I said with a smirk.

"Oh, thank you, sweet baby Jesus," she gushed, snatching the cup and taking a large swallow. She closed her eyes and I was immediately jealous of her blissful expression. At this point, caffeine wasn't for pleasure, it was sheer survival.

"Are you okay?" she asked, looking harder at me. "You, uh…kind of look like hell, Trev."

"Well, by no means should you sugarcoat it." I raised one eyebrow as I glowered at her. "I have slept exactly nine hours in the last three days. I have two finals tomorrow and have to work at four a.m. I haven't been able to play worth a crap lately and I'm fairly certain I'm close to being kicked out of my program. How are you?"

She slid the coffee cup back toward me. "Welllll, first off, I think you need that more than I do. Second, why are you letting them do this to you?"

We caught up after Thanksgiving and I'd given Charlie a version of what happened, only admitting to the fact that my parents needed some financial help so I had to work some extra hours. From our conversations, I assumed she'd also selectively shared her story, but we were each entitled to our secrets — at least until I had the energy to devote to the excavation of Charlie's past, which wasn't possible right now.

"I can't have this conversation," I said, waving a hand between us. "I appreciate you standing up for me, I really do, but I can only fight one battle at a time. Music theory wins today."

"I actually stopped to tell you it would be fun to hang out this weekend once finals are over. I'm not going back to Pella until Sunday and I, uh…have something for you."

I should not have enjoyed her blushing cheeks and instant shyness as much as I did.

"Charlotte Lydia, did you get me a *Christmas present?*" Her cheeks flushed a deeper red.

"It's not a big deal. Really, it's like, less than a big deal." She tripped over her words, and her backpack, as she rose from the table.

I grinned at her. "It's fine, Charlie. I have something little for you, too. And I want to see you before you leave. But you're back for J-term, right?"

She laughed — a cross between a snort and a sigh. "Of course. There's no way I'd stay with them for more than the three weeks they close down campus. No. Freaking. Way."

I laughed with her, but also dreaded the three weeks I would have to spend with my own parents.

"Then, I'll see you this weekend," I agreed. "Darcy and Sam want to grab dinner Friday night, so how about Saturday night is just you and me?" I had to work a shift in between, but I could sneak a few Red Bulls from the bar to keep me going.

She nodded and smiled, her eagerness to find a moment just for us giving me hope I knew was dangerous, but wanted anyway.

Now, the only issue was the gift I lied about having.

***

Dinner with Charlie, Sam and Darcy was a few Casey's pizzas set out on the floor of the girls' dorm. I convinced them we needed breadsticks too, so they convinced me to pick up the pizza.

"Were three larges really necessary?" I asked as Charlie dug up some paper plates.

"I can eat an entire large by myself," Darcy replied with a shrug.

"So can I," Sam agreed. They bumped fists as Charlie and I exchanged skeptical glances.

"They don't believe us," Darcy said to Sam, crossing her arms over her chest.

A silent exchange between them had me concerned about where this was headed.

"Shall we wager?" Sam challenged while Darcy grinned. "Winner chooses terms."

I lifted an eyebrow as Charlie caught my eye, nodding sarcastically. There was no way they could each put down a large specialty pizza.

"Done," I confirmed. "But you have a half hour to eat the whole thing."

"Done," they said simultaneously.

I dropped onto the beanbag chair and dug into my sausage and green pepper pizza, grabbing a breadstick as well.

"Then, go!" I shouted, hitting the timer on my phone. Pizza tops flew open and groans of cheesy appreciation filled the room as Darcy and Sam stuffed their faces. I was surprised anyone would want to eat that fast. Casey's pizza was meant to be savored. Every gooey inch was perfection.

Engrossed in the madness happening in front of me, I didn't see Charlie coming. She snatched the breadstick from my fingers, dipped it in marinara and took a bite.

"Hey!" She grinned and proceeded to take a piece of pizza from my box.

"If they have to eat one each, you're sharing, Trev," she said, settling in next to me.

"Don't look so happy about it," I replied, leaning forward and biting off a chunk of breadstick while it was still in her hand. She tried to look salty, but couldn't maintain, finally giving up and grinning at me.

"Just face it, you think I'm adorable," I teased.

"Come after my food again and you'll see just how adorable I really think you are," she said with a fake smile as she batted her eyes at me.

The four of us got lost in an episode of NCIS and before I knew it, there were chest bumps, high fives and "HOOAHS" everywhere. Darcy and Sam were doing everything from the Tebow to the John Cena. It was ridiculous and in the midst of their celebration, my phone timer went off.

"We WIN!" Darcy shouted. "That means we pick the terms." Her sneaky, conniving tone had me on high alert.

"We sure do," Sam said, grinning at me and rubbing his hands together. I looked over at Charlie and she seemed just as wary.

"Out with it. What do you want? Do we have to streak across campus or something?" I was joking, but really hoped that wasn't it.

"Oh, no. Nothing so deviant as that," Darcy chided, her mischievous tone not lost on me. "What we want is pretty simple actually."

"Yeah," Sam agreed, nodding. "All you and Charlie have to do is kiss."

"Excuse me?" I said, just as Charlie said, "Fine."

"What?" we both directed at each other.

"You're okay with this?"

"Are you not," she replied, looking both offended and amused.

My brain couldn't put the words together. I simply stood and stared at her. Finally, I said, "Out, both of you," to Darcy and Sam, who stood silent, watching us like this was an episode of The Bachelor.

I turned, and shouted, "OUT, BOTH OF YOU." I wasn't unkind, but I wasn't waiting on them either. Darcy glared and Sam winked as they passed by.

Once the door closed, I spoke. "You know they cooked this up, right?" I asked.

Charlie rolled her eyes. "Obviously. But, really, we were getting there anyway, so what's the big deal?"

She was being far too nonchalant about all this.

"The big deal is I told you the first time we kissed, you'd ask for it. You can't get out of my edict through this ridiculous wager." I crossed my arms over my chest and looked down at her, unimpressed with her efforts.

We stood in our traditional standoff, eyeing each other, waiting for the other to break. I was full, tired and sated in the knowledge that Charlie did indeed want to kiss me. She wouldn't win today.

Finally, she stomped her foot. "Argh! Why does this have to be a thing? Why does everything have to be a thing with you? Why can't we just get it over with and figure out what it means later?"

A slow grin spread over my face as I closed the distance between us. I held up one hand and after a moment, she raised hers to meet it. Our fingers sat alongside each other's and then folded over the other's palm.

I looked down into her nervous gaze and spoke softly but firmly. "We can't 'just get it over with' because there are moments in life you don't waste. There are seconds that will forever imprint on your memory and your soul. No matter where life takes you, you will recall them in an instant. I want to remember the smell of your perfume, the color of your shirt, the taste of your favorite lip gloss and the feel of your tongue in my mouth. I want to know this kiss is one you'll tell your friends about even if I'm not the guy you spend the rest of your life with. I need to know you'll spend the rest of your life remembering me."

She looked hypnotized, her gaze unfocused but her grip tight on mine. I stared down at her in silence until finally, she snapped her head back and forth, and said, "What do we tell them?"

"Oh, I think they heard us," I said as I projected my voice. "Didn't you?"

Darcy and Sam basically fell through the door as they opened it.

"You're ridiculous," Sam chided as Darcy said, "Ohmygod, *I'm* never forgetting and it didn't even happen to me."

"Hey!" Charlie argued. "It didn't happen to me yet either."

I snagged her hand once again, twisting my fingers in hers, and said, "*Yet* is the operative word."

CHAPTER

fourteen

I had exactly one hour before I was supposed to meet
Charlie and I was in the depths of hell. It was two in the
afternoon at the biggest mall in Des Moines on the first
Saturday in December.

There were people, children, strollers and madness
everywhere. I had no idea what to get Charlie and had
already wasted ten minutes staring at the information
sign, mentally crossing off stores I knew held no hope of
a decent gift.

I finally landed in Barnes and Noble. It was initially
out of need for coffee, but as I stood in line to order, my
eyes roamed the store. They landed on the journals—
leather-bound journals filled with blank pages waiting for
her.

I was suddenly impatient for the barista to finish. I
tapped my foot as I scanned the shelves, squinting while
I tried to guess what was on the covers and cursing my
out of date prescription. Finally, she called my name and
I quickly grabbed the cup, sliding a sleeve over the latte
and making a beeline for the correct aisle.

It came down to two options. One was dark brown leather, barely tinged in red and tied with a leather strap. The other was more of a light, yellowy tan covered in rows of bars filled with notes that didn't make a certain song I could pick out.

I debated for just a few minutes and went with the dark leather. It was up to her if she used it for the things she kept hidden or if she wrote songs again. As it were, she could do both.

I approached the cashier and she couldn't seem to wrap her head around my never-ending grin.

"Good gift choice?"

"Best gift ever," I said, nodding and congratulating myself again. Charlie would love it; I was sure of it.

I left Barnes and Noble and headed toward the food court. As I neared the exit that would take me to my car, I saw her.

"Mrs. Logan?" Charlie's mom was on her phone, standing off to the side of the main crowds. She looked up and the shock at seeing me was apparent.

"Trevor Adler?" Her blonde hair was pulled back severely, as it always had been. Her suit black and heels high, she was every bit the power lawyer.

"That's me." I stepped closer and smiled. "How are you Mrs. L?"

Her smile tightened. She always hated the nickname and I knew it. Charlie's mom and I never got along and I had my suspicions that the miscommunications after I moved had something to do with her.

"I'm doing well, Trevor, thank you. I'm actually meeting a client soon and was just confirming the restaurant, which actually appears not to be in the mall itself. Do you live here now?"

The quick glances to her phone made it clear she had more important things to do than play catch up with her daughter's old friend.

"I actually attend Rodgers with Charlie. We didn't realize it until our first week, but it's been great seeing her again. I'm there on a full ride for music." I loved the surprise that pulled her eyebrows high on her forehead, but more than that, I loved showing her music could actually amount to something.

"Well, that's quite wonderful," she said, her tone both placating and insulting all at once. "I didn't think the two of you kept in touch. I'm sure your parents appreciate the burden of tuition being removed." She failed to hide her condescension, setting her purse down so she could put her coat on.

Remembering Charlie's comments about how much her parents hated Katie being gone, I decided to touch a nerve for her as well.

"How is Katie doing? I heard she won't be making it back any time soon. That sucks," I said, keeping my face expressionless.

Mrs. Logan froze in the middle of reaching down to pick up her purse. Her head slowly tipped up and her eyes bulged while her mouth hung open. In all my years knowing her, I'd never seen her taken by surprise.

"Why would you say such a hateful thing?" she asked, the words barely there and choked with the emotion twisting her features. Pain etched in every line of her face as she straightened. I scrambled for words.

"Hateful? That's a bit extreme since I just mentioned your daughter not coming home for Christmas." I took a step toward Mrs. Logan and she recoiled as a single tear escaped her perfect facade.

"My daughter is dead. Katherine killed herself four years ago."

***

I don't remember what I said to Charlie's mom before she walked away or the drive downtown. I ended up parked in the ramp that's always empty at four a.m. when I show up for work, but was now full from the Saturday night crowd.

I sat there, my hands on the steering wheel but the engine off, trying to process what I'd just learned.

Katie is dead. My best friend's sister is dead.

It was one thing to picture Katie off in Paris, following her dreams an ocean away with the possibility I would never see her again. But now, I realized she was wiped from the face of the earth. Her body buried somewhere, I didn't even know where, probably back in Muscatine. Her energy had gone back to the universe to become something new because she was no longer.

And then there was Charlie. It didn't all make sense, but it made more sense. What I couldn't understand was why. Why not tell me? Why hold back such a life-changing secret?

I tossed my glasses onto the passenger seat and leaned forward, resting my forehead on the cold rubber of the wheel. Tears burned in my eyes — for Katie and the realization that something drove her to this, for Charlie and the pain she was clearly still in, and for me, because I couldn't decide whether I was more hurt or angry at them both.

My phone rang and Charlie's name came up on the screen. I stared at the blueish light in the pitch black of the car, at the six letters I thought defined my best friend, but all I could think was I truly didn't know who she was. I didn't know this person who would lie to me about something so real and painful when I had given her every opportunity to confide in me.

I silenced the phone as I got out of the car. Shoving it into my coat pocket, I put my glasses back on, exited the ramp and found myself amidst the madness of Court Avenue. Couples holding hands, friends in bunches, everyone wrapped in scarves, hats and gloves to fight off the twenty-degree low for the night.

People talked and laughed around me, but I just walked. I walked block after block until I crossed the river and found myself in the East Village. As I passed Up-Down, Mike called out to me from the bouncer's normal spot in the entryway.

"Hey, man, you okay?" He scanned me up and down.

"Oh, yeah, I'm fine. Why?" They were the first words I'd spoken and I found it hard to speak. Between the cold and my clenched teeth, it felt like a hinge desperately in need of oil. I couldn't bring myself to move my mouth again to ask Mike why the owner of the bar was on security detail.

"Because your lips are blue, Trevor. Come inside for a few," Mike said, grabbing a handful of my coat and pulling me inside.

"I can't be—" I started, but Mike shook his head.

"It's early and there are only a few people downstairs. Just go sit at the bar and tell Hannah to get you some coffee. It's fine." He nodded toward the steps with an encouraging smile.

I attempted a smile in return and my face felt like it would shatter. As my glasses fogged and the warmth settled in, I realized just how cold I was.

Hannah was behind the bar, her purple hair bright as ever. She reminded me of Abby from NCIS, a lot of goth mixed with a level positivity that seemed unreal.

She smiled as I sat down, glancing up the stairs behind me. "Hey, Trev, long time no see," she said.

"It's okay, Hannah. Mike told me it wasn't optional for me to come down and get some coffee. I won't be here long," I assured her. The owners were sticklers about the over twenty-one rule, and for good reason. They'd built a booming business and the employees knew no one made exceptions. It just so happened Mike was one of the owners.

This time her smile was big and she nodded as she headed for the coffee station. "Black or a latte?" She tossed over her shoulder.

"Just black, thanks," I responded as I stretched my hands and tried to ignore the painful tingling in my legs. My phone rang and I sent Charlie to voicemail again.

Hannah set the cup in front of me and leaned into the bar.

"It'll be easier if you just tell me what's going on," she said, matter-of-fact.

My head snapped up. "What do you mean?" I stuttered out, struggling to maintain eye contact as she looked at me knowingly. Hannah had been working at Up-Down since before I started cleaning last year. She trained me on how to stock, clean and prep the bar, so we'd spent a few weeks getting to know each other. Now, she was like an older sister.

"Something is clearly up with you. You're never this quiet and I've never seen you look so…sad," she finished, her lips pressed together as she continued to study me.

"Have you ever found out something someone was hiding from you? And you thought something was wrong before, so you asked them over and over what it was and they wouldn't tell you, but then finally someone else did? And it was bad — really bad?" I stared into the dark coffee as I rambled. The porcelain mug burned my icy fingers, but I refused to let go. I needed to feel; I needed the numbness of the last few hours to subside in some way.

Hannah tapped her black nails on the bar for a moment before she spoke.

"You want to know whether you should confront the person who lied or not, that's what you're asking?" I looked up and nodded.

"I think you have a choice," she said. "You can either confront this person who didn't tell you the truth now, while you're still clearly processing what you learned, and chance making what sounds like a shitty situation way worse, or you can wait. Give yourself time to figure out what this means to you and maybe think a little harder about why they wouldn't have told you the truth. Then, when you do talk about it, you can go into the conversation seeing both sides. Because based on what you look like, I can only imagine what the other person has gone through to keep this hidden."

Hannah stepped away to take care of a customer, her purple hair and all black outfit drawing the normal random customer comments. I watched her deftly pour three beers while carrying on conversation, but my mind was elsewhere. Every time I thought of Charlie, my gut ached and my blood pressure soared. I wanted to yell. I wanted to accuse. I wanted to take back every ounce of effort I'd put into the last five months. Hannah was right. Until I could confront Charlie and give her the chance to actually explain, I needed to keep my distance.

CHAPTER
fifteen

Finishing the last chorus of *Jessie's Girl*, the crowd cheered and clapped. It was ten and they were drunk, which was good given my calluses now had calluses and my throat was scratchy.

"I'm going to take a quick break. Be back for my last set in fifteen." I propped up my guitar and headed for the bar.

My eyes itched, not used to my contacts or the late nights, but the bar was packed and I'd been encouraging them to drink all night. The more they spent, the better my cut was.

"You're having a great night," my mom said as I sat down. I eyed her glass and it was only water, so I relaxed and nodded. It had been almost eighty days, but it was still hard to trust her commitment to stay sober. My dad sat next to her, sipping a beer. As I sat down, he clapped me on the back, and said, "Nice job tonight, son."

I was taken aback for a moment and sputtered out, "Thank you."

"I'm surprised you guys are here. You've heard all these songs a million times. Heck, you taught me them," I said with a half-smile. It was meant for my mom, but my dad was the one who chuckled.

"It's good to see you up there. You know how to read the crowd, you're picking all the right songs and you've got them eating out of your hand," he said with a grin.

That look, the one where he wasn't clearly plastered and his smile was real, with nothing hidden behind it, was one I hadn't seen in a long time. The waitress set down my iceless water and I drained it in a few gulps, hiding my uncertainty at how to react to my dad tonight. These moments were rare and I'd learned not to put too much stock into them, but having him acknowledge me in any way that wasn't manipulative or belittling sparked hope inside me I couldn't ignore.

We carried on a strange sort of small talk over the next few minutes, ranging from new songs I should try to learn to how the Cubs might do next year. I finally started to relax, my parents acting like normal parents for once.

"I have to say, I'm looking forward to a few days off," I said as I motioned to the waitress for another refill.

"About that," my father said, leaning back in his chair. "I'm going to need a favor from you tonight, Trevor."

I closed my eyes briefly and tried to keep my voice level. "What do you mean?"

Mom's hand grasped mine under the table. I wasn't sure whether it was a warning or reassurance.

"Buddy's had a last minute cancellation and Stan heard you were back in the circuit. He called me earlier begging for you to fill in, so I told him you would." He held up his beer to signal for the waitress to bring him one, not bothering to find out what I thought about the arrangement.

"I've been playing for three hours. I don't have much left," I argued.

His eyes flicked to meet mine and I saw the change. The subtle darkening paired with the tick in his jaw conveyed I should shut the hell up and do what I was told.

"It's just one more show," my mom interjected. "They'll all be drunk. You know how Buddy's late night crowd can be. You'll be in and out in no time." She nodded, her eyes pleading.

"I've been playing every night for two weeks. You have to be close to what you need," I gritted out before taking another drink of my water, unable to keep my father's stare.

Over the rim of his bottle, he smirked. "Break's over, son. You better finish strong," he said, tipping his head toward the stage. Swallowing down my rage, I squeezed Mom's hand and did as I was told.

***

After last night's double-shift and a shitty night of sleep consisting solely of me wondering if Charlie's mother told her I knew her secret, I had to get out of my parents' apartment. Part of me wished Charlie would reach out again, but the other part still wasn't sure what I would say to her if she did. Katie's suicide had to be the worst time in her life, but I still didn't understand why she cut me out of it all. Or why *someone* would, considering Charlie thought I disappeared and not the other way around. And how did Katie dying lead to Charlie's abandonment of her dreams, of herself? There were just too many questions and I was still dealing with my own shit show of a life.

I headed for the door and was almost there when Mom called out, "I made breakfast!"

I closed my eyes and my head dropped forward, staring at the door for a second. *So close.*

Spinning on my heel, I made my way into the kitchen. With a cup of coffee in one hand and a spatula in the other, she flipped pancakes. Mom wore her Christmas robe. A threadbare, floor-length red fuzzy mess she'd been wearing every Christmas since I could remember.

"Merry Christmas Eve, Trevor," she chirped.

"Merry Christmas Eve, Mom." I forced a smile as I poured myself a cup of coffee and took a seat at the table.

"I'm making your favorite, just like I used to. You remember?" she asked, her spatula still in the air as she waited for my confirmation.

"Of course." What neither of us mentioned was I also remembered every year they were too messed up to realize it was Christmas and I made my own pancakes — or butter noodles, in the worse years.

"I talked to your dad, and he agreed to cancel your show tonight," she said as she handed me my plate. She stood tall, the pride in her accomplishment obvious.

"How did you do that?" I questioned, hesitant to celebrate until I understood the terms.

"It doesn't matter." She spun back around to the stove. "What matters is we'll have a nice Christmas."

"It does matter," I said, shoving back from the table and crossing the small kitchen. I put my hand on her arm and turned my mom toward me. "What did you do?"

She blew out a noisy breath. "I found his box of money," she whispered. "There's enough. You've made more than enough, Trevor. I see how exhausted you are. And I got my first paycheck last week. I won't let him keep forcing you to do this."

Without a second thought, I wrapped my arms around her and squeezed, my relief almost more than I could handle.

Her hand came up to my cheek and she pressed a kiss to my temple. The exhaustion was deep in my bones and knowing I didn't have to force the happy musician act for another night was almost enough to send me back to bed to sleep for the next week.

As I pulled away, she said, "Things will get better, Trevor. We'll take what you've given us and start fresh."

I paused, hesitant to rain on her parade, but ultimately decided the question was worth asking. "What makes you think he'll ever change?"

"Because I love him. And deep down, your father is a good man. Once things start to go his way a little bit, he'll be the man I married again." She looked so hopeful and sure. I wondered how many times she'd convinced herself of the same lie.

"Sit down, honey," she said finally. "Eat your pancakes and let's have a good day, okay?"

"Okay," I agreed, taking my seat.

My knee shook as my foot tapped rapidly under the table, but I smiled and told her stories about Sam and

Darcy, and the fact that no one could fathom how they were just friends. She laughed and laughed when I detailed Sam's Halloween costume, his horrendous but slowly improving fashion sense and Darcy's affinity for Fireball.

Hannah's purple hair and five-inch platform boots generated so many questions about everything from her religion to her parents, few of which I had answers for. My mom's total curiosity about what makes someone decide to dye their hair purple and wear diamond-studded dog collars had me genuinely laughing.

What I didn't talk about was Charlie or Katie. I talked around them both as if Charlie wasn't in my every thought and Katie being gone didn't tear at my soul. But my mom was smiling and I promised her a good day, so today would not be the day I reconciled my own issues, even though the only thing I wanted to do was lay these problems at her feet and let her tell me how to solve them.

CHAPTER
sixteen

January

The knock on my dorm door surprised me, given how quiet campus had been since I got back yesterday. January term, or J-term, was a time lots of students took off or used to travel. But there were classes on campus and the dorms reopened, which meant I was free from my parents.

"Come in," I yelled. I should have expected Charlie to show up eventually, but the sight of her magnified the ache I'd tamped down tenfold. I dragged a breath in, the air seeming to be devoid of oxygen as the room spun slightly.

Her hair was in one of those fancy braids all the girls liked once Hunger Games came out. I wanted to yank the elastic from the end and pull it apart—to mess it up and have her finally look on the outside like I knew she must feel on the inside.

Charlie shut the door and leaned back against it, her hands behind her and her coat still on. She stood there and said nothing; she just looked at me.

We stayed like that, in a silent stalemate that wasn't unfamiliar. In the old days, I always won these matches, but the look on Charlie's face was pure, angry determination.

She doesn't know I know. I couldn't decide whether that was better or worse.

I adjusted my glasses and tried to muster a fake smile, but couldn't.

"I'm tired, Charlie," I started, giving into the realities of where we were and the inevitable situation about to unfold.

"I spent the last three weeks working nonstop and the last twenty-four hours were the first peace I've had since finals. It's the first night I've slept in a bed and the first time I haven't had someone constantly talking to me or threatening my existence. I see you over there, pissed at me because I haven't talked to you, but life happened and I had to deal with it."

She pursed her lips and I watched her chest rise and fall as she tried to hide the deep inhale that kept her voice level.

"Life happened?" she asked as she pushed off the door. "You've spent the last five months coming at me, dredging up memory after memory, making me question every choice I've made for the last four years and when *life happened*, it was okay for you to just disappear?"

By the end, her voice wasn't level. Her face was red and her hands were shaking. I forced myself to stay in my chair when all I really wanted to do was cross the room, get in her face and yell my questions. I wanted the truth, no matter how I had to get it. No matter how selfish it was, I wanted her to own her story so we could move on and she could be the person I needed—the one who could help me overcome the bullshit of my life. Instead, we were here and it suddenly felt like the last five months had been all about her.

"And exactly what happened four years ago, Charlie? What is it you have tried so desperately to hide from me?" I asked, my indignant tone a reflection of my revelation.

Her mouth opened and then snapped shut as she crossed her arms over her chest.

I nodded, not shocked, but still hurt by her silence as I pushed myself up. I pointed at her with one hand while the other pushed my glasses up on my nose. "And there it is, Charlie. That's the magic question, isn't it? You're right, I have spent the last five months getting to you. And the thing is, *it worked.*"

I walked toward her, pausing only within arm's reach. "This," I said, waving a hand at her Ugg boots and perfectly coordinating outfit, "isn't you. It never was." She stood straighter, but couldn't hold my stare.

"You're hiding, Charlie," I continued, unable to care anymore whether she could handle the conversation this time. "And it isn't just me you're hiding from. Sure, I scare you, because I know the truth. I know who you are at the core. But when you're with me, you forget who you're pretending to be and you question why you're pretending at all, don't you? You're not hiding from me, you never were. *You're hiding from you.*"

She stared out my window, her bottom lip trembling, her eyes barely wet with tears she didn't bother to hide. I stepped a few inches closer and put my hand to her cheek. She jumped, but didn't pull away.

125

"You could just tell me, you know," I said softly, praying she would and this could all be over. We sat like that for a few seconds, and then she stepped away.

Clearing her throat, she swallowed down the tears and turned back to me, pulling a small box from her pocket. "I came here to give you this and yell at you," she said, tossing the box at me. "You are the one who screwed up this time, Trevor, not me. Don't try to turn this around. You never showed and you disappeared. You didn't answer my calls, my texts or my emails. What the hell?"

Rage simmered under every pore. I had to set the box down on my desk before I crushed it. The last three weeks wore on me like fine sandpaper, all of the finesse and patience I normally had for her ground away under my father's manipulations and the weight of Charlie's lies.

"I didn't answer your calls, your texts or your emails?" I repeated, over-exaggerating my tone and raising my eyebrow. She nodded dramatically in return, throwing her hands out.

"And I just disappeared?" I asked, clenching my fists and then forcing myself to relax.

"Yeah, Trev," she said, snapping her fingers. "Like, poof, you were gone."

I stood tall and crossed my arms over my chest, staring her straight in the eyes.

"Sucks, doesn't it?" I stated. "Now, try wondering what the hell happened to someone for four years instead of three weeks."

"I told you I tried," she said, her tone weak because she had to know her argument was as well.

"For how long? How long did you try? Because I tried for almost a year and by then, you had all but disappeared. None of your phone numbers worked, your social media accounts were gone, your email kicked back 'inbox full' messages…I kept trying. Did you?"

"I couldn't."

"But you won't tell me why, so we're right back to where we started, aren't we? Back at that place where everything is about you and what you need because you're the only person who matters, aren't you?"

She stared at me for a millisecond, then the door slammed behind her and I collapsed back into the chair, my head dropping into my hands.

It might have been an hour, or four, that I sat like that, forcing breaths in and out, continuing to have our screaming match inside my head. I yelled. She yelled. I said things I meant and things I didn't—things I should have and things I shouldn't have. Exhaustion finally got the better of me and I stood, ready to stumble to my bed.

But there was the box. The small little box wrapped in red paper with Rudolph's big red nose dead center. I tore at the gift wrap and shredded the thin cardboard lid. Nestled in tissue paper was a ring—my ring. A thick silver band inlaid with a large Onyx stone. I'd given her that ring the day we moved away and told her as long as she had it, I'd always be with her.

Under the ring was a folded up slip of paper. Charlie's looping script had scrawled: *Together again at last. Looks like you can have this back.*

I collapsed back down in the chair, now only able to wonder how I could feel so justified in my anger and so ashamed of my behavior all at once.

***

"What exactly did you do?" Sam asked for the fifth time since he'd arrived back on campus this morning. "How did this go from Charlie searching for you to Darcy telling me she'd like to throw knives at your picture?"

I shook my head. "Not worth discussing," I lied. "A better topic is you explaining the transformation from Samwise Gamgees to Rudy?"

Sam sat a little taller, a toothy smile stretching wide. His hair was no longer shaggy, but now had an actual cut, and in the four weeks since I'd seen him, he'd clearly lost about fifteen pounds.

"I didn't have much to do over break, and before I left, Darcy showed me some exercises to try, so I went to the gym every day and stayed away from my mom's Christmas goodies. Well, most of them," he said, giving his significantly smaller belly a rub. "I also talked my older sister into taking me shopping and got some kick-ass new clothes."

"Good work, man. And score one for older sisters with fashion sense," I said, putting up a hand for a high five he quickly returned.

"On the topic, you look, ah…a little worse for wear, my friend," he said, clearly hesitant to call me out.

"It wasn't the best break, let's leave it at that, okay?" I requested, giving him a look that plainly said I didn't want to talk about it.

Sam shrugged and started pulling clothes from his suitcase. Silence settled over our room, only interrupted by the sound of hangers, toiletries being put away and Sam's movements.

Charlie hadn't spoken to me in four days. We literally ran into each other in the cafeteria yesterday and she didn't even say, "Excuse me." It was as if I no longer took up physical space on the planet.

"You know," Sam said, interrupting my circling thoughts, "you two are the same."

"Excuse me?"

He sat down on his bed, and said, "You and Charlie, you're doing the same thing. You both have things happening you won't talk about, especially to each other. Yet, you push so hard to take care of each other, whether the other person wants it or not. It's obvious what you mean to each other, maybe even more now than you did when you were kids, but neither of you are willing to trust the other completely. And neither of you are fully trying to understand who the other person is now. You're like magnets, but you keep flipping over, so you're either pulling with all you have, or pushing with the same force."

"Did you take psych last semester?" I asked sarcastically.

Sam rolled his eyes. "I'm being serious, Trevor. You said you haven't practiced once since you got back, you aren't talking to Charlie and you look like you went on a coke bender over break—which I know isn't possible. You don't have to tell me what's up, that's fine. But tell her. You started this whole thing on a mission to find your best friend, so treat her like it."

"You don't understand, Sam. She's been lying to me for a long time," I argued, suddenly defensive.

Sam sat silent and stared down at his hands. Finally, he said, "I suppose you have to decide what matters more—the fact *that* she lied or *why* she lied."

I wanted to say I didn't care why she lied, but that was naive and selfish. The why was really the only thing that did matter. So I let his words settle over me, a thin layer of epiphany mixed with shame.

I sat with my elbows on my knees and my fingers loosely intertwined. Hannah's previous advice played over in my head again as well. I looked to my nightstand and stared at the ring I couldn't bear to put on or put away. I could have told Charlie the truth about my home life at any time in the last four months, just like she could have told me the truth about Katie.

As the reality became clear, my head dropped toward my chest.

"We all have our secrets," I admitted.

"Every single one of us," Sam responded.

PART TWO

CHAPTER
seventeen

Charlie

January

"Truth or dare?" Darcy asked.

We were sprawled out on the floor of our dorm room eating popcorn and wasting time until we decided what to do with the rest of our night. Or, better said, she was trying to decide as I alternated between wanting to scream at Trevor and wanting to break down and tell him everything. Everything except how I'd thought about him every single day since he left when we were fourteen and how seeing him the night of the auction was both everything I wanted and the only thing I couldn't handle. He could be my undoing—the only person who could ruin the carefully crafted house of lies I'd built and now depended on.

"Truth," I responded, already dreading the question.

"You always pick truth." She threw a small handful of popcorn at me and I attempted to catch a piece in my mouth, but failed.

"And you always pick dare," I countered as I swept my hand over the floor to pile the small kernels next to me.

Darcy smirked, a small twist of her perfectly pink full lips. It wasn't fair she was athletic *and* pretty.

I groaned in anticipation, which only earned me a face full of popcorn I should have seen coming.

"What's your hidden talent?" Her eyebrows popped up and down dramatically and her bright blue eyes blazed with curiosity.

I laughed and paused, debating my answer. Darcy had been a great friend so far this year and I clearly needed to stop depending on Trevor. She deserved a genuine response, not one of my bullshit answers.

"I used to play music and sometimes I'd write songs." I couldn't meet her eyes and when I looked down at my right hand, it was tapping notes on the floorboards. I flattened it and exhaled thoughts of Trevor—both good and bad, but mostly the guilty ones.

"Used to?" she probed. Unable to sit still for long, Darcy tossed a soccer ball in the air and bounced it around like it were a hacky sack from the inside of her foot to the top of her knee and back, looking like Alex Morgan.

"Mmmhmmm," I mumbled.

The soccer ball shot in the air and thumped against Darcy's forehead before she caught it. When she turned to me, a red welt was already fading.

"That's not an answer, Char."

"Why do you call me Char?" She'd been doing it for months, and while it didn't bother me, now seemed like a great time for clarity on the subject.

"Don't avoid the question," she chided. "And I do it because I'm not sure what to call you. Charlotte doesn't fit, but Charlie seems like he-who-shall-not-be-named's name for you, so to me, you're just Char." Darcy stared at me, one eyebrow arched, her resolve unwavering even between the hints of empathy I saw.

"Yes." I sighed. "I *used to* write songs and play music. As in, past tense, because I don't anymore. It's something we did together when we were kids, but it stopped before high school when he left and hasn't happened since."

"Even though I always see you scribbling in that notebook you keep next to your bed," she said, giving me the side eye.

She wasn't supposed to have noticed that.

"Truth or dare?" I tossed a piece of popcorn up and this time actually caught it myself.

I grinned as she exclaimed, "We weren't done. Cheater!"

"You want more answers, you wait your turn. Now, truth or dare, woman."

I prayed she wouldn't ask me anything about Trevor when my time came again. I hated knowing I would lie if she asked the wrong question, but I would.

Darcy gave me a tight smile, and said, "Dare."

"I dare you to ask Sam out," I said, tossing another piece of popcorn up and catching it.

Darcy's face instantly flushed, but like a wilting flower, she visibly drooped, collapsing into a heap on the floor next to me.

"Sam isn't interested in me." She wasn't sad, but she also wasn't relieved.

"How do you know? He looks amazing since he came back from break. He's sweet. He understands soccer and I'm pretty sure he loves Fireball as much as you do," I teased.

Darcy smiled and shook her head. "I don't think you've been paying enough attention there, baby cakes. I like Sam. I could maybe even *like Sam*. But, I'm pretty sure Sam plays for my team."

"He plays soccer now?" The question dropped from my mouth before I connected the dots. Darcy was laughing as I spat out, "Oh. Ohhhhhh. Are you sure?" I really hadn't been paying enough attention.

"Pretty sure. The guy has seen me half-naked and had more comments about the design on my sports bra than anything else." She tried to hide her frown and failed. Sam's evolving fashion sense and increasing flare for the dramatic was suddenly making a bit more sense.

"Dudes are dumb," I stated, wrinkling my nose as I shoved Trevor and his stupidly adorable glasses quickly out of my mind. I should be *more* pissed at him. I should *at least* be pissed at him. I should want to do anything except run directly to him. I didn't need him. I didn't need anyone. I was fine. Just fine.

Darcy almost snorted in agreement. "Dudes are most certainly dumb."

"Truth or dare?" she asked.

"Dare." I smacked a hand over my mouth and then immediately tried to take it back.

"No way, Jose," Darcy argued, "not happening. This is so awesome. I have to come up with something good."

The sinister smile on her face as she rubbed her hands together had me regretting any level of trust I assumed we had.

"You really don't have to come up with anything good. I mean, I didn't even make you actually do something. We could just quit. We could go to the Sigma party tonight and hang out with obviously gay Sam. We could just get the heck out of here and forget all about this," I rambled, praying something would resonate to get me out of my current predicament.

A slow grin spread across Darcy's face.

"I dare you to come with me to the Sigma party and be *you*. Dress like *you* want. Act like *you* want. Be whoever it is *you* want to be."

"What in the heck are you talking about?" My pulse was already rising. Trevor had eased me into some of my old ways, but this — this went against everything. It was utter rebellion. It was regression.

It sounded freaking amazing.

"Our first few weeks, I wasn't sure I could stick it out," she started. "You barely talked to me and when you did, it was obviously fake." I tried to cut in, but Darcy held up a hand, giving me her patented stare.

"But then *he* showed up," she continued, "and I feel like a whole new Charlotte came with him. I like her. I think you like her too, for the most part. So tonight, I want it to be about you being whatever version of you feels good—not the one he compares you to or the one who showed up the first day. That's my dare." Darcy stood up, holding out a hand.

"I dare you to be you, Charlotte Lydia Logan," she said with a satisfied grin. The gauntlet had officially been thrown down.

My inner competitor reared up and some part of me rejoiced. I got chills from my neck to my knees and I couldn't stop myself from smacking my palm to hers.

"I accept your dare," I said as she pulled me up to stand beside her. My confidence from three seconds ago already waned, replaced by an icy warning shiver down my spine. "But…I'm going to need some help."

"Come to momma," Darcy said, cackling as she dragged me toward my closet. I don't think either of us expected what I dug out.

***

With a drink in my hand and a bassline thumping in the background, I was happy. I was buzzed and didn't feel guilty, or like I was smothering something. I just…was. I bounced from foot to foot, reveling in the numbness, in the momentary bliss of feeling nothing at all.

Darcy grabbed my hand and led me toward the dance floor yet again. I held my drink high above my head, the signature red cup filled with crappy keg beer I drank for no other reason than it was there and I didn't want my moment to end.

I forced myself not to cringe outwardly when people brushed against me as we squeezed through groups of guys. One reached toward my ass and I whipped around. As our eyes met, I found myself face-to-face with a guy from our floor. It took him a second to register who I actually was given the outfit we'd cooked up, but as soon as he did, he yanked his hand away and put it up in surrender. One day in the hall, I'd overheard him saying I looked like a fun-hating prude, so my glare was pointed.

"Whoa, what happened to you?" he said, his mouth still on the floor.

"It looks like I found a way to stop hating fun," I started, a sweet smile stretching my lips. He nodded, his intrigue blatant, and took a small step toward me. "Because I stopped trying to hang out with judgmental, pretentious assholes who didn't understand real fun to begin with."

Darcy grasped my hand and with one final look at his startled expression, I walked away. We kept going until we hit the center and found a hole.

A dozen different retorts fired through my brain, all the things I should have said that would have been more impactful. I'd lost my edge. Trevor would have known exactly what to say to that guy. But Trevor wasn't here and I was. I needed to *be here*.

I took a slow breath in and shut down my inner monologue, letting the music fill the space instead.

"I love this song," Darcy yelled over the sound system in the Sigma basement. For as tall as she was, I was surprised by how graceful Darcy's movements were. We swayed, bounced and jumped all over our three-foot square. Guys approached, doing their worst white-man dance or half-grind, and we boxed them out, not even acknowledging their existence.

Never make eye contact; every college girl knew the rule.

With my arms up and head dropped back, I closed my eyes and let the music swallow me. It enveloped every inch until the beat of my heart matched the rhythm of my hips and my body moved on instinct based on the lyrics.

Songs I knew, when I could anticipate the words and use my body to convey the emotions, were my favorite. Florence sang about shaking it out and I waited for the next stanza—the one that tore at my being and made me jealous of how strong she was. The words erupted from deep in my soul when she declared she was done with her graceless heart. I screamed them out as tears burned the back of my eyes. Shoving them down, I blamed the alcohol for my wayward emotions.

Could I cut it out and restart like Florence declared she would? Tonight, Darcy had me believing it was possible.

We had dug through my closet, past the bright colors and chevron, and finally came to the few items I'd never brought myself to get rid of. A frayed denim cutoff skirt, cropped Metallica T-shirt I'd sliced open at the back and tied back together in multiple places, paired with combat boots. I'd thrown my hair up in a high ponytail and applied darker than normal eye makeup. It all had me feeling outdated and in my own skin at the same time.

My hair was shorter in high school and having it off my shoulders and away from my face was oddly freeing. Like I'd removed the mask I wore every day and the air in my lungs was fresh, not filtered through an invisible barrier I kept between me and the rest of the world.

"You're having fun, aren't you," Darcy accused as she grinned at me, her face right in front of mine as she hollered the words.

"Of course I'm having fun!" I yelled back, happier still that it was the truth. I gestured off the dance floor and she nodded, grabbing my hand as we wound our way out of the madness. She clinked cups with guys and girls alike, seeming to know everyone.

"You know, you think too much, Char," she said as we climbed out of the basement. "You just need to chill and let things happen."

"Wise words from a drunk girl," I threw over my shoulder, laughing as I wobbled a little. I stumbled and a guy coming down the stairs grabbed my shoulders, standing me upright again. His hands gripped me — unfamiliar hands inside my personal space — but then he was gone. I never even looked up at him, yet I was frozen. I stood on those steps, unmoving, until Darcy nudged me from behind.

"You're fine, girl. You're just fine. You gotta keep moving," she said softly into my ear. She squeezed my hand and my chest loosened a fraction, then retightened. It ached and the debilitating pain spread quickly as I tried to inhale and exhale the panic back down. I nodded and forced one foot above the other until we were out of the cramped staircase and I could breathe normally again. Then, I realized Darcy had not only seen my panic attack, she'd recognized it instantly and knew exactly what to do.

I turned and stared at my roommate. How did she get in? I hadn't made the decision to let her in, yet here she was, challenging me to face my fears without knowing what they even were — reminding me who I was without ever knowing me.

It's okay for someone to know you. It's okay to feel okay.

The counselor's words echoed in my head. Calm statements from a lifetime ago. Words I hadn't thought of since I was fifteen and they forced me to sit on her overly plush couch with her matching throw pillows and bookshelves covered in self-help titles.

"Char?" Darcy questioned, pulling on my hand.

"Sorry," I said, shaking the thoughts away as my head snapped back and forth. "Drinks?" I asked, desperate to return to where I'd been just five minutes prior.

"Um, duh!" she chirped, pulling me toward the keg in the kitchen.

"Well, well, look what the cat dragged in," I heard just before an arm draped over my shoulder. Sam's ruddy face dropped between Darcy and I and we both leaned in and pecked him on the cheek.

"Hey, Sammy!" Darcy whooped. "We need drinks!"

Sam cut between us, grabbing our glasses as he went. "Of course you do. Charlie! Looking good, girl. I like this early two-thousands throwback thing you have going on tonight. And Blackest will always be my favorite album." He grinned up at me as he pumped the keg and poured fresh glasses, nodding hello to the guys in the kitchen.

"Thanks, Sam. You're looking pretty suave yourself tonight," I countered, accepting my now full cup.

He did a little shoulder bob and then leaned in. "Do you think this works, though?"

I looked over his head and tried to suppress my smile as Darcy slapped one hand over her mouth and motioned to say, "See!".

"It's part lumberjack, part posh, and I like it!" I assured him. Sam pulled at the gray scarf he'd wrapped around his neck and smoothed his hands down his flannel shirt, but finally relaxed.

"I saw it in Men's Health and decided I could rock the look," he said with a wink. I couldn't help but agree.

"OHMYGOD! Are you Charlotte Logan!"

WHO SHE WAS

Her shrill voice sliced through the air and I slowly turned to come face-to-face with Sarah Peters, no one's favorite Muscatine High cheerleader and the last person to have claimed to see Katie before she died.

CHAPTER
eighteen

I froze. Every ounce of light-hearted, carefree Charlie seeped out of me in an instant and I was flung back to a time I never wanted to remember again.

Sarah Peters swore she was one of Katie's best friends when it all happened. She wasn't, but she wanted attention and she got it. The media interviewed her while she cried, talking about how amazing my sister was, how happy Katie had obviously been and how there was no way she could have done this to herself. Sarah didn't know shit. No one knew what Katie had been through except me. No one saw my sister unless she was put together and perfect, except me.

The air stayed in my lungs, sticky and attached to my interior like mold on expired food. I would either die without oxygen or explode and yank her bleached hair from the roots.

She kept talking, and I watched her mouth move. Her lips asked if I was okay and how I was handling everything I'd been through. She said I hadn't changed a bit. But I couldn't respond. I couldn't even blink. Then, I felt someone wrap an arm around my waist. With one inhale of his cologne, the room was filled with more than just her and I.

"You know, everything is really great, Sarah, and it's been a long time, but we really have to go. This was just a quick stop. We'll see you later," Trevor said with a quick wave, swinging us around and shuttling me toward the door.

At the last second, he veered right and we went down a deserted hallway. He gently pushed me up against a wall and asked, "Charlie, are you okay? Charlie, talk to me."

He had one of my hands gripped in his and the other was on my cheek. He was so close, I could see the smudges on his glasses and the freckle on his bottom lip.

"You're mad at me," I breathed out, the alcohol, anger and lack of oxygen spinning my head and making me close my eyes.

He exhaled in an irritated huff. "Maybe I am. And maybe I miss you."

My eyes popped open. "You miss me?" I whispered. "Because I miss you."

He nodded, the hint of a smile pulling at the corner of his lips.

"My heart hurts," I whispered. My mouth moved of its own accord. I couldn't stop the words or move my eyes from his as I said the things I knew I shouldn't. "It hurts, Trevor. And the only time it doesn't hurt is when you're here. I know you're mad at me and I don't understand what's changed, but it doesn't matter because all I can think about is what it would feel like if you held me and how the world would change in an instant if you kissed me. And I need you not to be mad at me anymore.

I can't do this without you. You're here now and I'm just so tired of pretending."

He looked down at me, his eyes searching mine. For the first time since he showed up, I couldn't read him, but it didn't matter. He was still here and that meant I wasn't alone.

I pushed up to my tiptoes and leaned toward him, my eyes flicking back and forth between his and his lips. I heard his sharp inhale right before Trevor pulled away from me.

"I—Charlie—we can't…one thing at a time and that's not the most important issue at hand," he stuttered out before yanking off his glasses and rubbing a hand over his face.

"Did you hear what Sarah said?" he finally asked before putting his glasses back.

I'd so quickly forgotten Sarah, but now that moment took over my mind. Her face, her moving lips, her questions. Trevor's rebuke of my kiss certainly stung, but my brain couldn't process both events at once. The alcohol had my thoughts in a jumble and I wasn't thinking about Trevor or Sarah. The only person I could think of now was Katie.

"Not really," I admitted, stepping back until I hit the wall, letting it support me and wondering what my sister would think of the mess I'd made of myself tonight.

"But everyone else did," he said.

My mind was foggy and I could only stare. I forced myself to rewind through those few minutes and watched Sarah's mouth move until my brain fully registered the words.

I can't believe Katie's gone. I don't know how you've managed to deal with her suicide so well.

I wrenched myself away from Trevor and bolted down the hall, shoving my way out the back door before I puked up everything I'd drank.

I hovered there, somewhere between being sick again and completely shutting down.

Hands gripped my hips and stopped me from ending up face-first in the mess I'd left in the yard.

Trevor pulled me to stand and stuffed my arms in his jacket. He yanked gloves from the coat pockets and helped me pull them on. Zipping the coat, he stooped down and looked me in the eyes.

"I can't find my phone and you clearly don't have one," he said, gesturing to my tiny skirt. "I need you to stay here for two minutes while I tell Sam and Darcy we're leaving. I need you not to move, okay, Charlie?" I nodded absently, my mind refusing to settle as he rushed away.

Katie's gone. She said Katie's gone out loud. They know. They know I'm a fraud. They know I shouldn't be here. She should be here. I shouldn't be here. They won't want me here anymore.

With that last thought on a loop, I stumbled down the back steps toward the swinging gate.

***

I moved quickly, my short legs determined to carry me away from that tragedy. I pushed forward with such focus, I didn't hear him call my name or his pounding feet. Finally, a hand on my shoulder stopped me.

Trevor's glasses were falling off his face, his breath short puffs of white as he looked down at me, clearly pissed off.

"Damn it, Charlie, I told you to stay there!" he scolded.

I ripped my arm away from him. "You can't tell me what to do, *Trevor*."

His full name was now like a swear word — a set of syllables I reserved for certain circumstances simply to make a point.

His hands came up to his head, threading into his hair before he turned away from me.

When Trev turned back around, it occurred to me he didn't have a jacket.

"Where's your coat? It's freezing, you idiot."

His shoulders dropped and his face had "What the fuck?" written all over it.

"What?" I tried my best to be condescending without falling over.

He pointed at me and waited. Finally, I looked down.

"Oh." I turned my red face away and looked sideways at him.

"Can I please walk you home, Charlie?" he asked, his patronizing tone blatant.

"I can walk by myself. I don't need you," I groused, charging forward once again.

It's a lie. You're a lie. You can't do this. You'll never be her. The voice in my head refused to shut up.

"Of course. You don't need anybody, that's perfectly clear. You're handling things just dandy." Trevor was talking to himself, but intentionally loud enough for me to hear — I was sure of that.

I wrapped my arms around myself and focused on the sidewalk in front of me. Square after square, I looked one more ahead. I had to cross one more street and then

148

campus, then I'd be at my dorm and away from all of them. In the safety of my room, finally, I could break. I could fall apart, let Charlie go yet again and put Charlotte back in place. It didn't matter if they knew; they didn't understand. It didn't matter. I just needed the time to make myself right again.

Trevor trailed behind me the whole way, not saying another word. He followed me into the building and up the elevator to the third floor. I dropped my keys twice before he picked them up and unlocked the door, letting us in.

The door clicked shut and we stood there in the dark. The lump in my throat grew, the repressed agony bubbling to the surface at a rapid rate.

"Katie's gone." The words were barely a whisper. My tongue and my lips formed them and on my exhale, they were so small. "Katie's gone and I'm a liar. I'm a lie. It's all a lie. Katie's dead and now they know. You know. Everybody knows it's all a lie. Everybody knows I'm a lie." The admission was a rush of breathy sound handed over to the darkness I forgot wasn't empty.

"Too fast. Too much." It was a strangled admission and as soon as I whimpered the words, I crumpled. My body folded in on itself and I was on my hands and knees, the sobs rocking me back and forth as I gasped for air and screamed with soundless cries.

My fingertips gripped the floor while my abdomen stayed concave, unable to allow more than a shallow breath of air to pass.

He pulled me backward, my world turning upside down as I hovered on the balls of my feet and then fell into Trevor's lap.

His cologne was there again. I didn't know exactly what it smelled like, but it was guitar strings, tacos, secret handshakes and comfort. It was safe, and I turned into him, curling into the tightest ball while I gripped his sweater and sobbed for her, for me and for everything I'd lost along the way.

His arms around me, murmuring unintelligible words but letting me know he was there, Trevor gave everything and asked nothing. He held me, brushing away the strands of hair that came undone from my ponytail and softly encouraging me to stay with him.

The ache didn't end and neither did my tears until he started to sing.

The words were unfamiliar. Unable to piece them together, I just let his voice wash over me. I pressed my ear to Trevor's chest, listening to the song and slow beat of his heart as it pushed blood from place to place in the body of this boy who refused to let me go.

"Why are you still here?" I whispered, my voice choked and hoarse.

"Because I need you just as much as you need me, Charlie Bear," he whispered.

***

Every part of me hurt. The bed was so uncomfortable and as I stretched, I realized why. My pillow was Trevor's chest and my bed was my dorm floor.

My head throbbed as I extricated myself from him, already missing his warmth but needing a toothbrush and pain killers more.

I tiptoed across the room and closed the bathroom door. As I put the toothbrush in my mouth, I finally looked in the mirror. My hair was sort of in last night's ponytail, I had more mascara on my face than my eyes and indentions from Trevor's hand on my stomach.

I brushed out my hair as I tried to piece together the night's events. It was like a dream, bits and pieces flitting in and out to the point where I couldn't guarantee all of it really happened. But my swollen, red-rimmed eyes were real and Trevor was here, so I knew I couldn't hide anymore.

When I emerged, face thoroughly scrubbed and sweats in place of an outfit I should have never dug up from the past, Trevor was sitting on my bed.

"Morning," he croaked out, stretching his arms above his head. "How are you feeling?"

I shrugged. "As long as thoughts are optional, I'm still miserable."

"You were impressive on a whole new level," he said with a teasing smile.

I could only muster a quirk of my eyebrow as a vague memory of my attempted kiss surfaced. He'd stopped it and I was grateful.

"I haven't seen that shirt since we snuck out and tried to convince a bouncer at a club downtown we were eighteen when we were barely fourteen."

"I told you you should have let me do the talking." I lowered myself into the chair at my desk one inch at a time.

"Mmmhmmm," he replied as he watched me.

We sat quietly for a few minutes and I silently bartered many things to get my headache to lessen and my stomach to settle.

"We need to talk, Charlie," Trevor finally said.

I didn't open my eyes. I couldn't look at him.

"How long?"

He was quiet for the most agonizing thirty seconds in history. I had no idea he was even at the party, let alone in the room. But he hadn't been fazed by Sarah's words last night. He knew I would break when I heard them. He had to have known she died, though I hadn't the foggiest of how.

"Since finals."

He knew she was gone and I hadn't been the one to tell him. Guilt and shame were equally oppressive, each layering onto my hangover, sending bile into my throat as waves of nausea ripped through me.

"So, we need to talk," I repeated back to him.

"Yeah, I think we do," he agreed. "You need to explain some things, and so do I. I also need to apologize for disappearing these last few weeks. That's why I came to the party. When your mom told me—"

"My mom?" Of all the options, that was not one I expected.

"Yeah, I ran into your mom and it just happened. I didn't know how to process what she said, but I shouldn't have run from you."

"No. I should have told you to start with, but there was never a good time. You were either irritating me to death or making me feel *so much*...or eventually, just letting me feel like me again. I didn't want to admit the truth."

I finally forced myself to look at my best friend. He regarded me with everything except pity. It was the one emotion I'd come to expect from every person who found out my sister swallowed a bottle of pills three days before Thanksgiving. Every single one of them looked at me with nothing but pity, except Trevor. He looked at me and just understood.

He pushed up from the bed and came to stand in front of me, finally squatting to my level.

"You're going to be okay, Charlie. I promise you that."

"But how do you know?" Tears burned behind my eyes. Hope begged me to believe him and fear scoffed at the notion.

"You're here and I'm here and we're going to do this together," he promised.

"But your sister didn't die." It was whiny and it was weak but it was how I felt.

Trevor looked at me, sadness drawing his features down until I wondered if we would both cry.

"No, my sister didn't die," he said, reaching out to take my hand. "But I think my best friend almost did and since I've never had a sister, she's the most important person I've ever known, so I'll do anything I can to bring her back and keep her here."

"I'm so sorry," I whispered, unable to continue looking at him.

He stood, one finger coming under my chin to force me to look up at him.

"You had to do what you had to do," he said. "I wanted to be mad at you. I tried to stay mad at you. But eventually, I realized there are times we all make the wrong decision for the right reasons. I just want to know your reasons so we can move on from this together, okay?"

I nodded and watched him leave, wishing I had the strength to ask him to stay.

CHAPTER
nineteen

February

He knows.
But he's still here.

I woke up every day to those two thoughts and still wasn't sure which was harder to believe. Not telling him the whole first semester was agony and a debate I had with myself daily. Anxiety had me on edge for so long, so afraid he would hate me once he found out, now I had no idea what to do with myself. My thoughts weren't consumed with what could go wrong, now they were a mess as I wondered for the first time what might go right.

Every morning, I also had a message from him, generally left hours before I woke up while he was already at work. Sometimes he included snippets of songs he was writing and often he'd send memories, our favorite songs and silly phrases only the two of us understood — like the time he called one of the lazy bartenders who left him extra work a kumquat face.

WHO SHE WAS

I burst out laughing when that one came through, hiding my face in my pillow so I didn't wake Darcy. In fourth grade, we misheard an older kid call another "twat face", and for years, we swore kumquat face was the ultimate insult, and we were so cool for being the only ones who understood.

The only problem was once I'd read the messages and the day began, I was still Charlotte Logan and this was still my life. Every day my friends knew the truth became harder to face. The lies I'd told and continued to live felt bigger and my commitment to them less solid. I knew why I had to stick to it. I knew I needed to do this and it was the right choice. *I knew it was.* Yet the questions lingered on the edges of my mind.

What if became a torturous game I played in the middle of the night when memories became nightmares. In the darkness, I could rewind it all and nothing would be as it was now, except Trevor and I would still be here together. This time, we'd both be in the music program. He'd be writing, I'd be playing and we'd perform together after the juries. We'd sing one of our songs. Our parents and Katie would cheer. We would finally become more than friends.

It would be the kiss that set the bar for all other kisses — the one Trevor promised me after Darcy and Sam's little plot didn't work. It wouldn't be my first kiss or our last, but it would be the only one that mattered and the barometer for every other.

He hadn't come near me though, not in that way, since before finals. We were strictly platonic, outside of his minimally flirtatious messages — messages I would have never considered flirtatious if I hadn't wanted so much for them to be.

I slammed my journal shut, cursing my attraction to Trevor and my overly attentive friends. "I need you two to stop looking at me like that," I said, frustration finally getting the better of me.

Darcy and Sam sat on her bed, whispering in low tones, obviously discussing me. It was what they'd been doing for two weeks, giving me side looks and stopping their conversations when I walked into the room.

"We need to talk about this," Darcy said, her tone soft, sympathetic — close to getting her punched in the face.

Sam nodded as I shook my head, disagreeing.

"We absolutely do not need to talk about this because there is nothing to talk about. By now, you've both googled it, read the details and you know what I know. My sister is dead, end of story." I pushed off the bed, shoved books in my backpack and pulled on my warmest socks to go under my tall boots.

"But how are *you*?" Sam asked. "That's what we're really worried about, Charlie. We're worried about you."

I shoved my arms into my coat. "Don't, Sam. I'm fine. It was four years ago. I've been fine and I'll be fine. I didn't tell you because I didn't want you to look at me exactly the way you both currently are. This didn't happen *to me,* it just happened, and I've dealt with it."

"Have you?" Darcy accused, standing up and striding across the room to my closet. She threw open the door and grabbed a handful of hangers. She held up one piece after another from Banana Republic, The Limited and Nordstrom Rack before dropping them in a pile at her feet. Pieces mostly chosen by my mother and dutifully worn by me.

"Are these really you, Char?" she questioned. "Because when I told you to be yourself, you picked a ripped up vintage Metallica shirt. You chose to be Gwen Stefani for Halloween. I don't see how these clothes are you. You hate every single class related to your Poli Sci major and told me you *used* to play music. Trevor was right — you're two different people right now and that's not healthy. We just want you to be you, whoever that is. Whoever you want to be."

I looked between them — Darcy's eyes pleading with me to just be honest, with her and myself, and Sam acknowledging the necessity of a double life while reminding me, without a word, what embracing your truth could do. He was so happy, so filled with joy all the time. His style was still a work in progress, but his outlook was always rosy and I was so envious. He hadn't even officially come out, but he was trying to find himself, to let his truth be seen and test the waters of an authentic life.

My truth wasn't pretty, though. My truth wouldn't set anyone free. My truth was a trap.

I sucked in a long breath. "I need you not to do this," I said, forcing my tone to stay level. "I need you both to *back off*." The last two words came out with unexpected force, a shrill threat I didn't intend to make that had their heads snapping back.

I snatched my backpack off the floor, put it on and almost ran out the door, my hands gripping the shoulder straps tightly as I tried to stop them from shaking.

***

157

Trevor waited outside the library and the sight of him calmed me in a way that should have bothered me more. I had depended on no one but myself for so long, I both longed for and hated the idea of being affected by another person. I walked the plowed path between the piles of snow toward his familiar smile and tried to forget what just happened with Darcy and Sam.

"They mean well," Trevor said as I got within a few feet of him.

I rolled my eyes. "Sam already texted you, didn't he?"

He shrugged. "We're all worried about you."

"I don't know how many times—"

"You're fine," he cut in, sarcasm tightly woven into each word. "We all know that and none of us believe you. You don't believe you."

"Can we just go study, please?" I was annoyed and unwilling to acknowledge his statement.

Trevor grabbed my elbow as I tried to move toward the door and spun me around, saying, "Nope, we actually can't. Because we've done homework every night this week and it's Saturday afternoon. We're getting out of here. International Relations or War and Peace, or whatever boring ass thing you're dealing with today can wait."

I trudged alongside him toward the lot across the street where he kept his car, feigning annoyance when I was secretly ecstatic to get away from the schoolwork Darcy was right about me hating. "And where, pray tell, are we getting out to?"

Trevor grinned the impish look he'd been giving me since we were in kindergarten and he started smuggling an extra fruit roll up into his lunch to give me when my mom refused to let me have anything resembling fun kid food.

"Don't worry about it. Just let me handle today," he said with a wink.

"You have no idea how okay I am with that idea." I tossed my bag into his backseat and tucked myself into the front. I'd depended on my control of every situation in my life for so long, the idea of relinquishing it was heady. It bubbled up a giddiness I hadn't felt in years. As a small smile spread across my face, Trevor's eyes met mine and I saw his relief. Every day, I was shocked by how well he still knew me when I didn't feel like I even knew me.

We sat in the car for a minute, letting it warm up before Trev took off toward downtown. I'd gathered it was his favorite part of Des Moines, and it was generally where we went together.

"You haven't said much about your parents lately, is everything okay?" I didn't miss the way his hands clenched the steering wheel tightly.

"They're fine. Mom's working at a local grocery store in the floral department," he responded, his voice uncharacteristically tense.

"And she's doing…okay?" Her drinking problems were no secret between us. By the time we were old enough to realize her "naps" were really the end of a drunken stupor, we'd already learned to steer clear when she had her "adult juice".

He gave me a sideways look as he said, "As far as I know. I haven't seen much of them since Christmas break."

We lapsed into silence only broken by the stereo.

"What about your parents?" Trevor asked.

"What about them?"

"Well, your mom has always just been…your mom," he started. "And your dad was cool once. I never really understood what changed for him, but one day, he liked me, and the next, I was a pariah. So I guess I'm asking how it all affected them?"

"Not you, too" I said, shaking my head. Why did he have to go so far back? I couldn't think about my dad before, when he sang along to the radio with me and cared about my dreams. Before Katie was gone and nothing I did was good enough anymore.

"Me too, what?" Trev asked, pulling into a parallel spot on the Grand Avenue bridge.

"I need you not to make everything about her," I responded. "My life didn't revolve around her before and it doesn't need to now."

"Right." He turned to face me. "Except it kind of did."

"It did not."

One eyebrow slowly rose above the thick black rims of his glasses.

"Katie was everything your parents wanted her to be and the more she conformed, the more they expected of you and the further you rebelled. So, sorry to break it to you, but she was a pretty big part of who you were."

I crossed my arms over my chest and stared out the front windshield. It was a rare February day that was chilly but not freezing, and the sky was the brightest blue. The sunshine glinted off the gold of the Iowa State capitol dome, making it look deeper and more vibrant than usual.

Trevor didn't wait for my response or indulge my sulk. He opened his door and I scrambled to unclip my seat belt and follow him. I had to take a running leap to get over the snow pile and onto the sidewalk, walking quickly to catch up with his long legs.

"Will you at least tell me what we're doing?" I asked as he pulled a stocking cap from his jacket and covered his dark hair.

"We," he said, gesturing to his left, "are going ice skating."

He didn't give me a chance to argue my inability to walk without tripping over something, let alone balance on a razor blade. Instead, he grabbed my hand and yanked me under the awning of Brenton Skating Plaza.

CHAPTER
twenty

I smacked into the railing, again, and did my best to stay upright. Laughter bubbled up as my feet scrambled for purchase below me and Trevor flew past. He turned with ease and skated backwards away from me.

"Show off!" I yelled, still laughing at my total inability to stay upright.

"Talent isn't showing—whoa!" A kid came out of nowhere and Trevor lost his balance, arms akimbo as he fell backward onto his butt.

I skated toward him in small slices, my hands out. From above him, my smile grew with every second he couldn't get up.

"You were saying?" I asked.

He scowled up at me and held out a hand. "A little help, please?"

I extended my hand, and seconds later, found myself sprawled on the ice next to him.

"You're lucky I didn't hit my head on the ice," I scolded as he laughed. "I could have gotten a concussion and you would have spent the rest of the night in the ER with me."

"Oh, like that time you wrecked your bike and swore your ankle was broken?" He rolled to his knees and pushed to stand.

"Hey! It could have been and it would have been your fault. You're the one who said I wouldn't ride down the Turner Street hill."

"And Charlotte Logan never turns down a challenge," he said, rolling his eyes. "For the record, I carried you for five blocks."

"You liked it," I accused. I'd liked it. I knew my ankle wasn't broken and told the nurse as much as soon as Trevor went to call my parents.

I tried to go from my knees to my feet and only slipped back down once before I wobbled my way to standing.

"Last one out buys hot chocolate," Trevor called, already a stride ahead.

"Cheater!" I pushed forward, skating and not stomping over the ice for the first time.

I got to the rink edge just behind Trevor and immediately laid into him.

"You totally slowed down! You aren't supposed to try to let me win," I grumbled.

"I didn't let you win, you're still buying the hot chocolate," he said, his voice hollow. "But, ah…this could get awkward."

"Awkward? Why?" I looked past him and froze.

"Because I'm pretty sure your mom hates me and that look on her face confirms my suspicion." My mother stood on the edge of the check in area, her annoyance clear in her tapping boot and crossed arms.

We quickly removed our skates, turned them in and pulled on our boots. I kept looking up at my mother and her scowl deepened with every second she waited for me.

"Time is money, Charlotte," she'd always said, the epitome of efficiency. *"Never waste either."*

I took the first step toward her and Trevor hung back. "Come on," I hissed, "don't be a wussy." My hands were shaking inside my coat pockets and there was no way I was going alone. I was fairly certain I knew what she wanted and didn't know if I could handle it.

He huffed out a quick breath and matched my stride. Just having him beside me made each step easier to take.

"Mom, what are you doing here?" I asked as we approached.

"Well, hello to you, too, Charlotte," she responded, grimacing. "I'm doing quite well, thank you for asking."

"I'm sorry," I started again. "Hi, Mom, how are you?"

"Hello, Mrs. Logan," Trevor said, his usual disdain for my mother absent in his quiet and oddly deferential greeting.

She didn't acknowledge Trevor in any way, but that was normal.

"Charlotte, you need to come with me," she said. "Your father isn't well and I need your help. I've been calling you for the last two hours and thankfully can track your iPhone since I still pay the bill."

My suspicions were confirmed and a snake of apprehension shimmied down my spine.

"We don't need to discuss particulars out in the open for the world to hear," she hissed, glancing past me for the first time to direct her icy glare at Trevor.

"Obviously Trevor knows. You don't have to pretend here," I said, keeping my voice low.

"Oh, I am well aware your little friend now knows our family tragedy. I'm not concerned with him at the moment. You know you're the only person your father will respond to when he's like this and I am at my wit's end. Let's go." She turned and walked away, her face already pointed down at her phone.

I looked between Trevor and my mother's back multiple times. I didn't want to go; I wanted to stay. But this time, staying was running and I didn't want to run anymore.

"Go, Charlie," Trevor interrupted my circling thoughts. "If your dad needs you, you should go."

He reached out and squeezed my hand as my mother called my name yet again.

"Go, and we'll talk when you get back," he encouraged.

"It might be a few days, but hopefully not." His eyes widened in surprise and his mouth opened to ask a question I couldn't answer.

"I'll explain later," I echoed his promise and turned to run after my mother, dread already filling the space that laughter had filled only moments ago.

***

With every mile we drove, closing the distance between me and Pella, it seemed a new memory forced its way to the surface. Scenes I'd long buried clawed their way into my mind, stealing the joy of my day.

As my mother worked, her earpiece in and a stream of conference calls I only half heard floating around me, I was catapulted back in time.

My dad played his old Beatles records on the beat up player in our basement, telling me stories of the concerts he'd been to while swearing there was a time when my mom had been fun.

My dad grinning at me when I told him I wanted to learn to play piano, before the fight ensued with my mother over his desire to buy me lessons.

Me, Katie and Dad on a secret adventure at the ice cream shop while he made us swear not to tell mom.

But those memories were the decoys. They were only the setup for the real pain. Before Katie was even gone, my dad changed. Trevor was right about that. I was too young then to understand what happened, but he was either very happy or very unhappy — it was always an extreme. He swung us in the air, ran around the backyard, bought every toy we'd ever dreamed of and indulged our every whim — or he lashed out, yelled, didn't want to play with us anymore and all he and mom did was fight.

I took a chance when I was twelve, in an attempt to reconnect with him again, and told my dad my secret — that Trevor taught me how to play piano and guitar, and I was really getting good. I even learned to play his favorite song, *Hey Jude*. I thought he would be proud. Instead, he yelled at me.

His big hands gripped my small shoulders and he shook me, his face so red. *"You will not waste your life, Charlotte. You will not allow that boy to distract you from making something of yourself. You don't have time for silly dreams — life is hard and you need to do something that matters."*

He threatened to tell my mother unless I stopped. Tears streamed down my face as I promised I would, but behind my back, my fingers were crossed. I couldn't stop playing. My father had just confirmed music was the only thing I had besides Trevor and I refused to let either of them go.

Do something that matters. The idea of what "matters" was so obtuse. It was hard to define, but everyone knew what it felt like to matter. I wanted to matter. In fact, that was all I'd ever wanted. I wanted to be important, to have my dreams encouraged, to know there were people who believed in me. I had mattered to Trevor, and he was taken away. I thought I'd mattered to Katie, but she lied and then left me to face them alone. I'd wanted so desperately to matter to my parents, especially my mother, who never really tried to know me, let alone understand me.

She and Katie were always closer. They talked about college and law school. They had real conversations. I was simply spoken to. I was too loud and too honest and too much for my mother. I was everything she couldn't handle.

Two years later, after Katie was gone, my mother sat me down and in her no-nonsense way, explained my father was bi-polar and we had to do everything we could to help him. I hadn't realized it then, but when she said "we", she really meant me. As much as he was disheveled and distraught, she was the epitome of order and control. She never understood why he couldn't simply make the decision to be better, as if being bi-polar was a matter of will and not a chemical imbalance.

As we pulled off highway sixty-five and made our way into town, my mother hung up the last call and finally addressed me directly.

"I know this isn't easy for you, but I need you to do whatever necessary to bring your father out of this. It's a waste of his energy and entirely unproductive," she stated.

"Oh," I said with a defiant snort, "well, for a minute I thought it actually mattered that it isn't easy for me."

We stared at each other, both shocked by my outburst. I started to fidget, my fingers tapping melodies onto my thighs as I stared straight ahead.

"Of course it *matters*," she gritted out, her perfectly styled and sprayed hair barely moving as she turned to look at me. "But you need to look at the whole and not the parts. Your father needs to go to work. He needs to function. He needs to understand that just because this happened to us doesn't mean he should hide from the world and fall back down this hole again."

"This?" I questioned, the anger I normally kept locked away spreading into my mind and out my mouth. "*This* what? By *this*, do you mean his daughter committing suicide? Because I don't think there's a rulebook for how you need to handle something like that. Or if there is, nobody shared it with me."

The words weren't fully out before she swerved to the right, coming to a screeching halt along the two-lane road.

"You listen to me, Charlotte Lydia Logan," she spat, inches within my face, the droplets actually spewing from her painted lips in my direction. "Your father was a brilliant lawyer and a man I was proud to call my husband. I have done everything I can to help him. I sent him to therapists. I moved to this godforsaken town to get him away from all the questions and prying eyes of Muscatine where everyone knew us but we actually had friends. I built a brand new practice he was supposed to be a part of *by myself* because someone had to put food on the table and put you through college. I have done *everything* and my daughter also died that day. It's time for him to just deal with it and stop using this illness as an excuse."

She sat there, fuming, her dark eyes a mirror of mine. But there was no feeling in them, not anymore. She'd never been one for overt emotion, the role of divorce lawyer suited her well. But now, she was made of ice — a cold, spiteful woman I generally feared more than hated. I didn't want to hate her. I wanted her to look at me the way she used to look at Katie. That was all I'd ever wanted.

"Fine, I'll do it," I said, averting my eyes. "I'll do whatever I have to because I want to help Dad get better."

Taking a deep breath, she turned back to the road and pulled back out.

"Thank you," she said, her voice low. "I would also like him to be better."

It was the first time I'd ever heard her admit she cared at all. I assumed she had to, given they were still married and she had made all those concessions, but her whispered words of gratitude both surprised and worried me. If she was truly concerned, what would I find when we got home?

Deciding to use this momentary show of emotion to my advantage, I asked the question I hadn't been able to answer since August. "Did you keep Trevor from me after Katie died? Did you lie to him and make him think I didn't want to talk to him?"

I expected her to tense up, to get angry even. Instead, she sighed. Her whole body drooped as she didn't even bother to lie. "Yes, I did. It was for your own good."

"My own good," I repeated. "He was my best friend. I needed him. I begged you to call his parents, to use your connections to find him. You let me think he abandoned me." Tears burned my eyes, but I wouldn't give her my tears, she didn't deserve them. Her betrayal was more than painful. It was the final crack that broke apart the fissure in our relationship.

"That boy distracted you. His parents were deadbeats and he was going to drag you down with him. I refused to let that happen to you." She twisted her fists as she gripped the steering wheel.

"*That boy?* That boy is the only person in my entire life who has ever wanted me to just be me. The only person who's ever wanted me to be happy — to be whole. *That boy* loved me, more than you apparently."

Her signal clicked in the tense silence as we turned onto our street. She pulled into the driveway and put the car in park as I seethed in the seat next to her.

"Charlotte, you are my daughter, and of course I love you, but you have never listened to me and up until the last few years, you never took life seriously. Until you have children of your own, you cannot understand the choices I made."

I waited until she turned to face me. She looked so satisfied with her answer, as if it should pacify me and make everything fine.

"What I know is no one who actually loves you follows it with the word 'but'."

I didn't wait for her response. I got out of the car and went inside to face what she wouldn't.

CHAPTER
twenty-one

My hand shook as I reached out to grasp the knob. I turned it in tiny increments, acid from my stomach roaring up my esophagus and sending tangy bile into the back of my throat. I swallowed it down, breathing through my nose while reminding myself it was my dad in there. No matter what state he was in, it was my dad and I wouldn't leave him to handle this alone.

"Dad?" I called out as I stepped into his bedroom. My parents had separate bedrooms from the day we moved to Pella and his was always closest to mine. There were days when that was a comfort, and days when it was pure torture.

"Baby?" he responded, his dark silhouette perking up in bed. A small lamp cast a low white glow over the room.

I forced a smile. "Yeah, it's me, Charlotte."

He was silent for a moment. "Oh, of course. Hi, Charlotte," he said, the joy of his previous response absent.

The tears from moments ago threatened again and a thick feeling lodged in my throat, but I refused to let this go downhill already.

"I started my International Relations class this semester and you won't believe it. I have Dr. Grayson, just like you did!" I almost choked on my fake enthusiasm. My parents met at Rodgers during their undergrad, both pre-law. It was one of a dozen reasons I ended up there.

"Is that so?" he asked, already sounding disengaged. "Is he still wearing the same old brown sweater every day?"

Taking his response as an invitation, I made my way across the small space. I cleared a pile of clothes from the single chair in the room and perched on the edge.

"He is." I forced a short laugh. "And now it's missing a button. Second one down. But he just buttons the other three and doesn't seem to mind."

That garnered an actual chuckle from him — a magical sound that used to mean root beer floats and tickle fights. "Sorry to break it to you, honey, but that button has been missing since the eighties."

"But the real question is if he always smelled like mothballs and mint gum?"

"He most certainly did. Some things never change." His smile lingered for a moment, giving me a smidgen of hope.

The darkness of his room could only be a contributor to his melancholy, so I stood and went to the window, pulling back the blinds.

"It's a gorgeous day today. The sun is shining and it finally got a little warmer."

"Charlotte, no!" he yelled. His terse command shocked me and I whipped the curtain back in place, but didn't get it all the way closed. A ribbon of bright sunlight filtered through the room and dust flecks swirled in the air. The beam cut across my father's bed, where he sat amidst the pile of blankets in sweats and a T-shirt so rumpled it was clear he'd been in them for some time.

His hair stood on end. It normally laid flat, a trendy businessman's cut that made him look younger than forty-six. Right now, he looked sixty, his face sunk in and pale. He refused to meet my eyes, so I continued to survey the room.

Trash piled on top of his dresser — take-out containers, dirty dishes and who knows what else. Self-help books littered his bedside table, their spines unbroken, likely meaning they'd come from my mother. Clothes were strewn everywhere, but there were no photographs — not of me, not of Katie.

"Dad, you told me at Christmas you were going to go back to Dr. Thompson," I said softly.

"I don't need you telling me how to cope," he snapped. "Your mother does that enough for the whole world." He paused, his hands clenching into the covers. "And Dr. Thompson wants me to take those damn pills. They make me feel like a zombie. I can't think. And...I-I can't remember."

I stilled, knowing exactly where we were headed. Him needing to remember meant I had to remember.

"What do you need to remember?" I asked. My hands trembled and my legs could no longer hold me upright, so I dropped back into the chair.

WHO SHE WAS

"She's fading, Charlie. Katie is fading and I can't bear it," he admitted, unchecked emotion turning his last words into a soft cry.

He rarely called me Charlie anymore — only in moments of weakness, when Katie wasn't Katherine, this girl we were all supposed to just move past. The one my mother spoke of like a long-lost cousin and not their daughter.

Goosebumps rose over my skin and I once again cursed my sister's name. Accusations flew through my mind.

How could you be so selfish?

How could you do this to me, and them?

Why was it okay to take your life and mine?

With a small shake of my head, I cleared those worthless thoughts and refocused on my father. He was here and he needed me.

"Dad, we have photo albums of pictures. And I made you that slideshow last year so you could play it whenever you wanted from your phone. Katie isn't fading. The medicine is helping you stay here, in this moment, with us. We need you. *I* need you," I admitted.

Those albums were the end of me. They were the end of Charlie—the girl who lived life on her own terms and wanted to change the world through music. It was hard enough to go through the pictures and see my sister's perfect life—her trophies, medals, straight A report cards and top tier friends—knowing it was all a lie. But then, I had to watch both my mother and father look at those pictures. I had to watch them as they blinked back tears, shared whispered memories as they ran the pads of their fingers over her matte-finished reflection. I watched them yearn for her and knew what I had to do.

"My little girl is gone. It just isn't the same," he argued.

I leaned back and let my head rest on the chair, swallowing down tears. "It's never going to be the same," I replied, the sting of his words nine lashes over the wide-open wounds I carried.

We sat in silence for another minute or so while I tried to find a way out of the current spiral.

"I, uh…you won't believe who I found at Rodgers. Trevor Adler, do you remember him?"

"Of course I remember him," my father scoffed. "He was a good kid, but was always getting your priorities mixed up. Please tell me he hasn't gotten you back into music. We've talked about this. That isn't a career."

I closed my eyes briefly and justified yet another lie. I'd told so many of them, it wasn't even worth crossing my fingers. "Of course not. I haven't done anything like that in a long time. You know I'm focused on becoming a lawyer. I want to make you proud."

He finally rose from his bed, a satisfied smile stretching his pale lips. "That's good. I'm sure you'll be just as good as Katherine would have been. Or at least close. She really would have been great."

I bit the inside of my cheek and let the metallic taste linger on my tongue so I didn't release the words it held.

"I think I need a shower," he said, defeat rampant in his tone. "Can you excuse me?" he asked, tilting his head toward the door. That was the Logan family, always polite even in the midst of a crisis. But a shower was progress and I would take progress in any form— progress got me the hell out of here.

"Sure, how about I pick things up a little while you're in there?" I offered. My mother wouldn't come in this room unless forced and it clearly hadn't been touched since I cleaned it at Christmas.

He shrugged. "I'm sure your mother would like that. You can tell her I'll be out for dinner."

As he walked away, I barely heard him mutter, "She wins again."

The door to the adjoined bathroom closed and I crumpled back in the chair, silent tears trailing down my cheeks.

Katie was gone and I was trapped.

***

I unlocked my door and found the dorm room empty. Part of me wished Darcy were here, to give me someone to talk to about anything and everything that wasn't the last twenty-four hours. But with the constant internal chatter swirling in my head, I wouldn't have made for a very good companion.

Between my mother's barbs and father's constant reminders that, no matter how much I tried, I'd never compare to Katie, I questioned what the hell I was doing with my life. How had I allowed it to come to this? I looked back on the last few years and they were a haze — a twilight time I wished I could wake up from.

I tossed my backpack in the corner and dropped onto the bed, saying, "You know exactly how you got here." Visions of drunk nights, times I never came home and classes I skipped to hide from the stares of my classmates galloped through my mind. My parents' disappointment, anger and then ambivalence stung like a slap, even after all this time.

The first few years of high school were much better forgotten. Too bad I now thought about the future more than I ever had and wished I could have those early years back.

I grabbed my pillow, intending to pull it to my chest, when something fell off and landed on the floor. Leaning over, I reached down to pick up the oversized red envelope. As soon as I flipped it over, I saw his familiar scrawl.

Happy Capitalist Day, Charlie!

I erupted in laughter, the sound unexpected even as it came from my mouth. Starting in middle school, Trevor and I made fun of Valentine's Day for being so obviously fake and profit-driven, then I stopped acknowledging it completely. It hadn't occurred to me it was already the fourteenth as I excitedly ripped open the seal.

I knew what I'd find before I pulled it out, and was already grinning.

Drop it like it's hot was written in perfect print letters across the CD face, and I knew what was etched on the back. It would have to wait, though. If I knew Trev, the best was yet to come.

I turned the envelope upside down and shook it, my grin growing when a business-card sized valentine dropped out.

Roses are red, grass is green, this isn't actually a valentine, because clearly, I'm mean. Professor Snape stared up at me, his sneer perfectly situated to communicate exactly how thrilled he was.

I giggled as I dug in my purse for my phone.

Charlie: Roses are red, violets are plum, I didn't get you a valentine because this day is dumb.

I hit send and immediately took the CD to my laptop. Thankfully, it still had a drive. Darcy's MacBook Air, which I was insanely jealous of, didn't. I popped it in and let it play, turning the volume up as far as it would go before sitting back down on the bed.

Piano chords filled the air, Beethoven taking up the empty space around me and quieting my overactive mind. I could imagine my fingers on the cool porcelain keys as my body swayed, playing along with him. The notes filled each dark and empty crevice one at a time, layering over each other and forcing out every emotion, except what he bid me to feel. In these few minutes, I was Beethoven's captive and I couldn't have been a more willing participant.

My phone chirped beside me and I unlocked it, eager to see Trevor's response.

Trevor: Can't argue with you there. Things go okay with your dad? Glad you're back!

I hesitated. We'd exchanged a few messages while I was in Pella, but I wasn't sure I was ready to tell the whole story, and to adequately explain the absolute clusterfuck of my life, I would have to.

That said, I refused to lie to him anymore. I wanted to tell Trevor the truth. I wanted him to understand where I'd been and beg him not to give up on me even though there were days his pushing forced me into territory I was uncomfortable with. My anxiety often reared its ugly head, and so far, he'd put up with it so well. I was terrified he'd label me a lost cause before I could get my act together.

Charlie: It's as okay as it can be for now. Where are you?

Trevor: FAC. Juries are at the end of this semester and I'm so far behind.

Charlie: K. I'm here if you want to drop by after.

Trevor: Plan on it.

I smiled at the phone, relieved to be back here and near Trevor—to have a moment of normalcy. Then, another message popped up.

Trevor: Listen to the CD, Charlie.

Charlie: I am! :P

The music continued to play and eventually, I sat up. I pulled the leather-bound journal Trevor gave me recently out of my dresser drawer and out from under my socks, holding it lightly between my fingertips.

He'd handed it to me last week, utterly nonchalant, and said, "Write in it. I don't care what, just write in it."

I had been writing in it—sometimes my thoughts, other times snippets of lyrics my mind wouldn't let go of. I reached for a pen off the desk as the song changed. No longer were the piano greats wooing me into relaxation, now it was a wooing of a different kind.

The guitar chords began and I heard Trevor clear his throat before he began to sing.

Honore
It's all changed
Pull your car up to the porch
And take all your things
To the other side of town
It's been strange
Having you around since the autumn days
Kept you tucked away
Honore

Honore
Around your waist
Were the hands that held you up
But you didn't want to dance
The music seemed to sound like it moved too fast
Dizzy from the ground
That underneath you sways
Oh, how you've always claimed
Honore

You didn't want to dance
Music seemed to sound like it moved too fast
Dizzy from the ground
That underneath you swayed
Oh, how you've always claimed
Waiting for the words to break
More stories you couldn't shake
Honore

I hit the back button and let it play again. The lyrics were deceptively simple, yet wrought with hidden meaning. They were his message to me, his reminder of days long past.

Honore Street was a real place in Chicago. We saw the sign at an intersection on a class trip and spent the whole drive back to Muscatine making up stories about the woman named Honore and what she'd been through to have a street named after her.

We had sat scooched way down in our bus seats, whispering of her dramatic life. Trevor spun this elaborate tale about how she was a ballerina who ended up torn between her abusive boyfriend and the best friend who'd been there for her through it all. She would run to her friend, but always went back, until one day she finally left the boyfriend for good. She went into hiding and gave up her dreams of dancing so he would never find her, but in the process, she walked away from her best friend as well, not wanting him to be caught in the middle any longer. In the end, the boyfriend did find her, and she was killed.

Trevor finished her story and I silently cried for this woman who never existed, but whose life was so tragically sad.

I listened to his low voice one more time, watching my screen saver swirl as I cried again for her. I hadn't cried for so many years and now it happened constantly. Trevor stirred a pot of emotions inside me I thought long dry—a barren wasteland, eviscerated by Katie's choices and my reactions. He made me feel, and while some days, emotion of any kind was welcome, others it was slow torture. Today, it was agony.

Honore was my story. I knew that's what he was saying. He was telling me I had a choice to make and it didn't have to be the one she made. Without pushing or pressure, he was asking me to make my choice and telling me he'd be here for me no matter what. The only problem was I didn't know if I could do it.

Trevor now knew part of my secret, but he didn't understand the depths of my pain. My guilt. My shame. The debt I felt I had to pay every single day to make up for what I'd done.

CHAPTER
twenty-two

March

I had my head buried in my polling workbook. The statistical analysis of polling, to be exact. And the fact that our voting system was utterly jacked up was a struggle for me to read, let alone stay awake for.

My phone started chirping, the text sound ringing over and over as I dug it out of my purse.

"Good grief, woman!" Darcy shouted from her side of the room. "Put a leash on that thing and figure out where the fire is!" She was already by my side as I finally located the phone at the bottom of my bag and unlocked the screen to find messages coming in rapid-fire from Sam.

You have to get over here NOW.

He's lost his mind. He's destroying his side of the room.

He won't talk to me, but I can't call and I'm afraid to leave him.

I didn't give Darcy time to fully read over my shoulder before I shoved my feet into the nearest shoes and grabbed my jacket.

"Stay here," I commanded as she rushed behind me.

"The hell I will." She pulled a hoodie on and followed me out the door. We ran across campus to Millen Hall, taking the stairs two at a time to their room on the sixth floor. Darcy had no problem with the impromptu workout, and I should have, but adrenaline rocketed through my system and nothing would keep me from getting to Trev.

There was only one person who would drive Trevor to this kind of behavior and anything involving his father was never good. By the time we were in middle school, Jonathan Adler had taken a liking to anything in a bottle. Off the booze, Trev's dad was a great guy. He was an artist, a hippie always wearing a big smile and ready with a joke. But give him anything to drink and his eyes were shadowed, darkness and anger emanating from him in waves everyone could feel. He was mean to Trevor and worse to his mom, but similar to my own father, his mood took abrupt turns and you never could tell what you were walking into.

We approached their door and I heard something crash to the ground. I turned to Darcy and put one hand on her chest.

"I need you to stay out here and keep Sam with you," I said. She started to shake her head and I pushed my hand harder. "Darc, I'm not asking. *I need you to do this.*" My own tone, suddenly so strong and sure I barely knew it as mine, shocked both of us. She nodded slowly and I withdrew.

I turned and reached for the door handle. Much like at my parents, emotion ricocheted around my mind and heart, but now they only held concern and fear. I'd been so wrapped up in my own tragedy I never stopped to really push Trev on how things were for him. I knew they were bad. I heard his offhanded comments and deflecting answers and *I knew it*, but I'd been too selfishly absorbed in myself to do anything about it.

Not anymore. I would get him through this.

I jerked the knob around and stepped through. With one tilt of my head, Sam flew behind me and out the door, only pausing to give my hand a squeeze on the way past. I leaned back, pushing the door closed and flicking the deadbolt.

Trevor stood at the window, his fingers digging into the frame. His head hung down, but every muscle in his back was bunched and taut. His knuckles were white and his breath ragged.

"Talk to me, Trev."

He didn't move. I gave him a minute and took a few steps closer.

"What did he do?"

Trevor spun around, his face twisted and red. His glasses slid down his nose and he ripped them off, flinging them across the room without hesitation. I didn't move my eyes from his or react in any way. I wouldn't show him, but he was acting more like his father than he'd ever want to admit.

"What did he do?" he sneered. I felt the rage emanate from him and I was scared.

I took another step forward, and said, "You heard the question. We both know your father did something, but you have to tell me what before you destroy everything in here." I forced calmness into my voice, but not pity. Never pity. Pity was for people who merely existed, not those who survived. Trevor was a survivor, whether he believed it or not.

Trevor reached out blindly and his hand connected with his guitar neck. He lifted it, and without further thought, I dove for them both, my hands wrapping around his forearms as I screamed, "No!"

As I expected, the pounding started on the door as Trevor stared down at me. His eyes were glazed over and wild, he wasn't seeing me. He wasn't even here.

"Just give it to me," I demanded. "You will not destroy something you love."

He let go, and I shouted, "It's fine, back off," to our friends, who were frantically trying to get inside, while Trev began to stalk around the room, muttering something I couldn't understand. I caught, "I don't love it that much."

I put the guitar back on the stand and waited. He thought he was the patient one, and there was a time when he might have been, but not anymore.

I counted fifteen passes back and forth before he finally stopped. Trevor stared straight ahead, seeing something I couldn't.

He turned to face me, and said, "I'm going to kill him." Grim satisfaction brought an uncomfortable calm into the small space we shared.

"Before you decide to spend the rest of our lives incarcerated for killing an asshole, tell me what happened. I'm not letting you out of here until you do," I threatened.

He laughed, which I expected. But the dark, hollow sound sent even more unease into my gut.

"I am small but mighty," I countered, pushing as much sass as I could muster into the statement. "And Darcy and Sam will call the police if you leave here. Won't you?" I asked, raising my voice and banging on the wall. I got two *thunks* in return and Trevor looked like he could kill me instead.

"Talk."

Both his hands were in his dark hair, yanking at the roots as he bent over and tried to maintain control. From that position, he finally said, "I went to see my mom. She called me last week and asked for money. For the first time ever, I said no."

Trevor stared at me, letting the silence hang between us. Guilt radiated off him and it took every ounce of my willpower not to go to him. I'd told him to stop giving into them.

"I told her the truth — I don't have it and I can't get it, not if I'm going to pass my freshman year of college. So, I went to check on her, to make sure things were okay. And I wanted to let her know it was almost spring break and I needed to come home since the dorms are closed."

His voice was muffled, directed at his knees. Trevor squatted down and laced his hands behind his head.

"I walked into the floral area where she works, and I knew. She was wearing a turtleneck and a ton of makeup, with one wrist in a brace. It's fifty degrees outside and we both know she's the first one to throw on her Birkenstocks and a dress as soon as spring shows its face.

"When she saw me, she could see I knew," he continued. "She started making excuses — that's all she ever does. *He hurt her and she made excuses.* I let this happen. If I hadn't said no, this would have never happened. He's never gone this far. It's my fault he went this far."

Unable to stop myself any longer, I took quick steps toward him. Trevor's anguish took him over in a wave. His lip trembled and his eyes glassed over. His chest shook and just before he fell back, I reached out and pulled him to me. His knees hit the ground and he buried his head in my stomach, wrapping his arms tightly around my body.

We stayed like that. Him taking short breaths, shoving down the myriad of emotions I understood all too well. Me staring at the ceiling and running my fingers through his hair, knowing exactly what I needed to say.

The words were wrapped in barbed wire, deeply embedded and hidden in a back corner of my soul. I'd never uttered them aloud and pulling them from the depths I'd pushed them to was like playing operation with a fist full of razor blades. But for him, I would do it. He needed to know that while our stories weren't the same, I understood too well what he was going through.

"I knew Katie was taking uppers," I said to the swirling ceiling fan as I gnawed at my cheek. The metallic ting of blood and the salty taste of tears coated my mouth. I wasn't sure which was real and which was a memory.

"What?" His voice was raspy and thick with checked emotion.

"I caught Katie taking Adderall. More than once," I confirmed, forcing myself to continue. "I confronted her, told her she had to stop, and she wouldn't. I told her I'd tell Mom and Dad, and she told me she stopped, but I caught her again. It was to the point where I could look at her and know she was amped."

I paused, unwelcome memories threatening my resolve.

"The last time I caught her, I got mad," I forced out, the truth coated in acid as I spat it out as quickly as possible. "I told her she was a fraud and she'd ruined my life pretending to be perfect. I told her if they knew the truth, they'd hate her as much as they hated me." The words stole the air from my lungs and it took everything in me to stay upright and draw my next breath.

When I finally looked down, Trevor was staring up at me. The pads of my fingers dug into his shoulders and I tried to pull away, but he captured my hands and stood.

"Why are you telling me this?" he asked. His gaze had softened and I shook my head.

"I didn't tell you to make this about me," I countered. "I told you because you need to know you can't save someone who doesn't want to be saved." I said the words, but still couldn't bring myself to believe them. I told him the truth that should have set us both free and wasn't surprised when he didn't buy it either.

He stilled and released my hands.

"You can't—"

"I can," I interrupted. "Katie made a choice and your mother is making a choice. Either of them could have gotten help and they continued choosing not to. You can't save her, Trev. She's an adult, and this is her choice. It's a choice she keeps making, over and over."

I still believed I could have saved Katie. Had I just been nicer, more understanding and a better fucking sister, I could have saved her, but Trevor's mother was a battered woman who'd chosen this life for nearly twenty-five years. She would never leave Jonathan.

The pacing began again and instead of standing still, I started cleaning up his mess. I found his glasses and popped a lens back in place. I stacked textbooks and sheet music. I folded clothes and remade the bed.

I was pulling the blanket up when he broke the silence. "Can we get out of here?"

I walked toward the door, turned, and extended my hand. He took it and we stepped over our collective roommates, not acknowledging their string of questions. We walked down the stairs, out the doors and into the sunlight without another word exchanged.

***

Trevor had been silent since we left his dorm. He'd even let me drive. I knew he needed space, so I stayed quiet — at least on the outside. Inside, my own demons raged. So much guilt and shame over not being there for Trevor mixed with anxiety, panic, and surprisingly, relief, over finally telling someone the truth — the whole truth.

"Why do you love being down here so much?" I asked as we walked the downtown riverwalk. Out enjoying the lamb of March, bikers, dog walkers and joggers warned us of being on the left and we tucked closer to the brown grass. The air off the river was brisk, but the sun on my face was welcome.

I watched him consider the question as his eyes scanned over the outdoor amphitheater, iCubs stadium and new hotels.

"They took something neglected and broken and brought it back to life," he responded. "There was a time when no one came down here. It was filled with empty buildings, old warehouses and bail bondsman. This area was unwanted and forgotten. Then the city, the community and the state all banded together and brought it back. Now, it's beautiful and vibrant and filled with life. It's something people want. It's something they didn't even realize they were missing until it was here."

Anger simmered inside me, directed solely at Trevor's parents. He didn't deserve to feel this alone.

We continued to walk, the silence between us comfortable. We followed the trail across the river behind the stadium and then headed west toward Gray's Lake.

"She left me a letter."

I clamped my mouth shut as my chest exploded in pain. The space under my left breast was on fire, my lungs frozen.

A strong hand shoved my head toward my knees and Trevor whispered in my ear. "Breathe through it, Charlie. You brought me back, now stay with me."

My hands were on my knees while he massaged the back of my neck and continued encouraging. Finally, the spasms slowed and I could expand my lungs. The leftovers from an attack were like an instant bruise. Each time my left lung inflated, I winced, but at least I could breathe.

"Slowly," he warned as I stood. The world tilted as my equilibrium reestablished.

Trevor kept my hand as we started walking again, this time deviating toward the main parkway and back toward the car.

"She left you a letter?"

"I've never opened it," I responded, enjoying the feel of his fingers wrapped around mine.

"Never?" He turned to face me, his mouth still hanging open in shock.

"You do look like Jim from The Office." Random laughter helped quell the anxiety of admitting my secret aloud.

Trevor grinned and used two fingers to jiggle his glasses, giving me a haughty look. He'd taken his hand away from mine to do it and I missed him immediately.

"He's a total dork, you know," I said, razzing him. "You should just tell people you look like John Krasinski because he's just hot."

"Avoiding the question."

I exhaled deeply, rolling my eyes as I started forward again. I needed to move.

"It's in my purse, zipped into the inside." I gripped the small bag at my side. "They gave it to me after it happened and tried to force me to open it. They wanted answers and justifications and to take the last piece of her away from me. So I told them I burned it without reading it. My parents didn't talk to me for a week after the funeral."

"Why haven't you opened it?"

"What could it possibly say?" I ground my teeth together. That was a lie. It was a lie I'd been telling myself for four years.

"You're afraid."

"I hate you."

"You do not. You love me because I call your bullshit," he responded, a small smirk making him look adorably conniving.

"Why do you have to be such a pain in the ass?" I bumped his shoulder with mine as I chuckled at his antics.

His arm wrapped around my shoulders and his cologne filled my nose. Spicy and sweet, with hints of citrus. I wanted to bury my head in his chest and stay there.

"Because you wouldn't love me otherwise," he said, pressing a kiss to the top of my head before I playfully shoved him away.

I hated the space between us. Two football fields of inches separated us and I despised them. But since Trevor found out about Katie, anything that had begun between us had disappeared. That kiss was the first sign of true affection I'd seen.

I couldn't blame him. Finding out from my mother and not me had to be a low point in our relationship, but I hoped we could go back to where we'd been.

"I don't know where to go during spring break," he said, cutting into my thoughts. "Before...all of that...I was going to go back home, but I can't. I don't think I'll live there ever again."

"I don't want to go to Pella either," I agreed.

"You never told me what happened with your dad," he said as we neared the parking ramp.

"Is it gut Charlie day? I thought this was about you?" I was only partly joking. "Why all the soul-baring discussion?"

He shrugged, a sad smile twisting his lips. "Because you're finally willing to have it and I'm trying not to react to my own shit."

I stared up at the blue sky, puffs of clouds and sunshine promising a spring we knew would get buried in more snow any day now.

"Fine, but this is it for today," I groused, amping up my pout and getting no response.

He nodded and leaned back against the light pole.

Now, it was my turn to pace. People moved past us, faceless humans who trudged through their own tragedies every day. How was mine so different?

"My dad gets really depressed. It started before Katie, but after, it was really bad," I started. "It's why we moved to Pella. He started acting crazy — or crazy according to my mother. It took a long time before they finally told me it was bi-polar disorder. The only thing that would calm him down after Katie died was to talk about her and I got nominated to do the job because it was just too hard for my mom. It often got to the point where he wouldn't leave his room and it took me weeks to get him to agree to go back to his therapist. Then it would be longer yet to get him back on his medication."

I'd been staring at the ground and flicked my eyes up to meet Trevor's. He was in the same place, with the same understanding look.

"My mom wanted him to work. She thought if he worked, he could occupy his thoughts with something else. So between me and the therapist, we convinced him to take the pills and eventually, he did get better. He started working, seeing clients, being normal." I hated the hope. I hated every time he smiled at me and I thought he saw *me*.

"But it never lasts," I admitted. "He always stops the pills and it's a spiral to rock bottom. At that point, he won't leave his room, he hates my mother and he barely tolerates me. But I'm the only one who can get to him, so it's my job to persuade him to rejoin the land of the living. Every time I go back there, it's a new nightmare. I never know what he'll be like or who I'm dealing with."

Trevor sat silent for a few seconds and then abruptly pushed off the lamppost and held out his hand. "We'll come back to all of this, but I just got the best idea and I think it's going to solve both our problems. Do you trust me?" His face was sincerity and love wrapped in hope and I put my hand in his without hesitation.

"Of course."

Trevor grinned, and declared, "I need to take you home. I've got a guy I need to talk to."

CHAPTER

twenty-three

We walked down a quiet hallway, and I whispered, "Are you sure this is okay?"

Trev laughed and rolled his eyes, not lowering his voice at all. "It's an apartment building, Charlie, not a hospital. And of course it's okay. I have the keys and we did pay for it."

I scowled as I trailed behind him, my overnight bag and backpack both stuffed to the brim and getting heavy.

"Mike rents it out all the time, and for the next seven days, it's ours. Just relax!"

"You haven't been this giddy since Heather Johnson kissed you during recess," I teased.

"She was pretty!"

"She was barely okay."

"It was fourth grade."

"She had a boy haircut and wore Minnie Mouse necklaces." I snickered, secretly still hating Heather for knowing what Trevor's lips felt like on hers, even if they were his fourth grade inexperienced lips. I could still feel his kisses on my neck from Halloween. I would bet he wasn't inexperienced anymore.

"Oh, look. We're here!" His relief was obvious as he shoved the key into the lock. I stifled a grin at his back.

Trevor pushed the door open and gestured me inside. The apartment was gorgeous. I dropped both my bags in the entryway and went directly to the windows. We were in a corner apartment and the Iowa State Capitol was filling the glass.

In the inky night sky, the gold dome and ornate architecture filled the space above the East Village high up on the hill. It was just a building, it shouldn't have looked so enchanting, but I wanted to climb to the top of that dome and press my face against the small glass panes of the rotunda. I wanted to look down on this place that could have been rejected, discarded and forgotten, but was reinvigorated and brought back from the brink instead. Trevor was right to love it. You couldn't help but be affected by this city and the hope it promised.

He came to stand beside me. "Pretty stunning, right?"

"This is gorgeous."

"You are gorgeous." I turned to him and we both wore the same surprised expression. He looked like he wanted to take it back and I just wanted him to say it again. As I stood there in my beat up Chucks, ripped jeans and one of his sweatshirts, I wanted him to tell me again I was gorgeous. Me — Charlie.

Trevor stared down at me, his dark eyes so familiar, yet now filled with so much more. There were memories I didn't have, pain I didn't understand and desire I knew too well.

He reached up and brushed hair away from my face, tucking it behind my ear. I was utterly still as he traced from my temple down my jawline. I'd just started to close my eyes and lean toward him when he abruptly stepped away. I felt the empty space where he used to be immediately. It was a void that left me feeling more than abandoned, I felt adrift. Like a balloon he'd suddenly let go of.

"This is, ah…just a one bedroom, but the couch pulls out. You take the bed. It's around the corner." Trevor stood awkwardly in the center of the small living room facing away from me.

"You sound weird." His departure was still stinging. I didn't know whether I was supposed to be Charlie, his best friend who called him on his bullshit, or the girl he'd just rejected.

Trevor had his back to me as he looked up at the ceiling. He slowly turned and said, "I know what we started, but things are different now and we have to deal with that first."

"*We started?* I don't know that *we* started anything. And what do you mean things are different? My sister died, that doesn't mean you shouldn't kiss me. Actually, it probably means you should kiss me." I clenched my fists at my sides, digging my nails into my palms so I'd stay where I was and not leap into his arms like I wanted to — not show him what it was like to be kissed by me.

He gave me a sarcastic smirk and shook his head. "That right there is exactly why I won't. Because I told you you would choose me. I won't be your escape. You won't use me to get away from everything you've been through, no matter how much I'd like to let you, because right now, I'd love to escape my own life. We'll walk through it together and at some point, I'll be your choice, not your alternative."

So many responses rolled around my brain, but each one stopped before it touched my lips. I kept opening my mouth to rip him a new one, but in the end, I knew he was right. Finally, I clamped my lips back together and stomped off to grab my bags. My "room" was actually part of the main space, separated by a partition wall.

"God help me," I heard him mutter as I tossed the bags onto the bed. I got a sick satisfaction out of knowing this was just as hard for him as it was for me. Navigating a lifelong friendship turned something more amidst the shit show that was each of our lives...*ay yi yi* — it had disaster written all over it.

"No one can help you, buddy," I yelled over the wall. "You're stuck with me for the next seven days and I won't hesitate to remind you this was your idea."

***

"I can't move," I said with a sigh.

"I don't want to move."

"Best. Pizza. Ever."

"Seriously."

"Did we save any for leftovers?"

"Are you for real?"

We stared at each other from opposite sides of the linen clothed table and started to laugh hysterically. Collectively, we'd had twenty-five dollars between us and Centro had the best wood-fired pizza in town, bar none. So, for tonight, we'd pretended to be classy as we ordered waters and the biggest pizza we could afford while still leaving a decent tip.

We exited the restaurant and walked toward Sculpture Park. It was chilly, but not terrible, so our jackets and gloves were just enough.

The Nomade lit up the sky. Set apart from the other sculptures, the man made of letters rose from the darkness. He hugged his knees, half his face missing. The letters were in no particular order, or so Trevor said when I asked earlier this week during one of our many walks downtown. Trev believed they were the pieces of the Nomade's journey, the elements of who he was and the memory fragments he collected along the way.

From the side, his arms hugged around his knees. But from the front, you could walk right into him. You could stare at his insides, looking up through each individual hole in his body and the empty space where his heart and mind should be.

"Can we go in?"

Trevor pulled back. "You've never wanted to go in."

I stared up at the Nomade and wondered what the artist went through to get him here. What did he dredge up from the painful archives that inspired him to create this man of mystery, who said so much and so little?

"I want to tonight. Can we?"

"Of course," Trev responded, leading the way. We stood in the middle of the sculpture, staring at the messy welds, both trying and failing to count the letters.

One moment we were both staring up, and the next we sat on the cold ground, facing each other. The longer I looked at Trevor and thought about where we were and who I was again because of him, the more I realized it was finally time. In this place, under the organized chaos of the Nomade's protection, I would tell him the whole truth. Trevor deserved it and we couldn't explore whatever was between us until I did.

"You've never asked me outright to tell you what happened." I didn't allow my eyes to dart away like I wanted to. I refused to hide anymore.

"It wasn't mine to force. I told you we'd talk when you were ready." Trevor managed to mix anticipation and sadness into one comforting expression that only confirmed my decision. I scooted to the middle and laid back, putting my palm upright between us. We partially covered the inlaid lights shining up into the statue and the sudden darkness sent a shiver up my spine.

Trevor mimicked my position and threaded his gloved fingers through mine. Instantly, my anxiety lessened. This would hurt, but I wasn't alone and I'd be stronger for it.

I closed my eyes and felt it again, memories I'd buried so deep I hoped to never resurface, shredding my insides as I pulled them from the depths of me. The thought of the arguments I'd had with Katie and the way my parents changed, left gaping scars I'd only pretended healed.

"You remember how my parents were growing up," I started, not waiting for him to confirm the statement, "they were quintessential lawyers — overly-analytical, type A, always reaching for the next goal. My dad still loved music though, and for the longest time I thought he was my champion, that he would keep Mom's skepticism at bay. But, eventually, he, too, refused to fight the battle anymore. I didn't understand it at the time, but he'd been fighting bi-polar episodes since his mid-twenties. They were usually short-lived and he wasn't a depressed bi-polar, he was hyper. He got wound up and that made him a lot of fun for a kid. It also made my mother crazy that he lost control continuously."

"As it was, Katie was the oldest and the perfect daughter. She had a four point oh and loved law dramas and discussing cases with them. She was popular, studied all the time, volunteered at an at-risk center for kids and seemed perfectly thrilled to be a little mini-me to my mother. For years, they cut me with small insults, relentless jokes about my ridiculous music dreams, and finally, threats to force me to give up music."

"Threats?" Trevor interjected.

"They told me we wouldn't be allowed to stay friends if I kept pursuing music, because you were bad for me and put insane ideas in my head," I said, allowing zero emotion in my voice, though the thought of those yelling matches still sent my blood pressure skyrocketing. "The news that your parents were leaving and taking you with them almost incited a party at my house."

Trevor harrumphed from beside me, but left it alone.

"It was the end of our eighth grade year that I first caught Katie…" I kept talking, but the memories were so vivid, the scene played behind my eyelids.

I opened her door without knocking, which I knew would piss her off, but it didn't matter. "Hey, Katie," I said as I walked in. She clearly didn't expect me and dropped the bottle of pills, spilling them all over her bedspread.

"Get out! Just get out!" she screamed at me, swiping at the pills with a look of sheer terror on her face.

"I can help you, I'm sorry—"

"Just get the hell out of my room, Charlie. NOW!"

I backed out and closed the door. Katie never swore.

"I came back later, when she was gone, and searched her entire room for the pill bottle so I could find out what it was. As far as I knew, she didn't have any prescriptions and she wasn't on birth control. Even then, I knew what that pack looked like from our ridiculous sex-ed classes. Of course, I didn't find it, but I did start paying attention.

"She was in the midst of finals and I was watching closely. She barely ate anymore and instead of realizing something was wrong, my idiot mother complimented her on how thin she'd become. She freaking praised her for starving herself. And she stopped drinking coffee, yet still studied endlessly and only barely slept.

"It was the night before her AP Chem final, which was a class she shouldn't have even been in as a junior, when she fell apart."

I knocked lightly on the door, afraid of another meltdown, and Katie yelled, "What? I'm busy," back at me. I took any response as affirmative entry and quietly shut the door behind me.

"Hey, can you help me—"

"No!" she yelled. "I cannot help you. I can barely help me!"

Katie's light brown hair, typically so perfectly styled, was in a disastrous knot on top of her head. She was wearing an over-sized sweatshirt that had to be our father's and ripped sweats. I'd never seen her so disheveled. She sat on her bed, surrounded by two different textbooks, a workbook and her laptop. Notecards were scattered around her and she looked at me with bloodshot, glassy eyes, clearly on the verge of breaking down.

"Maybe I can help you?" I offered. "I could quiz you with your notecards. Maybe you just need another person to go through it with."

"You don't want to help me. You hate me." She spat the words at me, her lip trembling.

Guilt filled me. I could see she was drowning and our parents would never think to pull her out.

"I don't hate you!" I argued, stepping closer. "Just because Mom and Dad hate me and think you're perfect, doesn't mean I hate you. You're my big sister. I love you, Katie."

Katie leaned toward me, and mock-whispered, "You want to know a secret? I'm not perfect. I'm not even close. You know what keeps me going — these." She yanked the bottle from her bag and shook it. "Without these, there's no way I maintain this GPA, do all the volunteering and be part of all the extra-curriculars they tell me I have to have to get into college. Without these, I'm nothing."

She dropped back against her headboard and I stepped to the side of the bed. I took the bottle from her slack fingers. Adderall was scrawled across the label.

"What is this? It didn't come from a pharmacy."

She laughed, an empty, lifeless sound.

"No, no it didn't come from a pharmacy. It came from a kid at the center where I volunteer." Katie suddenly sat up, gripping my wrist like a vise. I tried to pull away and she only pulled me closer as my wrist bones crushed together.

"You won't tell anyone about this," she hissed. "We're sisters and sisters trust each other. You've got to swear. SWEAR IT!"

"I-I swear. I do. I promise," I said as I pulled away and she finally released me. "But maybe you should stop. You're not okay. You don't look good and you're acting a little crazy. I'm worried about you."

"Don't worry about me. You'll see eventually. Growing up sucks and you do what you have to. I'll be fine. I'll make it. I always do."

She wasn't looking at me anymore. She looked through me, sadness thick in the air around us, making me wish I'd never burst into her room.

CHAPTER
twenty-four

"Her finals were over and summer began. I knew you were leaving so we spent all of our time together. I mean, I still paid attention, but Katie seemed like she was doing okay," I explained, guilt my constant companion whenever I thought of those months. I should have been there for her and I wasn't.

The cold concrete seeped through my coat, but the idea of moving an inch was inconceivable. I stared up at the inside of the Nomade's head. The letters arced and swirled, looking like they were twisting together, trying to give me the answer to questions I was afraid to ask.

Trevor squeezed my hand and I realized I'd stopped talking.

"As soon as school started again, I knew she was taking them. Her eyes were always bloodshot and she never left her room. She was either a fidgeting mess or a focused disaster. Mom only harassed her because she wasn't putting enough effort into her appearance, which only made it worse. Instead of getting up at five, she started getting up at four so she could shower and spend an hour becoming the made up, flat-ironed beauty they expected.

"It was mid-September when I confronted her again," I said.

No one was home and Katie was in the kitchen. This was as good as it was going to get.

"Hey." I sat down at the breakfast counter, facing her.

"Hey," she responded, filling her glass with water from the fridge door.

"You're doing it again, aren't you?" I asked, hesitant at the potential backlash.

Her eyes flipped up to mine, first shocked, then narrowing in anger.

"Why do you care? You need to stay out of this. I never should have told you. You're too young to understand." She stood taller to add to her condescension, even though she wasn't much taller than me.

She tried to walk away, and I warned, "I'll tell them. I'll tell Mom and Dad."

In a second, Katie was in my face. "You will not!" she screamed, the threat clear in the way she gripped my shoulders so her nails bit into my flesh.

"Katie," I pled. "I don't want to tell them. But I don't want anything to happen to you. You don't eat. You never sleep. You can't do this to yourself. I hate seeing this happen to you. You need help. It doesn't have to be Mom and Dad, but you need to get help. I don't want to lose you."

Tears I swore I wouldn't cry slid down my cheeks as I looked up at her. I knew this was bad, but I truly thought she could handle it. I believed she could stop.

Katie's eyes softened and slowly filled. A single tear trailed down her cheek before my big sister pulled me into her chest. It was the tightest hug, and she whispered, "I know, Charlie Bear. I love you, too. And I'll stop. I know I need to stop, and I will. I promise."

"We stayed like that for a few minutes. I felt her tears in my hair and clutched her tighter. I tried to silently tell her I would be there for her, even though I didn't understand what I was there for or what the problem really was. It turned out, it didn't really matter what she said, though. She couldn't actually stop."

I stopped talking and felt the wetness on my cheeks, cold trails that slid over my jaw and down my neck. My voice changed, thick with emotion and my clogged sinuses. I felt Trevor start to sit up, and quickly said, "No, just stay."

He lay back, his grip on me tighter now than before, as if with one hand he could hold me here. In some ways, he did tether me to the here and now, but in others, he took me back to places I told myself I'd left behind.

"The last time, that's the time I'll never forgive myself for," I forced out. "It was mid-terms and I'd known for a while she'd lied and was using it again, but she did everything she could to hide it. I think maybe she used less, but I couldn't be sure. My parents were at some benefit and left us money on the counter for pizza. I went to order it and the money was gone."

I knocked and opened Katie's door to find her in the center of her bed, just like always, surrounded by books.

"What's up?" she asked, without looking up. She'd been trying so hard to keep herself level around me, as if I couldn't tell she was constantly up and down and everywhere all at once.

"Where's the pizza money?" I asked. "I'm hungry."

"What money?" she responded, nonchalant.

"The pizza money we both know Mom left on the counter. She made both of us come in to the kitchen to see where she put it. Don't lie to me, Katie. I'm a freshman, not a moron."

She glared up at me. "I need it. Can you just make a sandwich?"

"For what? For the pills you promised me you'd stop taking?" I crossed my arms over my chest and silently dared her to lie again.

Katie shoved up off the bed, coming to stand in front of me. "You don't get it and you never will, Charlie. Because as much shit as they give you, you're allowed to be whatever you want. They threaten, but they won't make you stop music. And they won't force you to get perfect grades. Probably because they don't care where you go to college or if you even go. But they care about me and I'll never be free until I do what they want and get the hell out of here."

It didn't occur to her how much her words would hurt me. She looked down, the disdain she held so reminiscent of looks I got from my mother and anger spurted from my soul like a fire hydrant, dousing any inkling of compassion I had for my sister.

"They care about you," I repeated, watching the light come on when she knew what she'd said.

"No, Charlie, I didn't—" she started to backpedal.

Katie reached for me, but I stepped backward and couldn't stop the vile flood of filth that poured out of me. "Oh, you did, Katherine. Perfect Katherine," I sneered. "But you're a fraud, aren't you? Without your pills, you're nothing. You can't be what they want and when Mom and Dad find out, they'll hate you, too. Just like they hate me. They'll look at you with the same disinterest and disappointment they look at me with and you won't be able to handle it. What will you do then, perfect Katherine?"

She stared at me, her mouth hanging open, shock freezing her features. Simply the idea of it terrified her, and for a second, I actually felt vindicated.

"Don't tell me I don't get it. I get it just fine," I spat at her.

"She came to my room a few hours later and it was clear she'd had a breakdown. We talked for a long time about what it was like to be her and what it was like to be me. For the first time since you left, I didn't feel totally alone anymore and I think maybe she felt that way, too. Eventually, Katie agreed, no matter what happened, she couldn't go on like she had been. She said she'd stop and she'd get help, without telling Mom and Dad, and I agreed to keep her secret.

"Four weeks later, my dad went in to wake her up and she was dead in her bed. My sister intentionally overdosed because I guilted her until she stopped taking the pills and she ended up with C's in two of her classes.

"My sister is dead because I told her they wouldn't love her anymore if she wasn't perfect and she believed me."

Before the echo of those awful words disappeared, Trevor sat up and pulled me into his lap. He leaned back against the sculpture and tucked my head into his chest.

"This isn't your fault even partly, Charlie," he said as I hiccupped through massive sobs. My body convulsed with the magnitude of them, but Trevor kept talking as he stroked my back. "You can't believe that. Something was wrong with Katie and you did your best to get her to stop and ask for help. Those were her choices to make. And your parents should have seen what was happening. This was their responsibility, not yours."

I cried for a long time, soaking the outside of his jacket, and wouldn't be surprised to have torn holes in it with the grip I kept on his chest. His arms stayed tight around me and I knew he was talking, but I heard none of Trevor's words. All the terrible things I'd been saying to myself for years swooped and swarmed inside my mind. Like insects, the thoughts multiplied, buzzing so loudly, I could hear nothing else.

This is your fault.

She's gone because of you.

You did this.

I screamed inside my head, but the words were muffled whispers. "I didn't mean to. I didn't want her to die. I didn't think she even remembered. We both apologized for that night. She swore she wasn't mad. I just want her back."

Over and over, I muttered my apologies into Trevor's arms until my energy was depleted and I could do nothing but stare out into the rest of the park.

It could have been minutes or hours, I had no idea, but finally, I could speak.

"No one knows," I said between sniffles. "I've never told anyone I knew what she was doing or that I said those things."

"They didn't need to know," he said. "It helps no one for you to tell them."

I nodded, but wasn't so sure I actually agreed.

"Is that why you've never read her letter?" His question was low and hesitant. "Are you afraid she blames you?"

Fresh tears fell as the guilt forced me into an even smaller ball, protecting myself from the truth. Trevor took my silence for affirmation, and he was right.

He set me down beside him and turned so we faced each other. Taking his glove off, he wiped away the tears that continued to fall and tucked my hair behind my ear.

"You need to read it, Charlie," he said. "You can't really start to grieve until you know what she thought, instead of what you think she thought."

I swallowed down the counterpoints I'd been reciting to myself for four years. I knew they were all bullshit. I was here because I knew I couldn't do this anymore.

I searched his face—his familiar face. Trevor's beanie hid most of his brown hair, with only a few longer locks poking out around the edges. Big brown eyes sat behind his geek chic black plastic rims, looking at me with nothing but concern.

For years, I'd borne this alone. No one, not even the therapist they forced me to, knew about the pills or what I'd said to Katie. But now, it was different. Now, I no longer had to face the raging, tumultuous waves I'd been tossed in for so long alone. Trevor had thrown me a life preserver and all I had to do was keep holding on. The idea of trusting him was both terrifying and thrilling, but hope was a dangerous emotion. Hope could hurt you. But If I could trust him, we could make it. Together, we could survive. He made me believe that.

"Can you do it?"

"You want me to read it?" Confusion knit his brows together.

"To me. I want you to read it to me. Because I don't know if I can do it." There was no way in hell I could. The idea of even touching that letter nearly sent me into a tailspin.

He sat silently for a moment, and then nodded. "Okay. I can read it to you. Do you want to do it here, or go home?"

"It has to be here. Now. By the time we get home, I don't know if I'll still be able to do it." I shoved my purse at him and slid backward on my butt until I hit the sculpture. I needed space. I needed air. I missed her so fiercely, but I could not be so close to my sister right now.

I let my head drop back and I stared up inside the Nomade's mind again. My eyes unfocused as the lights shining from the ground lit up the white letters making them blur together. Maybe everyone's mind is ultimately like that: a mess of hope, regrets, worry and fear — sentences filled with words made of letters we only pray we can put in the right order to do good and not harm.

The whizz of my purse zipper seemed to echo in my ears, followed by the crinkle of the envelope as he unfolded it, the light rip of the corner and the slice of his finger along the edge of the seal. He pulled the letter out and I squeezed my eyes closed, begging for the memories to stop and words to quiet so I could just listen. Then, I prayed once again my sister didn't die hating me.

CHAPTER
twenty-five

Dear Charlie Bear,

First, and most importantly, this is not your fault. I know you think it is, so just stop it, because it isn't.

There's no way for me to truly explain the choice I've made except to say I'm lost. I don't know who I am anymore. If I'm honest, I'm not sure I ever knew who I was. I was always the person someone else decided I should be and never fit in this skin. Our parents, my teachers, coaches...I should have been able to stop it, to control this like I tried to control everything else, but I can't. And I'm so tired. The idea of what it would take for me to dig myself out of this hole is simply too much. I can't do it.

It's not an excuse. I know this will hurt you, and Mom and Dad. I wish I was stronger.

I wish I was like you.

I bet that one caught you by surprise, didn't it? But it's true. I wish I had your strength, your resolve, your passion. I wish I had a tenth of your heart.

It's really important that you hear what I'm about to tell you, so please focus. Stop crying and really focus. Read these words and hear my voice inside your head.

Don't ever lose yourself.

Life is hard and you will have to make so many decisions that aren't fair. Decisions you know will hurt someone. But ultimately, you have to protect yourself. You have to stay true to who you are. I'm not saying you shouldn't trust people, you should. You should love, and make so many friends, and live the biggest, best life ever. But make sure it is your life. The one you want.

Mom and Dad aren't bad people. I love them, just like I love you. They wanted me to have a great life and I won't fault them for my inability to stand up and say the one they wanted for me wasn't the life I wanted for myself. And I want to apologize, because until recently, I didn't fully understand my part in your pain. I would have never intentionally made it harder for you, and I don't think Mom and Dad mean to either. Try to understand them, just like you always want them to understand you. See them as people, not just your parents.

But, no matter what, promise me—right now, Charlie, I want you to say it out loud and know I can hear you—promise me you will never give up on your music. I don't care if you do it for fun or a job, don't let anyone take it from you because it's your soul. You play and it changes the people around you. It changed me. Listening to you play will forever be my favorite thing, even when I did it through the wall between our rooms and you never knew I could hear you. I could always hear you.

I will always be listening for you.

I love you, Charlie Bear, and I hope someday you can forgive me.

Katie

***

We didn't speak for the longest time.

Trevor sat on the ground holding a four-year-old letter from my dead sister, staring at her handwriting in the way I stared at her slack, lifeless features during her wake — like it couldn't really be her and I couldn't believe I was actually there.

I felt like the emptiness of the Nomade was now filled with Katie. The letters around me were her words, her warnings and her pleas. She was all around me and I couldn't be there anymore. I stood up, mumbling, "I need a minute." I walked away from Trevor and the Nomade. I walked away from the two men who'd sheltered me in my time of need because I needed to breathe without feeling like she was watching me, waiting for me to lose it.

I stumbled down the crisscrossing sidewalks of Sculpture Park, but Katie's voice followed me. I couldn't outrun her. I couldn't get away. I had to accept that she'd never go back inside that little box I'd shoved her into.

I stood in front of a horse made of driftwood and absently contemplated how I could both see through him and every piece of him. I wondered if I had made an effort not only to see through my sister's lies, but to see her for who she really was, if I might have gotten through to her. If I could have saved her from herself.

I didn't leave the confines of the park. I didn't want Trevor to worry about me and I knew he could see me from his position still inside the Nomade. He paced as I walked, always vigilant but never leaving the sculpture.

I walked the outer edges of the block and heard Katie say, "Promise me you'll never give up on your music."

Fresh tears flowed as new waves of guilt lapped at the shores of my heartache. I didn't intend to give up music. In fact, I needed it. I craved it. I longed for it with such ferocity, I dreamed every night of songs I never allowed myself to play.

I hadn't made a conscious choice to become my sister and take on her life. It happened in small increments that left the real Charlie Logan cast aside, like a discarded doll no one needed or wanted anymore.

First, I'd rebelled, because once the visitors stopped and it was just the three of us, I was invisible. I cried out for attention in every wrong way possible — I got drunk, I skipped class, I got stoned. I did anything that numbed the pain and kept me away from their unbearable silence or intolerable arguments about who should have done something or seen something, because they didn't know I did and had.

I'd tried to find Trevor, and then resigned myself to the fact that he, just like everyone else, had abandoned me. I still couldn't believe my mother had kept him from me when I needed him the most.

When I was failing every single class, the school finally persuaded my parents to send me to a grief counselor and I'd said the things I needed to say while blocking her out entirely. On the last day, she gave me the only piece of advice I paid attention to. She said the best thing I could do for myself was to talk about my sister if I needed to.

When the time came and I could finally talk, the only person who wanted to listen was my father. He would listen endlessly. Her death sent him into manic episodes and it seemed like he needed to listen as much as I needed to talk. He would laugh with me as we joked about Katie's fondness for cherry-flavored everything and fake a scowl when I made fun of the polka dot glasses my mother hated and she adored. It felt good to talk about her, to remember her and celebrate the person she'd been. In those moments, I didn't hate myself quite so much.

The problem was anytime I tried to talk about me, he glazed over. If I talked about me and music, he got angry and it became apparent I was still a disappointment. So I stopped talking about me, and I never talked about music—I only talked about what he wanted to. Then, I mattered. The warm body in front of him who could talk about his dead daughter mattered.

I stopped dying my hair and let it grow out. I traded in my combat boots and old rock band T-shirts for stylish, boring clothes I hated, but she would have loved. And I told myself it just made it easier for everyone. I told myself I was honoring my sister and helping my parents heal. I told myself to say the right things and do the right things and it would all be okay.

I told myself lies, and Katie wouldn't let me lie anymore.

I looped back toward where Trevor stood, just in front of the Nomade, his eyes on me and the folded envelope in his hand. As I approached him, he tried to hand me the letter and I shook my head, keeping my hands buried deep in my pockets.

"She told me I had to live my life, the one I wanted," I said to him, "and until I can say I'm doing that, I can't take her letter back. I won't."

PART THREE

CHAPTER
twenty-six

Trevor

April

The only good part about my job, outside of the money, was the fact that no one else was in the building at the same time I was and it gave me time to think. I took another sip of my extra hot coffee and hoped the caffeine hit before the mop bucket filled with water.

Charlie still wouldn't take the letter back. It had been two weeks since our night in the Nomad when she finally told me the truth and took the massive step to open Katie's letter. She declared at the end of the night she couldn't take it back until she was living her life, the one Katie wanted for her. I had a hundred questions about how she was going to do that and what she even wanted for her life, but panic layered just below her resolve kept me from asking.

Every day, I approached Charlie hoping the resolve had won, and every day, she still looked terrified. She'd taken to dressing a little more less like Katie, but I could still see her apprehension over being too loud, too opinionated or too much of anything at all. If any of us asked her opinion, she had to second, third and fourth guess herself to know whether it was what she really thought.

So, now Katie's suicide letter was in my top drawer, under my socks, until Charlie found herself. What she didn't understand was she'd never left, she'd only been ignored and neglected by everyone who should have loved her—most of all, herself.

A forgotten mourner is who she was. Back in January, once I initially processed through Charlie's lies, I spent weeks scouring the internet trying to understand what happened to her and how we ended up here. Charlie's parents barely paid attention to her when Katie was alive, so it only made sense they wouldn't think to help her grieve through the process. Now, all these years later, she still hadn't found her way through that black void. She'd tell you she did, but shoving something down and taking your sister's life as your own to help your parents cope wasn't grieving. It was about as far from grieving as you could get.

I sloshed the mop back and forth as my mind raced around the possibilities of how I could help. Scenarios popped up and faded away as I dismissed them, finally realizing there was only one true option: music. I had to get her back to music. Katie had begged her to do it, and Charlie missed it. I knew she did. She carried the leather-bound journal I gave her in her backpack every day now. She wrote in it constantly and I assumed at least some of it was lyrics.

She'd always loved playing more than writing, even though she wrote great songs. As I quickly finished mopping and started stocking the fridge, the plan solidified. Now, all I needed was a little bit of luck and her not to freak out when I asked for her help.

On second thought, I needed to accept she would freak out and have every possible counterpoint already prepared—yes, much better plan.

I was running it through one more time when I heard a crash up near the back door. Glass hit the cement stairs and tumbled down toward the four-player Pac-Man console as I quickly debated my options. I decided not dying was the best policy, so I lowered the mop to the floor, making as little noise as I could, and crept quickly toward the bathrooms. I texted Mike and Paul, the owners, and then dialed 911 from the stall, letting the operator know I was only a few blocks away from the station and a break-in was occurring.

I had just shoved the phone back into my pocket when the bathroom door slammed open. I jumped and a man in a ski mask shouted for me to come out.

I quickly made my way into the main room.

"Give me the money," he said, his voice muffled. "All the fucking money!"

"Th-there isn't any money. It's all gone. They deposit it every night," I stammered. I hadn't been that scared initially, but the light glinted off the matte black metal of the gun in his hand and I could think about nothing but the fact that I wanted to live.

"Bullshit! Clear out the token machines then," he demanded, gesturing toward them with his handgun and then pointing it back at me. My hands raised automatically and I stepped backward.

"There isn't any money!" I screamed back at him, mentally calculating that I had maybe twenty bucks in small bills in my wallet. Nowhere near enough to make someone who'd gone to these lengths happy.

"Hey, get down here!" the man yelled back over his shoulder. Footsteps pounded down the stairs and as soon as the man turned the corner, our eyes connected.

I watched my father's eyes widen and then narrow from beneath the mask as he pointed a Glock at me. He was pointing a gun *at me*—at his son. I saw only his eyes, but read every word loud and clear. He was here for a reason and it didn't matter what happened to me.

"You said there would be money, man!" the first guy shouted, breaking the shocked stare down between us.

Jonathan charged the bar. "There has to be something here! Give it to me, goddammit!"

His words were slurred. He was drunk and the tone of his demand was one we both knew would spur me into action. It was violent and promised repercussions if I didn't listen. I dove for the register, hating myself as I grabbed the cash the bartenders always left in case of rotten fruit, or some other random bar need as they opened.

"It's a hundred bucks, maybe," I said, the cash landing in a pile and scattering over the bar.

I tried to step away and he grabbed the front of my shirt, yanking me within inches of his face. I could smell the whiskey and his perspiration. I could see the sweat spots on the mask and hear his deep pants of breath.

I hate you, I thought as loudly as I could. I stared him directly in his veiny, unfocused eyes and screamed, *I HATE YOU*, over and over.

"You never saw me," he hissed.

I was going to nod, but then I saw it — the guilt as he squinted and looked through me. I saw the realization that he held his son by the scruff of the shirt in a bar he'd robbed at gunpoint. He released his grip, and softly pled, "You never saw me."

"The cops will be here any second," I whispered, pissed at myself even as I said the words.

With that warning, he threw me backward and they fled. It was a half-hearted shove, but I let it take me to the ground and stayed there sprawled out while I wondered how I would ever explain this to anyone.

***

"Trevor, we really appreciate you taking the time to come down today," Detective Weber said for the second time this afternoon as he handed me a paper cup of water.

"Not a problem, Detective," I said, taking a sip of the barely tepid water and wishing the tiny interview room was a little bigger.

I'd sat in an uncomfortable chair in the corner for the last hour at the end of a table that took up most of the cramped space. Detective Weber's chair was pulled to the corner of the table, his knees only inches from mine, while Detective Taylor stood behind him next to a thermostat that had to be set on eighty.

"We'd like to run through what happened last week one more time, if you don't mind," Weber said, flipping through a folder he kept tipped just far enough toward himself so I couldn't see what he was looking at. "I know the patrol officer took your statement, but it would be great if we could go through it again."

"Sure." I shrugged. "I was working. Normally, I don't clean on Tuesdays because the bar is closed on Mondays, but they did a fundraiser the night before and Mike asked me to come in, so I did. I heard glass break and ran into the bathroom to call nine-one-one. I guess the guy saw my mop and came after me. He wanted money, but I told him there wasn't any."

"That's when he called out for the second guy?" Weber broke in.

"Um, yeah. The second guy came down the stairs and yelled at me. He pointed his gun at me and told me to get the petty cash from the register. It's there for emergencies, or in case one of the bartenders need to grab something from the store before we open. It's, like, less than a hundred dollars, and I told him that."

"Who did he sound like?" Taylor piped up.

"What?" Why didn't I think of that question? I'd come up with dozens of others and thought through them all after Weber called so I'd be ready. My palms were sweating and I forced myself to keep them loose in my lap.

"The guy you talked to, who did he sound like? Did he have a deep voice like James Earl Jones? Or maybe an accent?"

I looked to Weber and he seemed nothing but interested in my answer. I was still processing how young he seemed and how strange it was that he was so nice. I got the good cop, bad cop thing — I'd seen NCIS — but this guy was way more very Special Agent Tony Dinozzo where Taylor was totally Gibbs. Except, I didn't much care for his version of Gibbs.

"I don't really know who he sounded like. Just a guy, I guess." I knew it was a dumb answer before I said it, but I couldn't come up with anything better.

"An older guy or a younger guy?" Weber pressed.

I didn't want to lie. I told myself the whole way down here I wouldn't outright lie to them unless they asked me straight if I knew the robbers. Then, I still had no idea what I'd say, but every time I thought about ratting out my dad, bile rose in my throat and I heard my mother's voice in my head telling me he was my father and I couldn't do this to him — to us.

"He didn't sound old, but he seemed too big to be young," I said, looking over Weber's shoulder but not directly at Taylor.

"Trevor, we don't believe you're responsible for the Up-Down robbery."

Relief coursed through me and I felt my exhale in every cell of my body. I'd been terrified if I didn't give up my dad they'd suspect me of being involved and I had too much to lose. School. My future. My future with Charlie.

I opened my mouth to thank him, but he continued. "The problem is the robberies haven't stopped."

I knew that, too. Mike hadn't talked about much else. He and his buddies owned quite a few bars in the downtown area and in the last week, two more of them had been hit. I could barely look him in the eyes every time he walked through the bar, mumbling about why this was happening to him.

"Do you have any idea who might be behind these robberies?" Weber asked. I swallowed, my mind racing with all the possible answers when I knew there was only one right one. Thankfully, Weber kept talking, giving me more time to decide.

"You've worked at all these places, but we know you aren't usually there when they are open," he continued. "We thought you might have a guess. A distributor who's upset? Someone who got fired? An angry customer? Anyone? We'd really appreciate your help."

Options, he'd given me outs. "I really couldn't say, Detective." I kept my tone even. "I'm always alone when I'm working, so I don't see anyone."

"Is there anyone who knew you worked at all these places?" Taylor asked from the corner.

Damn it, man, shut up. "Uh, lots of people. Over the last year, I've rotated through all those bars. They have me train the new guys and tons of people know me."

"But only the Up-Down robbery was when someone was there and you said yourself you weren't supposed to be there. Who might know the schedules of all these bars? Who'd know your schedule?"

I tried to stop my hands from twitching while my toe tapped on the dingy linoleum of the room. "I have no idea. Why would I know that?"

Detective Weber piled up the folders in front of him and slowly stood, tapping the stack into an orderly group as he did. "Trevor, we really appreciate you coming down today. I know it doesn't seem like we accomplished much here, but even the small amount of information you gave us really helps. If you think of anything, even the tiniest detail, we'd really like for you to call us. I'd really hate for these guys to bust in somewhere and have someone be there. People could get hurt. In these types of situations, it's basically a guarantee it will happen eventually."

I nodded and made my way out of the small room. The hallway was at least ten degrees cooler, and while I should have been more comfortable, fallen officers now stared down at me, silently judging me for not telling the truth. Their framed pictures reminded me of what could happen if my father continued his spree.

The elevator, which barely fit two grown men, was too small and the walls were closing in on me. I dug my nails into my palms and forced a measured pace through the foyer of the police department main floor, until I was out the door and down the steps.

It was only once I was safely inside my car, with my seat belt buckled, that my hands started to shake violently. The only coherent thought I had was Weber was right.

Someone was going to get hurt and it was going to be my fault, regardless of which choice I made.

CHAPTER

twenty-seven

Charlie

"You need to turn him in." My chin rested on my crossed arms, which hugged my knees. Trevor pulled me out of the library earlier this week in near hysterics and we'd been having the same conversation each day.

I looked up at him sprawled out on his bed, his fingers laced together and palms behind his head. He stared at the ceiling, a muscle ticking along his jaw.

"It's not that simple and you know it." He wasn't mad at me for stating the obvious, but he did the same, and he was right.

We lapsed back into silence and I continued to watch him. We'd spent so much of this school year focused on me, but Trevor had gone through his own family hell and I wanted to help however I could. So, I sat with him, and for the last few days, let him stew, but he couldn't do this forever.

I reached down to retie my shoe and smiled to myself when I realized I was wearing my favorite beat-up red Converse. The fact that I'd put them on without second-guessing myself or changing three times reminded me I was making progress. I'd been able to transition a few things, mostly my wardrobe, over the past few weeks since we read Katie's letter together.

More jeans and T-shirts and less "preppy chic", as Sam kept calling my old look. I'd tried to talk more in general and be more open with Darcy about what I'd been through. I let Trevor delve a little further into my past and even went out shopping with Sam. I didn't buy any of the bright, eclectic clothes he kept tossing my way, but it was fun to try them on and let him make up stories about where I could wear them.

It wasn't all easy, though. Sometimes, I choked on words I wanted to use but knew would offend my mother. Many times, I had a real opinion about something in my classes that contradicted everyone else's groupthink, but before I could even raise my hand, my face flushed, my mouth dried out and my head would start to pound. I hated the fact that I'd conditioned myself to be so small and reclusive. I looked in the mirror and even I didn't know who I was anymore. But that didn't stop the reactions that were now ingrained in me—unless I was with Trev.

With him, I was just Charlie, and nothing else mattered. As I tossed ideas around about how to get him out of this room while he barely acknowledged I was there at all, we were good. We were taking care of each other and that felt right. I couldn't count the times this year he'd pushed me past my breaking point only to bring me back again, stronger than before. I needed to do the same for him now.

I leaned back against the bed and debated my next words.

"If you're not going to make a decision, then I'm done," I stated. I didn't turn around to look, but I heard his head shift on the pillow.

"What?"

I swiveled around and looked Trevor in the eyes, repeating myself. "If you are not going to make a decision and do something, then I'm done talking about it and we're getting out of here."

Trevor's eyebrows knit together and then popped high on his forehead. "And exactly where are we going?"

I stood and crossed my arms. "When's the last time you were in the FAC?"

"You seriously want me to care about school?" he argued, sitting up so we were eye level again.

"Yeah, I do, because what else do you have to focus on?" I asked, tilting my head to accentuate the sarcastic question. "You aren't doing anything but having the same conversation over and over and that doesn't change anything. I can promise you it won't. So, let's go to the FAC and you can get some work done. I'll help you. You're never getting away from them until you graduate."

He closed his eyes and took a breath. When he opened them, his frustration had receded a tiny bit. "Okay, lady on a mission. As long as you're coming, let's go."

We gathered our things and had just approached the elevator when Sam stepped into our path.

"Hey, guys! How are things?" Sam's chipper personality was in full swing as he bro-hugged Trev and full-on crushed me. I couldn't stop the giggle, and for that, I got a bonus kiss on the cheek.

"Looking pretty dapper today, Sammy," I said, complimenting his button down, gray tweed vest and deep purple tie. The evolution of Sam Murray was one I enjoyed watching. He grinned, and responded, "Thanks, sweets!"

"Where you two headed?" Sam asked as he shoved his keys into the dorm lock.

"Over to the FAC," Trevor replied. "We're going to work." His last words were accompanied by a small smile. I saw a similar conspiratorial one come across Sam's face as he responded, "Ohhh. Well, don't let me keep you, but Darc and I are grabbing dinner later, so you guys should meet us. We'll text details."

Waves were exchanged and we made our way to the FAC. April was fickle in Iowa, and the sky threatened spring storms, with biting wind and chilly temps. We didn't speak again until we were in the building, tossing our stuff into the room Trevor was lucky to snag last minute.

"Why did he look at you like that?" I asked as I rubbed my frozen hands together.

Trevor chuckled, the first positive sound I'd heard all week. "Before all this, Sam was helping me come up with a way to persuade you to do exactly what you just volunteered to do," he said, pulling his glasses off and wiping the lenses with his shirt hem.

I scowled. "You only had to ask."

"Really?" He looked genuinely surprised. I stopped and forced myself to think through the question.

"Well," I admitted finally, "maybe I would have. Maybe I wouldn't have. I guess I don't know. I keep thinking about this life I'm supposed to lead and I don't know what I want yet. I miss music, but I'm not sure what to do about it. I don't know what I'm ready for and don't want to lose what I've gained."

I was ashamed of these irrational fears. I knew they were ridiculous, but I couldn't stop them — I couldn't reason my way through them and I couldn't wish them away. As I stared at the piano, an ache built in my chest. My fingers demanded to be popped, something I hadn't done in years. They twitched and tapped on my thigh, my fingernails scraping across the denim just to occupy themselves.

I most certainly missed that piano, but the idea of actually touching it made me uneasy. I couldn't put my finger on the emotion, but it was a giant warning flashing in my mind, holding me back.

Trevor sat down on the bench and patted the seat beside him. I wanted to be there so much, I almost leapt at him. It was tight and we pressed close together to both fit.

"How you doin'?" He bumped his shoulder lightly against mine. I was fine. I was great. I stared down at the keys in anticipation of him playing while I chided my self-involvement and redirected the conversation back toward him.

"I'm fine, and this isn't about me. It's about you and what you need." I wanted the music to drown out his issues. I was not interested in discussing my own drama even a little bit. I had enough inner monologue for both of us.

He shook his head and sighed. "That's the part you've never really understood. I don't think there's ever been a time when it wasn't about both of us. Do you remember what I told you last time we were here?"

I remembered that night with a vivid clarity I wished I didn't. It was the one and only time I'd ever thrown a stool across the room and it was the first real breakdown

I'd had. Looking back, one might even call it a breakthrough. But I hadn't been the only one to confront my truth.

"You said you hated music. Why? What happened?"

Trevor leaned over, his elbows on top of the piano as he turned to me, shame and sadness written all over his face.

"My dad basically pimped me out for money. All his bar buddies would hire me to play and then they'd pay him, not me. I spent every weekend of high school playing dives and strip clubs all over Omaha and then Central Iowa. He did it again over Christmas. It's part of why I was a wreck when we got back in January. He used me...again. I don't understand why I keep protecting him. He isn't worth it and he's only made my life hell since we left Muscatine."

"We've both been through some shit the last few years, haven't we?"

"It appears we have."

"When you moved away, at first I thought it was inevitable that we'd find each other again." I remembered how much I'd missed him and my fierce loyalty to our friendship. I'd worn the ring he'd given me on a chain around my neck every day, most nights falling asleep with it clutched in my hand. "But then you stopped calling and I couldn't find you. Katie died and I thought you'd given up on me, too."

I paused, swallowing down the automatic self-disgust that didn't belong inside me anymore. "But you hadn't. My mom finally confessed to keeping us apart, you know. And even though you thought I abandoned you, you kept at me this whole year, not letting me stay in my self-built cage."

"Of course I wouldn't abandon you." He pulled back from the piano, looking ready to launch into a defensive rebuttal.

"Don't be offended, Trev," I chided. "I said that because I could see on your face you worried about telling me your truth. But you did, and I'm still here. Just like you're still here. We're on equal footing now, right? No more secrets?"

He nodded and held out his right hand. A few smacks, a few flips and a fist bump explosion later, we laughed together.

"Putting your dad aside, why are you here? Why are you going to school for music if it isn't what you want?"

Trevor stared at me. His eyes softened and a sad smile appeared.

"You," he stated.

"Me?" His gaze never left mine and I thought I might fall into his depthless dark eyes. They held so much emotion and honesty. I wondered if I did fall, would I ever want back out?

"I never loved music as much as you did, Charlie," he admitted. "But you loved it so much, it overflowed out of you and filled me up. Your passion was so intense, I couldn't stop myself from loving it, too."

Straight-faced, he looked at me in a way I'd never been looked at before, like he could see inside my soul and even though he knew what was there, he would still choose to stay.

"I kept taking piano and guitar so I could teach you." His words were barely above a whisper, but I heard the shake in his voice, giving away just how hard it was for him to admit these things. "I sang to make you smile. I wrote because there was so much inside me for you, I never knew how to say it any other way. You disappeared and music was the last piece of you I had left."

I couldn't look away from him. I searched his face for more, but Trevor didn't move except to allow the corners of his mouth to turn up and a knowing smile to overtake his features. His eyes crinkled at the corners and I wanted to reach out and remove his glasses, to take that small barrier between us away, but I couldn't move.

The breaths came and went and I knew what was coming. I knew what he would say if I didn't say something — anything — else. I didn't know if I was ready for that. I had no idea how I would react. Even though I wanted to reciprocate, and I knew he was more than my best friend and had been for some time, this was more than I could handle.

But I had no words; all I had were feelings. Emotions ricocheted around inside me and pushed from opposing viewpoints. If I did what I thought I wanted to do, it could change everything. Or it could just be the inevitable conclusion Trevor and I were always supposed to come to. Or I could ruin it all. Everything we'd built and how far we'd come together, I could ruin it all. I did that. I ruined things. I couldn't ruin this.

"Are you choosing me, Charlie?" he asked softly, his mouth inches from mine. My gaze flicked from his lips to his eyes as the war raged inside me, two halves fighting each other and both ruled by fear.

"I'm scared," I admitted, breathless and immobile.

"Me, too, but I'll never let myself be too scared to tell you the truth again."

Unable to make the final decision, I could only stare up at him and silently plead for him to take control of the situation.

Finally, Trevor pulled me in and pressed a kiss to my forehead, his lips lingering, making me wish I were stronger. "There's no time limit. I'm not going anywhere," he said. "I'd rather at least know the thought is in your head. How about we work on some music so I don't fail?"

"Mmmhmmm, yes, le-let's do that," I stammered, finally able to form a few words of my own.

He chuckled and I wanted to pop him in the shoulder like I normally would, but I was afraid if I touched Trevor in any way, I'd spontaneously combust.

CHAPTER
twenty-eight

Trevor

Charlie stayed next to me on the bench. Maybe I should have felt rejected, but I saw the look in her eyes—I saw what she was afraid to admit out loud, and just knowing she'd admitted it to herself sated me.

So, she stayed, looking at me expectantly, her eyes darting between mine and the keys, her anticipation actually making me excited to play.

I rested my fingers on the keys and let my mind wander, sifting through all the options until I landed on the piece that called to me. Beethoven's *Moonlight Sonata* was both comfortable and calming.

Inside me, a swirl of emotions twisted and turned on each other, fighting for space in my mind and heart. The future loomed in front of me like a magic eight ball. I couldn't control any of the outcomes, I simply waited for my fate to be handed down to me.

And I hated it.

My body swayed with the music and I felt Charlie moving with me. Her soft sigh was a content sound that made me feel like I was finally doing something right. The song built to its crescendo, still managing to sound light even though the notes hit my soul like arrows buried deep in a bullseye.

This song was always about sadness and regret to me. It was Beethoven's wordless apology for decisions he never made and questions he never properly answered. It seemed fitting for me and Charlie, sitting here together, both trying so hard to overcome our past, our parents and childhood fears.

"Do you think every parent screws their kid up?" I asked her.

Charlie stared out over the piano for a moment before responding, "I have to believe it's inevitable. They're humans. They were screwed up too at some point, and they are just doing what they know how to do. I've been thinking a lot about this since Katie told me to try to understand my parents, to see them as people, and the more I do, I see they were doing the best they could. I want to be mad and blame them for everything, but I can't. Some things, yes, but not everything. I made choices, too."

At eighteen, we shouldn't have to be thinking about things this deep, yet here we were.

"Do you want to have kids?" I asked.

She shrugged. "I don't know. I don't like the idea of doing this to someone else. I'd like to believe I would do it better and not make the mistakes they did, but I can't guarantee that." Charlie looked at me, such sadness in her eyes, and said, "I'm still trying to figure out what I actually want from this life. Heck, I can't even decide what to do with myself when I have an hour of free time. What are my hobbies? What do I want to do? I don't know. I only know what my sister would have done or what my mom would want me to. What about you?" she asked.

"I don't know either," I admitted. "It seems like such a risk. You don't know how you'll handle being a parent and you don't know what kind of kid you'll be dealing with. And then, I think about all these kids like us who don't have a person who understands them. They're alone out there facing shit like this...maybe they're eighteen or maybe they're eight. Who's taking care of them? Who's making them feel safe?"

"We're pretty lucky to have each other," she said, bumping her shoulder to mine.

"Yeah, we are."

We sat in silence for another minute before she said, "Play something else."

I started to reach for the keys and then thought better of it, turning to Charlie instead.

"How about you play for me?"

She sat straighter beside me, but her face paled slightly. A battle of excitement versus fear played out across her features as she gnawed at her lower lip, a crease forming between her eyebrows as she stared down at the keys. Her index fingers twitched in her lap and I knew she wanted to do it.

"It's okay, Charlie. The piano won't bite," I teased. Her eyes flicked toward mine and she stared at me like she didn't believe me.

After a few slow breaths, she finally reached out and laid her fingers over the keys. She sat there, so still, the pads of each digit barely skimming the tops of the ivory. Her eyes were closed and I waited for her to begin. I wondered which song she'd choose for her entry back into music.

I watched Charlie, the seconds dragging out. A tear popped from her right eye, trailing down her cheek. She opened her eyes and shook her head in tiny jerks back and forth as she vaulted from the bench and across the room. Her hands balled into fists at her sides as she continued to silently tell me she couldn't do it.

"It's okay," I reassured her. "You don't have to do this right now."

"I thought I could do it," she said, her voice trembling. "I wanted to. I wanted to sit next to you and I wanted to play, but I can't. I don't know that I'll ever be able to."

Coming around the piano, I stood in front of Charlie. I held out my arms, unsure of her comfort level, and was relieved when she stepped into my embrace.

I pulled her to me, and whispered, "You can't do everything overnight, Charlie. Just because we read Katie's letter and she wants you to doesn't mean you can undo years of change immediately. Give yourself some time. Cut yourself a break."

She nodded into my chest as she gripped my back.

We stayed like that for a few more minutes before both our phones chimed at the same time, likely a group text from Sam or Darcy. As we pulled apart, I kept ahold of her hands and applied gentle pressure, bringing her attention back to me.

"You're not doing this alone, Charlie."

She squeezed back. "And neither are you."

***

The end of the semester called for a celebration. It wasn't exactly the end yet, but it was close enough for us to declare the need for something more than crappy pizza or subs. Tonight, we were going all out and having sushi.

The four of us piled into my Honda and made the short trip to Sakari, one of the best sushi spots in town. We were just in time for their happy hour, which meant cheap rolls. Given we had about fifty bucks between us, cheap was good.

"Are you going to astonish the judges?" Sam asked me from his shotgun seat. I almost snorted in return, my eyes meeting Charlie's in the rearview mirror. We'd worked for a few hours today and she'd critiqued my main pieces, offering suggestions and helping me finalize my list of songs.

"He's going to absolutely kill it," she said, grinning at me.

The achiever in me wanted to kill it, but the reality was my heart wasn't committed. The longer this year dragged on, the less I wanted to spend hours at the piano. I loved music, but I didn't want to be a slave to it. I wanted to enjoy it, to let it take me away. But much like Charlie, that meant I had no idea where my life was supposed to go. Who was I if I wasn't here to play music?

A flick to my earlobe jarred me back to the present.

"Helllllllo…" Darcy howled in my ear, her fingers poised for another strike. "Earth to Trevor, we are all making lewd comments about you and you don't even have the decency to look embarrassed."

I swatted her hand away as I maneuvered into prime parking in front of Sakari. "Lewd comments, huh?" I questioned, unable to keep my eyes from finding

Charlie's in the mirror once again. She blushed and looked away as both Darcy and Sam laughed.

We made our way inside and once we were all seated and the rolls ordered, Sam grabbed his glass and clinked the side with his fork. As more patrons than just us paid attention, he ducked down a little in his seat, his face turning red.

"Nothing to see here, apologies," he said with an embarrassed laugh.

"Something to share?" I asked as he waited for the dining room to resume their conversations.

"I do, actually," he started, looking at each of us individually. "The last year has been the best one of my life and I blame it entirely on all of you."

All four of us laughed, but Sam suddenly got very serious. "When I got to Rodgers, I didn't know who I was or who I wanted to be. I had never fit in anywhere and no one had ever really wanted to be my friend. I'd insert myself into groups and play the funny, chubby guy who looked like a Hobbit, but we all knew I'd put myself there and hadn't been asked."

I caught Charlie's eyes and saw the same sadness I felt for our friend. Darcy reached across the table for him, but Sam pulled away, shaking his head.

"No," he said, "don't go doing that. This is a sad story with a happy ending." Darcy pulled her hand back and we all watched Sam expectantly.

"You all saved me," he started. "You asked for my opinions, made me feel included and didn't make too much fun of me for wanting to be in a frat. Even there, where the guys are great, they aren't you."

Sam turned to Darcy, specifically. "You're beautiful, Darc. Inside and out, you are the most gorgeous woman

I've had the pleasure to know." She blushed and mumbled, "Thank you."

"You helped me see I was worth the effort to be healthy, to feel good about myself and to let my inside be reflected on the outside," he said, smoothing his hands over his crisp, checkered button down. "You helped me find myself and show the world."

Darcy's eyes glistened with unshed tears and she blew a kiss his way.

"And you two," Sam said, turning to Charlie and me. "The last year hasn't been easy for either of you, but you relentlessly protect each other and showed me what best friends really look like. It may not always be pretty, but you always come back to each other."

I looked up to find Charlie staring back at me. Even today, we'd brought each other another few steps forward. We always came back to each other and I would always protect her. Today, she'd also showed me she'd protect me, even if just from myself.

While his comments weren't unwelcome, Darcy, Charlie and I looked at each other, unsure of where Sam was going with all this.

"I know, I'm rambling on, but I had to say all that to explain why I wanted to say this," he said, reading our minds. "I wanted to tell you all first I'm officially coming out. I'm gay."

We all looked at each other again during a brief moment of silence.

"Uh, Sam, we knew that," Charlie said first. Sam looked at her, confused, and then to Darcy and I. We nodded, shoulders and eyebrows up in wordless agreement.

Sam burst out laughing. "Of course you knew. Of-freaking-course you all knew, because you're my friends — my actual friends. Why didn't you say anything?"

"It wasn't ours to say anything about," Charlie said, reaching out to pat Sam's hand.

"Just like everything else that's gone on this year, things have a way of working themselves out," I tacked on.

"Though," Darcy cut in, "I will say, it is reassuring to finally have it said out loud the reason you didn't want me was a valid one." Her tone was haughty and her wink lascivious.

Sam reached out, grabbed her hand and laid a big, fat kiss on the top. "You'll always be my first lady, Darc."

"You bet your ass, Sammy," she returned, yanking him toward her and planting a loud, wet kiss on his cheek.

Just then, the rolls were delivered—platters of glorious seafood that had us battling chopsticks, wishing we were old enough for sake bombs and thankful to have each other.

CHAPTER

twenty-nine

Charlie

"What exactly are we doing?" I asked Darcy as she dragged me by the hand into Baskin Robbins.

The door dinged above us and a high school kid came out from the back. Seeing two college girls, he adjusted his ball cap and gave us a wide smile.

"We are taste-testing!" she exclaimed. "You said earlier you don't even know what kind of ice cream you like and that's basically a mortal sin, so we're here to find out!"

I laughed and shook my head in awe of her constant harebrained ideas. Ever since sharing my full story with Darcy, she'd been on a mission to help me find myself.

"So, we're taste-testing…" I took in the thirty-six buckets of ice cream behind the long glass counter. Darcy already had her face all but pressed to the glass.

"Yup. And we played our last game yesterday, so I can eat whatever the hell I want." She was nearly drooling.

"First, I need baseball nut, because, duh, it's baseball season," she requested of the guy behind the counter as he gave her a goofy grin. "And then, I want to try chocolate chip cookie dough."

The kid grabbed two tiny spoons and handed her the samples before looking at me.

"I, um…" I looked through the glass and was embarrassed by my inability to choose something. Katie always loved plain chocolate, she said it was simple and delicious, so why stray from perfection? I couldn't order chocolate.

"What's calling to you?" Darcy pressed. "Are you wild and crazy enough for Bananas Foster? Or do you go with staples like mint chocolate chip? Perhaps, you prefer a little caffeine in your dessert and want a Jamocha?" Her eyebrows popped as she sucked the ice cream remnants off her itty-bitty spoon. I shook my head as the kid ogled her like he was watching a porno.

"You know what I want to try…I want to try orange sherbet!" I declared. "And…rocky road! And give me some of that Cherries Jubilee!" With each order, something else caught my attention I now wanted to vet. It was strangely empowering to choose anything and everything.

The kid shrugged, indifferent to my self-exploration as I savored each bite of distinctly different flavors. The sherbet was just okay. I could see it being amazing in July when it was ninety-degrees, though. The rocky road reminded me of being a kid, when the Schwan's man would knock on our door and my dad would sneak us a few cartons of ice cream before my mom noticed. My nose wrinkled at the Cherries Jubilee, the texture of the mushed up cherries feeling wrong in my mouth.

Ten more samples later, I was not only full, but also declared my favorite — chocolate peanut butter.

"It's classic. Timeless, really," Darcy said, her expression dead serious. Then, she ordered a two-scoop cone of mint chocolate chip. After all those samples, I didn't know how she wasn't already bursting. With a wave to the poor kid who indulged us, we left.

We strolled along the sidewalk outside the shop while Darc inhaled her cone and found ourselves in front of a music store. From the outside, I peered into the shop and smiled at the kids wandering the aisles with their parents. I imagined they were picking up bow strings, reed oil and other necessities we music geeks knew all too well. I remembered sneaking dollars from my dad's change jar until I had enough for new guitar strings and then sending Trevor into the shop to buy them for me in case the owner knew my parents. What happened to that conniving kid?

"Let's go in," Darcy said, tossing her napkin into the trash bin before pulling open the door and doing just that. I followed her, but already felt the unease creeping in. Being in a place like this was dangerous. Music was still dangerous. With each tiny step I took forward, I still couldn't bring myself to reengage with that part of me.

I shoved my hands into my back pockets and silently followed Darcy around the store. Every now and then, she'd stop and ask me about something she saw, which I usually could explain. Then, we came to the back corner, where a baby grand piano was displayed in all its glory. The body was dark and shiny, the keys pristine ivory and brilliant black. It was utterly gorgeous and the very item I'd dreamed about from the first time Trevor taught me chords and let me loose on the beat up piano in his parents' basement.

"You can play it if you want to." The clerk appeared from nowhere at the end of the aisle and her voice surprised me. "From the look on your face, you know your way around a piano." She gave me a knowing smile and disappeared again.

I ached to play it and the same feeling I'd had in the FAC last week rolled around in my gut as it called to me, pushing and pulling all at once.

"Well, go on, at least get closer and stop looking at it like the darn thing is going to jump up and eat you," Darcy said, gently nudging me forward.

I reached toward the keyboard, but my breath hitched as a lump grew in my throat. I pulled back and extended just one finger, lightly running it over the keys without actually pressing them down.

For the first time, I didn't want to run. Maybe it was Trevor not being here with me. Maybe it was being an anonymous person in a shop, hidden away in the back. But I refused to waste the moment, so I slid over the bench and took my place in the center as an eerie calm laid over my frayed nerves.

I didn't make the conscious choice of what to play, I just played. John Mayer's *Slow Dancing in a Burning Room* filled the air around us. My foot pressed the pedal as my fingers floated over the keys. My body swayed and I started to sing. This song held so much symbolism to me. Me and Trevor. Me and Katie. Me and my parents. The walls burned down around us all in one way or another.

Goosebumps rippled over my flesh and I felt a tear slide down my cheek as air that had been trapped for years escaped my lungs. I pulled from deep in my diaphragm to push out the words and it was as if I'd unlocked a hidden door in my soul—a space I'd neglected and forgotten.

Darcy sat down next to me, lending me strength as I finished the song. When the last note faded, clapping erupted around us. Darcy grabbed my hand, a proud smile on her face as we took in the crowd I hadn't seen gathering.

"I think you can do a little more than kinda sorta play," Darcy teased as the crowd dispersed.

"I can neither confirm nor deny those allegations," I responded as I tried to calm my racing heart and understand the barrier I'd just torn down. I wanted to yank my phone from my pocket and call Trevor right this second to tell him, but something held me back. I wanted to bask in this moment, just me this time.

"Oh, I think you blew those allegations straight outta the water, love bug," she said as she pulled me up to stand. Dropping an arm over my shoulders, she added, "And I think we've had enough self-discovery for one day. What do you say we go Netflix binge something?"

I grinned, relieved to have some time to process the last hour, and wrapped my arm around her waist. "Add some Sour Patch Kids and popcorn, and you've got yourself a date."

CHAPTER

thirty

Trevor

May

In the week since I'd last been at the station, another bar
had been robbed. Detective Weber called me yesterday to
ask again if there was anything I could add that might
help them. My father was breaking into every bar I
worked in. He was stealing from my friends and
vandalizing their dreams. I couldn't let this go on; I had
to get some answers. If Charlie could finally face her
demons, sit down at a piano and play, then I could face
this.

As soon as she saw me, my mom said something to
the other woman behind the counter and rushed my way,
grabbing my arm and pulling me back outside.

"What happened, Trevor? I know that look and
something's happened," she said as soon as we were
away from the main entrance of the grocery store.

"Did you know?" Her head tilted and she looked at me in complete confusion. I searched my mother's face for any signs of deceit, but she genuinely looked baffled by the question.

"Know what? Honey, what is going on?"

"I spent two hours at the police station last week," I started, "where they questioned me about the robbery at Up-Down, but also the robberies of a few other bars I clean. They are denying it so far, but they think I'm involved somehow."

"How could they possibly think that? And why would I have known?"

"Because I was there during the Up-Down robbery, and so was Dad." I forced my face to stay neutral as anger raged inside me.

Her face paled instantly. "Your father? He robbed you?"

"At gunpoint, Mom. He broke into the place where I work in the middle of the night and robbed me at gunpoint with one of his loser friends. What the hell is happening? What is he in to now?"

She started to pace. In small circles, she walked back and forth. "I should have known," she muttered.

"Mom!" I interrupted. "What should you have known?"

"Obviously things have gotten bad," she started, shame already evident in the way she looked past me and not in my eyes. "You, ah...saw me, and I know that's why you haven't been home or come to visit me like you usually do. I've been working a lot so we wouldn't have to ask for your help and it only made him angrier that I was providing and not sitting next to him on the couch. Your father has been drinking a lot more, he wasn't working, and he was spending a lot more time at the track. At least, that's where I thought he was.

"A few weeks ago, a man showed up here during my shift and I thought he wanted to buy flowers. Once he got me away from the other girls, he grabbed me and told me if Jonathan didn't get him the money he owed, then he'd get it however he needed to. He made himself perfectly clear," she concluded, her fear of this man still evident.

If I thought I was angry before, the idea of my father putting my mother in a position to be threatened by his bookie sent me through the roof. My hands shook with the need to collide with the nearest hard surface.

"I went home and asked your father about it," she continued. "Of course, he got very angry, but in the midst of it all, he admitted he owes someone over twenty-thousand dollars. But he said he had a plan and he was taking care of it, so I needed to trust him."

"*Twenty-thousand dollars?*" I was incredulous. The number tumbled around in my head, and with each revolution, it only increased my fury.

"Mom, you don't have to trust him," I argued. "You have to *leave him*. How long are you going to let him do this to you? He's worthless, he's a drunk and he's an animal."

"Do not speak about your father like that." Her biting tone was just as surprising as her defense of him. My mother stood taller. She looked up at me and down on me in the way only moms can when they're disappointed.

"You're serious?" I struggled to keep my voice down. "After all this, you're yelling at me for calling him what he is? My *father* held me at *gunpoint* and has made the police think I have something to do with his crimes. What about me? What about what he's doing to me and my future — does that not matter to you?"

The stone exterior of the grocery store was looking more and more enticing. I had to focus on the fact that I couldn't pass juries with broken hands. Like Charlie said, I had to graduate. A degree was the only way to truly get out of there.

"I know you don't understand, Trevor, but he's my husband and I made a vow. For better or worse. I can't just leave, he needs me. I just need some time to help him get sober again. If we can get out from under this bookie and maybe get out of town, start over somewhere, it will get better. He'll be the man I married again. I know who he really is under all this."

What started strong ended as hopeful wishes as she kept pacing.

"What about me? What about the fact that your son needs you?" I finally asked the question I hoped I wouldn't have to ask — the statement she should have made, not me.

She stopped and stared at me before donning the saddest smile I'd ever seen. "Trevor, you've never really needed me. You are stronger than your father or I have ever been. I know you've spent more years as the parent than the child, but I need you to walk away from this. I need you to let me handle it. I'll talk to your father. I'll get him to stop."

She wouldn't directly ask me not to turn him in, but she came close.

I looked up and over her head, swallowing down the painful ache burning in my chest.

"No, Mom, you're wrong," I finally said, my voice thick with emotion I could no longer contain. "I've always needed you, I just never mattered enough for you to pick me."

She kept talking, but I turned and walked away, unable to listen to the excuses or the lies anymore.

***

"Trev, you have to tell them," Charlie said again.

"It's not that simple. You don't understand," I argued. We'd been going around in this circle since I found her alone in her room and explained both my call with Detective Weber and the conversation with my mother.

"What's there to understand? It's either you or him. If you don't tell the detective, they'll pursue you. You're the only lead they have. You said it yourself, he isn't worth protecting!"

She was right. I knew she was. Yet, the longer I thought about it, the less I thought I could actually do it. Why was it at this moment all I could remember were the good times? I didn't think about high school. Instead, I thought about elementary school, when he taught me how to fight back against the bullies that made fun of my glasses. And how he'd carry me on his shoulders around the county fair and let me pick out any game I wanted. We'd play until we won the biggest prize they had. Every memory that surfaced reminded me of the man I wanted to protect, not the one who'd committed this crime.

"What about my mom?" I asked, throwing my hands in the air. "What if he takes it out on her? And what will she do on her own if he actually goes to jail?

She's never been alone. She all but begged me not to turn him in. Will she hate me? Will she never speak to me again? These are all very real possibilities, Charlie!"

He was my father. Bastard that he now was, he was still my father and that meant something. I paced the length of her and Darcy's room, letting the distinct differences between the two halves occupy my mind and not the endless list of scenarios and questions this choice generated.

On Charlie's side, everything had its place. There was nothing on the floor and there was no clutter. She sat at her small desk and watched me walk, letting me process while she clenched her teeth to hold back what she wanted to say. I could see the effort she put into staying silent. Everything was about control with Charlie.

Darcy's half was chaos. Posters of the women's national soccer team were crookedly hung on the walls, practice paraphernalia was scattered all over the floor and papers were strewn across her desk. A vase filled with dead flowers and no water sat on her dresser. Makeup, jewelry and clothes were everywhere, but it all stopped at the line that marked Charlie's side.

"Do you know what I ask myself all the time?" she finally said. "I ask myself, if I would have told someone about Katie's problems, would she still be here?"

"You can't compare these situations," I countered, pissed she would make this about her. "I see what you're saying, but they are in no way the same. You were trying to save someone. If I do this, he could go to jail. And if he doesn't go to jail, he could do something much worse to me or my mom. I don't know if there is an actual positive outcome here."

Charlie stood and came toward me, unwilling to relent. "And if you don't do this, he could hurt someone else. Detective Weber warned you it was possible and the longer this goes on, the more likely it will become. You have to take care of yourself, Trevor. This has to be about you and your life. You said it to me — you're the kid. They should be protecting you, not pimping you out to play music for their friends, taking your money and making you lie to the police for them. You have to think about you, because your parents have made it abundantly clear they won't."

"Is that what you're doing?" I argued, my fear and anger getting the better of me. In that moment, I hated her for saying those things aloud, for putting words to my shame.

"Are you taking care of yourself?" I pressed on, knowing I shouldn't. "Because to the best of my knowledge, you're the pot calling the kettle black."

Charlie took a step back from me, her face going blank but her eyes widening. I should have stopped. I knew I needed to, but I couldn't. There was too much hurt and way too much anger. It wasn't meant for her, but it had nowhere else to go and she wouldn't leave me alone.

"It's been weeks since you read Katie's letter and you keep living her life for your parents. You said you wanted to change, but you still look like her, you still mostly dress like her, you have her major and your parents actually encourage you to keep doing it. They should have taken care of you when Katie died. Your parents should have made sure you were okay and they didn't. They were so caught up in themselves, they forgot about you entirely."

Every piece of research I'd done to help Charlie was suddenly another weapon, a way to keep her from judging me and pushing me into something I wasn't capable of doing. Who was she to tell me what was best when she hadn't bothered to take care of herself?

"You took care of them and you never let yourself grieve for your sister. You keep going back to Pella and letting your father tell you how you'll never be Katie, but still, you deny everything you want for your life to be what they want so they'll love you. *They forgot you and you forgot yourself.* If I hadn't shown up at Rodgers, who would you be right now? Robot Charlotte, AKA fake Katie, with her perfect everything and life built on lies? Would you have ever opened that letter?"

Tears spilled from her eyes and tracked down her cheeks as Charlie looked at me in utter shock. I hated myself. I was a wretched human being, the most despicable form of life, and even though I knew it, I couldn't stop the filth spewing from my mouth.

"That's low. That's really low." Her voice was raspy with emotion.

I told myself to shut the hell up, yet my mouth kept moving. "You can't stand there and tell me I need to make this monumental choice without owning your own situation. If I drive to the police station right now, are you driving to Pella? If I give up my father, will you give up your sister?"

"You need to leave. You need to go now." Her words were barely audible.

She turned away from me and I stood there for a moment, my eyes closed as I berated myself for stooping to this level. I opened my mouth to apologize when Charlie whispered, "Get out."

CHAPTER
thirty-one

Charlie

Trevor's steps toward the door were heavy and loud. I waited for it to open, unable to do anything but drag ragged breaths in and out. The weight of his words was crushing, a vice grip on my chest that refused to relent. My knees shook and I was afraid I would crumble before he was gone, but I wouldn't let him see me like that. Not now and never again, not after that performance.

When his cold fingers gently wrapped around my forearm, both shocking and instantly angering me, I ripped my arm from his grasp and backpedaled across the room.

"Charlie, I'm sorry. I shouldn't have…I didn't mean…"

I looked into Trevor's eyes, ready to lash out, but the words stayed lodged in my throat as my shattered soul reflected back at me. He yanked his glasses off and rubbed a hand over his face then back through his hair. His brown eyes were surrounded by red spider webs, his face gaunt from the stress only deep anxiety can cause. I wanted to hate him, but I couldn't. I knew what he was going through.

"That's not enough, Trevor," I said, shaking my head. "I know you're sorry. I know you didn't mean it. But you said it. You said the things we're not supposed to say. The truths we know but are never supposed to use against each other." I stepped forward, wiping my nose and swallowing the agony stabbing me in the chest. I would not cry anymore.

"We're honest. We tell each other what we need to hear, but we don't do this." The longer I spoke, the more I believed in my own words and the reality of where we now were. "We don't destroy. We don't decimate fragile foundations and intentionally hurt each other. Don't you think we're already broken enough?"

His eyes pled with me to understand. His defeated posture begged me to see he would take it all back if I let him.

"Even though I eventually tried, I was afraid to call you when Katie died because I knew I was spiraling," I continued. "I knew it would eat you alive to watch it happen from across the state. You didn't have a license and you couldn't get to me. You couldn't save me then, Trev, and you can't save me now. You were wrong when you said we could save each other, we can't. Maybe my mom keeping us apart was the right thing. Maybe it's time we worry about saving ourselves."

His face pinched together. From his hairline down to his chin, it compressed into a confused mess of lines and edges.

"What are you saying, Charlie?"

What was I saying? Could I even say it?

Every piece of my tenuously stitched-together heart raged at me. The words scattered and reshaped in my mind, but the message was the same. Everything I'd craved, everything I'd wanted all these years, I finally had it. I wasn't alone anymore and I mattered. I had Trevor back, but I couldn't keep him like this.

"I can't need you this much, Trevor," I whispered. The pain of the truth brought my hand to my heart, as if I could protect it while I ripped it from my chest. "I can't hand you my secrets and my pain and let you take it away. If I do that, I'm no better off than the day before you showed up here. At least then I knew the rules of the game. Now…now we use each other. We lash out, we apologize…we push, we pull. But where are we really going? What are we doing?"

His mouth hung open and I saw the rebuttals forming behind his eyes.

"But we understand each other in a way no one else ever will. I fought to get you back. I'll always fight for you. Even tonight, you were fighting for me and I know that. It's what we do. I'm sorry I was such an asshole, you didn't deserve it and I know that." He stepped toward me and I immediately put additional distance between us.

"It is," I said, nodding as a traitorous tear snuck out and trailed down my cheek. "It is what we do and we can do it again, just not right now. I'm not saying I don't want to be your friend any more, I'm just saying we aren't helping each other by living in the past. You need to go and we need some space to decide who we want to be, not who we were."

"For how long?" he asked, as if a specified length of time was obvious.

"I don't know, Trevor," I responded honestly. "I won't avoid you. I'm not mad at you. But I have to learn to stand on my own and you have to trust yourself. You have to make the choices you need to make, and so do I, regardless of each other. Maybe even in spite of each other."

He stood there, his mouth open and head shaking back and forth. He stared at me like I was speaking French and he had no clue what I was talking about.

These words felt right. I'd put so much into him and his opinions, into wanting to please him and let him soothe the hurt away so I'd feel whole again, I'd allowed myself to depend on Trevor instead of myself. Being able to sit at that piano with Darcy and play in front of those people reminded me I could do this alone. And after today, I needed to make sure I did. I couldn't hand my self-worth over to anyone else, it was mine and mine alone.

"I-I'll see you at juries, how about that?" I asked, struggling with his expression and the pain I knew I was causing after everything Trevor had done for me. "It's in two weeks and I promise I'll be there for the post-performance. I wouldn't miss it. I swear."

He nodded, but his gaze was empty. He trudged toward the door, only stopping to pull a thin, folded envelope from his jacket pocket and set it on the small table where we threw our keys. I watched him turn the knob, but before he opened it, Trevor spoke without looking back.

"I miss you already."

Without waiting for my reply, he slipped out the door and I was left with nothing but silent emptiness.

I lowered myself to the ground and stared at the closed door. I didn't cry; there were no tears for this because it was right. There was no question it hurt. It tore at my fragile heart and I wished the words weren't the truth. But if we could do this, if we could exist separately and still feel whole, then maybe we had a chance.

***

"Alright, move over." Darcy shoved at my right side with both hands and after I re-situated myself, flopped down on my twin bed. We both stared at the ceiling, the taupe paint just as boring as always.

"We need to talk."

"If you're going to tell me I need to talk to Trevor, don't. I'm not—"

"Pfffft," Darcy cut in, "he was being a total douche canoe and I don't care if he was dealing with his own crap, he had no right to say those things to you, even if they were somewhat accurate. As far as I'm concerned, your decision to put some space between you is well-timed. There's been way too much testosterone in here lately."

I dropped my head to the right and stared at her, unable to decide whether I should roll my eyes or shove her off the bed. Darcy gave me a half smile and pursed her lips in a kiss.

"You love me. And no, I was not going to say anything about Trevor. We need to talk because I have an idea, but first, I need to tell you a story."

I shimmied on the bed, making myself comfortable, and then smirked, thrilled to have a conversation not centered on me. "Okay then, let's have it."

Darcy stayed in her position, her hands clasped on her abdomen.

"I want to tell you this because you've been honest with me and shared your story," she started. "You know I have two younger sisters and my parents are divorced, but what you don't know is how hard their divorce was on me. I was ten, Mallory was six and Shea was three. First, I thought it was my fault. I thought if I could have only helped more, or made it easier on my mom, then she would have wanted to stay.

"Then, I got really mad. I was mean to the girls and my parents. I acted out and eventually walked out on soccer practice after some choice words with my coach. It was actually her who persuaded my parents to send me to a counselor."

"Like a therapist? They did that to me, too. It was worthless." I rolled my eyes, but Darcy cut off my annoyance.

"Then you weren't listening." She kept her tone level, but as Darcy turned on her side to face me, her expression was sad.

I mimicked her position and backed up so I pressed against the wall, the firm coolness of it comforting.

"During my mandated sessions, Denise told me two things I'll never forget," Darcy continued, "two things that helped me get past what happened and move on. The first one she had to say at least a hundred times, but it took until the hundredth for me to hear it. She told me there is no wrong way to feel. There is a wrong way to act, but not a wrong way *to feel*. She said my emotions were mine and no one was allowed to invalidate them, least of all me. And she constantly reminded me I couldn't control anyone else's emotions so they weren't allowed to control mine, especially not when their control was in my own head since their responses were ones I made up instead of verified."

I nodded, tracking her logic while internally commenting on how impractical that expectation was. Other people didn't let you feel the way you wanted to feel. That wasn't the way the world actually worked. If it were, my mother would be banished by now.

Darcy kept talking. "Second, she told me what I wanted mattered. She sat there, on her fluffy brown over-sized chair I always wanted to steal and put in my bedroom, and told me if I didn't take care of myself, no one else would. It wasn't that they didn't want to, it was because I hadn't shown them who I was or what I needed. If I didn't know me, no one else would either."

Darcy paused, and in an uncharacteristic show of emotion, turned to me so I saw the glisten of tears in her eyes. "I can easily say she's the reason I'm here. Because without her, I wouldn't have admitted how much I missed soccer and I wouldn't have told my parents all the reasons I thought they got divorced, which were none of the actual reasons they got divorced. If I hadn't pushed them, I don't know that they ever would have thought I was old enough, or strong enough, or *whatever* enough to handle the realities of what they went through."

Darcy spoke so calmly about her personal tragedy. I could see in the strain of her eyes and hear in the thickness that crept into her voice that the memories still stung, but she sat there and talked about it, not hiding her truth from me.

I thought over her words and the idea of allowing my emotions to surface made me nauseous. It was a layer of goosebumps followed by an ache in my gut, culminating in bitter acid in the back of my mouth. Telling my parents what I'd done and how I felt had me physically pulling away from Darcy, flattening my back against the wall and wishing I could disappear into it, away from her insane notions and fairy tale solutions.

"I don't want to invalidate what you're telling me in any way, because I'm honored you would share this, but your parents got divorced and my sister died. That's a really different set of circumstances." I struggled to maintain eye contact as I spoke, and only her short snort of acknowledgement brought my gaze back to hers.

Darc's lips quirked up and amusement danced in her eyes. "You're right, Char," she said, her tone now a bit patronizing. "My sister didn't die, but that doesn't make what I just said any less applicable to you. Which brings me to my next point." Darcy rolled off the bed, miraculously landing in a light crouch before coming to stand. She held out one hand and waited, her eyebrows lifted and head cocked.

I took it and let her drag me across the room until I stood in front of our full-length mirror. Darcy stood behind, yet almost beside me, her hands resting lightly on my shoulders. We looked at each other through the glass, such intense opposites in every way, yet bonding over life's unavoidable pitfalls.

"What do you need, Charlotte Lydia Logan?" Darcy asked.

I looked at her, perplexed and suddenly self-conscious. I tried to step away and her grip went from gentle to gorilla. She locked me in place, her eyes boring into mine through the glass.

"What do you need?" Darcy asked again, this time enunciating each word. "Forget Trevor. Forget your parents. Forget your sister. Forget me. Forget Rodgers as a whole. Right now, right this very minute as you look at yourself in the mirror, *what do you need?*"

I stared at myself, scanning from my bare feet up to my perfectly straight hair. "The mall," I blurted out. "I need the mall."

Darcy grinned over my shoulder as I felt a sweep of tingles from the back of my neck to my knees and a ridiculous sense of relief.

"To the mall we shall go," she declared. "Thank God for divorced parents and twice the spending money."

***

Darcy's whistle was low and long, followed by, "Wow, Char, you look *hot!*"

The stylist swiveled the chair around and I could only stare for the first minute. I reached up to finger my short, black hair and a smile crept over my face. I stifled a giggle as pure joy flooded in. I looked nothing like me and everything like me.

The stylist delivered on exactly what I asked for. The bob ended at my chin and had a light stack in the back. She'd texturized my thick, wavy hair and then added a mixture of product, giving me choppy, beachy waves. I wanted to run my fingers through it, scrunch it up and shake my head around. I wanted to dance around the room so everyone knew just how happy I truly was.

The eight inches of light brown hair scattered around me was a skin I'd shed, revealing my true self.

The stylist stepped away and Darcy stood behind me, much like she had a few hours ago. "Seriously, so hot," she said with a wink.

I shook my head and laughed. "It wasn't about hot, Darc, it was about me. Katie said I had to live my life, *the one I wanted*, and if I'm going to figure out who I want to be, the first step is recognizing the girl in the mirror."

I spun around and stood. Darcy pulled me into a short, tight hug and I returned the squeeze. It wasn't until she'd let go that I realized it had been a long time since I'd been bothered by someone's touch.

I settled my tab, happy my mom wouldn't think twice about seeing a charge from the salon on her card, and we exited out into the main portion of the mall.

"Where to next, boss?" Darcy asked, her arms spread wide, a mischievous grin on her face.

"You're just loving this, aren't you?"

She slung an arm over my shoulders. "Oh, hell yes. This transformation is going to be epic."

We laughed together as we meandered through the mall, eventually finding ourselves in one of the department stores.

I stood in a giant dressing room strewn with clothes from every end of the spectrum — professional gym goer, mini-skirt party girl, Bohemian peasant, leather-bound freak...Darcy brought it all to me in hopes something would feel right.

She poked her head in again, and asked, "Nothing?" I shook mine in frustration and she came inside to join me.

"What's the problem? Talk to me." Darcy stood tall, her face serious. She gestured toward herself with both hands, like I was one of her teammates and we were on the pitch.

"I don't know. It's all just...someone else." I fumbled to find the right words and ended with a harsh exhale. "I'm...I'm like a blank slate. It's been so long since I really thought for myself and made my own choices, I find myself reaching for all the things I'm certain aren't me simply out of habit. I need to start fresh with something new. I can't dress like I did when I was thirteen because I'm not thirteen anymore, but what does eighteen-year-old Charlie wear? I have no idea!"

"I get it," Darcy said, nodding. Her brows knit together as she looked through me instead of at me. Finally, she perked up. "I've got it!" she exclaimed. "Get dressed, we're getting out of here."

Once I was properly clothed again, we almost ran through the mall — or at least that's what keeping up with Darcy's long legs felt like to me. She paused for a micro-second outside American Eagle and pointed up. "This is what we need. They are all about the basics."

She grabbed my hand and we walked the store, her piling item after item into my arms. Eventually, there was a shove toward the fitting rooms, where I dropped the pile and started hanging things up on the hooks around the space.

"Oh, stop it, you're just going to take it back off and put it on. Try. Them. On," Darcy demanded from her tiny space in the corner.

I grabbed a few things off the floor and began my fashion show. Forty minutes later, I emerged wearing black skinny jeggings, a white linen T-shirt and a gray asymmetrical cardigan.

"How's my blank slate feeling?" Darcy asked as she unlocked the trunk of her car.

"Like even though I don't know her completely yet, I like the girl in the mirror for the first time in a long time." As we'd exited the mall, I caught my reflection in the store windows and each time it was like seeing an old friend—one I'd dearly missed, but hadn't realized how much until she was back.

I pulled Darcy in for the biggest, tightest hug. "And it's because of you. Thank you, Darcy. Truly. Thank you."

"All in a day's work, baby cakes."

CHAPTER
thirty-two

Trevor

"You know, I don't think I'm a fan of sullen, morose Trevor," Sam chided from across the table.

"What? What did I do?" I stammered, pulled from my racing mind. I'd promised Charlie space, but not being near her, not talking to her, was torture. I wanted to explain, to apologize a hundred more times for the horrible things I'd said. She didn't deserve any of it and while I didn't want to believe her, I knew there was truth in her logic. I wasn't even sure how I got here. What started as a ploy to get answers had so quickly morphed into her being the person I wanted near me always.

Sam's gaze flicked upward as he shook his head. "I've been trying to talk to you about how much I don't want to go back to the middle of nowhere Minnesota and how much I want to stay in Des Moines but have no idea where I'd work, live, or how I'd survive, and you're not listening at all. If you want to talk to Charlie, you should save us both and just go talk to her."

"She said she wanted space and I'm trying to respect that, but I'm honestly afraid she's going to disappear again. This time, because she thinks she has to," I admitted.

"Do you really think she'd do that? Especially given how far she's come with your help?"

I drew random shapes in my notebook as I pondered the question. It was the same one I'd been asking myself for days. Had I really helped her or had I pushed her too far, too fast? I knew Charlie was stronger than she gave herself credit for, but who was I to judge how she coped?

I sighed deeply. "All I wanted was for her to be happy. And I suppose if she needs me to get lost so she can be, that's what I should do."

"Bullshit." I looked up to find Sam staring at me from across the table.

"Excuse me?"

He drummed his fingers on the tabletop, one eyebrow arched. "I said *bullshit* because that's what that answer is. You've spent this whole year fighting your way back to her and now you're just going to give up when shit gets real? No way, I won't let that happen."

"And what exactly do you propose I do about it? She said she wants me to keep my distance and I don't want to disrespect that."

"She said she'd be at juries, right?" I nodded. "Then you have your platform. It's time for the grand gesture."

Now, it was my turn to give him the deadpan stare.

Sam reached across the table and grabbed my shoulder. "This is the classic white knight scene, my friend. This is Richard Gere in the limo climbing up the fire escape in Pretty Woman. It's Heath Ledger singing

Can't Take My Eyes Off of You in the stadium. Patrick Swayze telling a room full of socialites how one of them changed his life before declaring, 'Nobody puts baby in a corner.' This is the moment you use the grandest stage to explain yourself so she can't ignore it or run from it."

"You're devious and a damn genius, did anyone ever tell you that?" I couldn't shut down my wide grin or the wheels spinning in my head. Sam had given me the nudge, but I already knew exactly what I needed to do.

Sam smirked and brushed at his shoulders. "A time or two."

Sam's gloating was interrupted by my phone. I expected it to be another call from my mother, which I would send to voicemail just as I'd done with the last seven, but this number was blocked.

"I've gotta get this, but the ideas are already swarming. Thanks, man!" I swiped across the screen as he waved goodbye and took off.

"Hello?"

"Trevor? This is Detective Weber."

"Hello, Detective, what can I do for you?" My heart was already racing. Maybe I shouldn't have deleted all my mom's voicemails without listening to them.

"I wanted to touch base and see how things are going. See if anything popped up over the last week you wanted to chat about."

"I, uh…don't think so, no." Except for the fact that I'd picked up the phone every single day to call him and admit everything. But that's no big deal, right?

"The thing is, Trevor, some new evidence has come to light and we'd really like to go over your statement one more time."

"New evidence?" I choked out. What if he changed his mind and now they thought it was me? I felt lightheaded and could barely stand the seconds of silence before his reply.

"Yeah, there was a quiet period since the last robbery, but last night another bar downtown was hit, and this time, someone was there. The owner, actually — Mike. And he apparently got into it with one of the robbers. Almost took the guy out, but he got away. Luckily, Mike only ended up with a black eye and some bruises."

"Mike was there?" The reality of what was happening finally sunk in. It was one thing when my dad was stealing things but not hurting people. It was different now. One of my friends had been hurt because of me. Charlie had been right all along, and I knew it. I had to tell them everything.

"Yeah, I'll come down right away, Detective. I'll be there in a half hour."

***

We were in the same stuffy room, but this time, it was just Detective Weber, and his tone wasn't quite as relaxed as our initial conversation.

"Trevor, I need to ask you a few questions."

I nodded. "Go ahead. I want to help in any way I can." My palms were sweating and the truth sat on the tip of my tongue, held back only by my guilt over what I was about to do.

"That's great, I really appreciate your help. Cases like this, ones that drag on, mean the county attorney is on my case and the bar owners downtown are getting restless. Nobody knows exactly where to expect these guys next and they just keep finding more to take. If they don't find money, then they steal high-end booze. They even took a computer from the last place. There's really no method to their madness, except you."

"Me?" Had my father somehow managed to implicate me further in all this?

"You're still the only common denominator, Trevor," Weber said, sitting back in his chair. "I've run down the employee lists, the distributors, the wait staff — everybody. And you're the only guy who shows up at every location sometime in the last year."

There was a moment of silence as Weber stared me down. His eyes bore into mine and the room was suddenly smaller, warmer and filled with air I could hardly breathe. I couldn't stop my head from dropping into my hands.

My father was stealing my future. He had finally found a way to ensure I never made more of myself than he ever could. I knew I had to tell Weber, I had to tell him now, but it was so hard to form the words.

"Trevor..." Detective Weber's voice was gentle and that surprised me. I looked up at him and immediately knew he saw the truth.

"I know you didn't do this, son, but I also know you know more than you're telling me. What did you say to the man who robbed Up-Down? We saw you exchange words on the surveillance video."

We have to save ourselves. Charlie's words echoed in my mind.

"I told him the cops would be there any second," I said, my voice thick and hoarse.

"And what did he say to you?"

"That I never saw him."

Weber leaned in, his elbows on his knees. "But you did. And you knew who he was, didn't you?"

My head bobbed as I whispered, "My father."

The rest of the conversation was a blur. I said things, signed things and told Detective Weber everything I knew about my father's gambling problems and the money he owed, which wasn't really much. I gave him my father's cell phone number, his car make and model and pretty much anything he asked for.

I felt like a giant traitor as I spoke, yet a massive sense of relief hit me when I walked down the police station steps. They would catch him or they wouldn't, but I did as much as I could to stop anyone else from being hurt by Jonathan Adler.

I wanted to call Charlie and tell her what I'd just done. I wanted to hear her congratulate me on making the right choice and have her ask me to come over to tell her how it all went down, but I couldn't. The idea of her not being a part of my daily life felt so wrong, but I knew this was short-lived. She promised we'd see each other next week at juries and I would tell her then. What just happened only reaffirmed Sam's suggestion. It was time for a grand gesture. It was time for me to trust her in all the ways I'd asked her to trust me.

Now, I had one more stop to really make things right and put these robberies behind me.

***

I knocked lightly on Mike's office door and waited for him to invite me in. I tried not to wince at the deep purple shiner he was sporting, but Mike being Mike, went right there.

"Think it'll get me some chicks?" He grinned until the movement caused him to wince.

"Chicks dig scars, not sure about black eyes," I replied. "And I don't think Maggie will appreciate your additional chicks."

"True, my beautiful wife would likely not appreciate that. What's up, man?" Mike smirked and settled back in his leather desk chair.

"I, uh…came to apologize." I forced myself to hold his gaze. I would be a man. I would be more than my father ever was and I would own this mistake.

Mike's face contorted in confusion. "Okay. For what exactly?"

"When I heard you'd lost your cleaning crew and approached you last year, you could have told me to get lost, but you didn't. I promised you I would always show up, I wouldn't lie to you, I would treat your bars like my own and respect your rules. You gave me a chance and a job, both of which I really needed."

"Yeah, and you've done everything you promised to do."

"I tried to." I struggled to find the right words. "But I lied to you after the break-in. I told you I had no idea who those guys were and that wasn't true. I did know one of them, but I couldn't tell you. I couldn't tell anybody."

Mike leaned forward, his elbows on the desk, and I could see his forced control. "And now?"

I stared at the ground and took a deep breath, blowing it out my mouth in a slow stream before looking back up at him. "And now I realize it doesn't matter how much I keep protecting him, my father will always find a way to fuck up my life if I don't do something about it. I told Detective Weber it was him and I'm here telling you, too, because I wanted you to know how sorry I am. And I know I need to find another job. I don't even expect you to pay me my last check. Consider it partial payment for what you lost, but please know I'm really, really sorry I let you down."

I stood, ready to get the hell out of there as quickly as possible, when Mike said, "Trevor, sit."

I sat, expecting him to berate me just like I deserved.

"When I graduated college, I had a teaching degree," he said. "My parents were so proud, they wanted me to change the world one high schooler at a time. They told all their friends how fabulous it was that I followed in the family footsteps. They were teachers, my siblings are teachers — it was a thing. The problem was, I really hated teaching. I hated lesson planning, high school attitudes and all the bureaucracy. But I did it for almost five years because I couldn't imagine how disappointed in me they'd be if I told them the truth."

"Okay." I was utterly baffled at the story's relevance.

Mike gave me a look that said, "Stick with me", and continued. "It was Maggie who looked at me one day and said, 'Michael, you hate your life and it's stupid. Your parents want to be teachers, so they are. You don't want to be a teacher, so what do you want to be?' It was the first time anyone had actually asked me what I wanted without already assuming the answer and I had no idea what to say. I spent the next six months trying to figure it out and still came up with nothing. Then, one day, my buddy Nick dropped onto my couch and said, 'I've got a crazy idea.' I quit teaching when that school year ended and never went back. Now, I co-own four bars and spend my days on the internet looking for old arcade games."

"It's always a girl," I said with an indignant huff.

Mike chuckled. "It is always a girl. Girls see the world differently than we do, but that's not my point. My point is we all make the wrong decisions for what we think are the right reasons in the name of our family. So, let me ask you this, did you give your dad keys to the bar?"

"No." I was shocked he would even ask.

"Did you tell him you'd be here and would help him rob me?"

"No."

Mike nodded and kept going. "Did you tell him how grand of an idea it would be to bust a window out at each one of my bars and steal my top shelf scotch?"

"Of course not!" I almost yelled. Now, Mike was smirking and I couldn't decide if I was okay with it.

"Then this isn't your fault and you aren't quitting," he stated. "You're a good kid and in the end, you did the right thing, even though it was a shitty thing to have to do. Now, go home."

"But—" I tried to argue, but Mike raised a hand and shook his head.

"I'm serious, Trevor. And actually, I meant to ask you if you'd like to upgrade a bit. I need a few bartenders for the summer. Know anybody else who wants to sling brews five nights a week for shitty tips and the potential of grabbing a few numbers?"

"Um, yeah," I stuttered out, still mind blown from the last five minutes. "My roommate and I both need jobs. And a place, actually, since I probably won't be welcome at home." I scratched my head, unable to process that, too.

"It just so happens I've got a vacancy at one of my properties on Ingersoll. Not as nice as the one you used for spring break, but it's got two rooms. If you need it, it's yours for a nominal monthly fee," Mike offered.

I stared at him, certain this was not actually reality.

He looked up at me, eyebrows raised. "We good here?" He gestured between us as he stood.

I started nodding like a bobble head. "Yeah, we're great. This is just not what I expected to happen."

Mike laughed and clapped me on the shoulder. "It's fine. Get back to me in the next few days and don't worry, kid. Life has a funny way of working itself out."

As I walked back to my car, I thought about his parting words. Charlie and I had both been through so much, yet we'd found our way back to each other just in time to be exactly what the other person needed. My future could easily have been stolen from me by everything my father had done, yet I was looking at a clean slate and the opportunity to be anything I wanted to be. It was time to make my choices. It was time to fight for what I wanted. I had a song to write and some big decisions to make.

CHAPTER
thirty-three

Charlie

"Which one are you less afraid of?" Darcy asked as she tapped the soccer ball from her foot to her knee and back again.

I dropped back onto the bed and groaned. "I don't know. I'm not *afraid* of either of them, I just know this is going to be super awkward."

That was an understatement. I'd spoken to my mom once since Valentine's weekend in a routine exchange that lasted less than six minutes and my dad only a few times. I knew he was staying on his meds and hadn't had a relapse since I'd last seen him. Mom had even given him some simple clients to handle to get him back to work. I was really proud of him, but I doubted they would be okay with me not coming home for the entire summer.

"So your mom, then?"

"Aaaargh, yes!" I threw a pillow at her for making me admit it. Darcy made a "told you so" face at me and went back to her drills, the ball alternately popping off her foot and knee.

"You said your dad is back at work, just invite him to lunch and tell him you're staying with me for the summer. My mom works at Blank Children's Hospital, so she's gone all the time, and my sisters are in camps all summer. We'll have free rein and you can make some decisions about what to do next."

"What does your mom do again?" I asked, trying to take us off the topic of me calling my father.

"She runs the Child Life program, which provides all kinds of services to kids who are in the hospital and their families. Art therapy, music therapy, human explanations of procedures, toy requests—you name it. But, I know what you're doing, and I'm not letting you off the hook."

Darcy tossed her soccer ball at me and I impressed us both by catching it and not ducking.

"You're learning, my Padwahn." She snickered as I sat up and tossed it back.

"Fine. Fine! I'll call him. How many days until the dorms close?"

"Five," she responded. "We've got the weekend and three more days. Then we're free!" With her arms in the air, Darcy ran around our room, whooping and hollering like the Weasley twins after too many butter beers.

I wanted to be excited, and the prospect of spending the summer with Darcy sounded amazing, but of course my thoughts drifted to Trevor. Over the last week and a half since we fought, I'd tried so hard to do more for myself. My hair, my clothes, even going back to that music store to play again — those were all small steps I took, and with each one, I had to stop myself from calling him. I knew he'd want to know. I knew he'd be proud. But as I accomplished each thing, I also knew I did it for me. I was sure it was my choice.

I'd reread Katie's letter a hundred times and what I finally understood was it wasn't just about playing music or making choices, it was about making the choices I needed to. It was about living my life without fear of someone else's judgment, even if it was my own parents' — *especially* if it was my own parents I feared.

"So, I should probably call him today." I groaned and fell back onto the bed.

"Not just call him, see him. Today. Now."

"Anybody ever tell you you're really pushy?"

"I consider that a compliment, actually. It translates into 'gets things done' on a resume." Darcy gave me a sassy grin.

"Have you decided what it is you want to do yet?" We'd talked a lot over the past few months about my wrong choice and her lack of choice around majors.

Darcy stopped playing with the ball and dropped into her desk chair.

"Not really," she said, sighing. "Soccer is the only thing I'm good at and it's ridiculous to think I could do it forever. I wasn't good enough to get onto a division one team, so at best, I could coach my kids' teams, assuming I want kids, which is also undecided."

"Why does it have to be so hard?" I groused. "I mean, we're eighteen years old and someone thought this was the moment we should decide our futures? Like we've amassed enough life experience to have a clue who we're supposed to grow up to be? I don't even know who I am now!"

"Amen, my sister. Preach!" Darcy threw up a hand and I laughed.

"Are you going to switch to a music major?" she asked, her tone a little more cautious.

"I don't think so." I rolled onto my side and propped my head in my hand. "I keep thinking about what it is I love about music and it isn't playing it for playing's sake. I don't need to be on stage and perform in front of a crowd. Actually, I'd prefer not to. I've always loved music for what's done for me. I love listening to song lyrics like some people love reading books. They are an escape, a connection to a person living a different life but feeling like I do in this particular moment."

I had to shove thoughts of Trevor from my head. I thought of music and I always thought of him. I thought of how much he had to do with my passion and what it meant to me to know he'd held onto that passion even when I'd abandoned it. It felt like he'd saved it for me, knowing I'd be back.

But Trevor didn't have to be the only person who understood me, so I continued, wanting Darcy to understand this part of me, too.

"I love hearing the individual instruments and what they bring to life in the song. Most of all, I love watching what it does for the people around me. I sit in concerts and I don't just watch the musicians, I watch the people watching them. I see when they tear up. I watch them press their lips together to hold back the emotions a certain lyric or set of chords has driven from their heart to their mind. Music heals. I think that's why I've avoided it this long. I didn't believe I deserved to heal after Katie died."

"Wow, Char." Darcy leaned forward in her chair, her chin in her hand and elbow on the armrest. "I've never heard you talk so passionately about anything before."

I blushed, feeling embarrassed, but also proud of myself. It wasn't easy to push out the last four years of thought processes, but I was trying so hard. And that was a moment of clarity for me. As I'd spoken the words aloud, I hadn't fully comprehended the idea that I did deserve to heal and I not only deserved, but wanted, to have music back in my life.

"So, back to your earlier question, I don't think I want to have a music major because I don't want it to feel like music is a 'have to' in my life. I stayed so far from it for so long, now I want to get reacquainted in my time, my way. Which is a really long answer that translates to me not picking a major. I guess I'm one of those liberal arts kids just wasting my education," I said with a chuckle. When I told my mom I was undeclared, she was going to lose it, but the idea of not making this choice sounded so much better than forcing one I didn't know actually fit. I had too much to learn about myself to select a major yet.

Darcy smiled at me from across the room, and said, "Look at my roomie, growing up so fast and making all these big girl decisions. You've come a long way this year, Charlotte Lydia Logan. I hope you know how proud I am of you."

"I didn't do it alone, Darc. I have you to thank for a lot of this," I said, so grateful for her friendship.

She winked. "Indeed, you do, but there's also this other guy I know who had a lot to do with it. I think he's missed you just a bit and is pretty excited your little sabbatical is almost up. Any messages you might like me to pass along to said gentleman?"

I paused, and then said, "You tell that boy our days of desperate times and desperate measures are over. You tell him I said it's time we both found our happily ever after."

"Oh," she responded, her head bobbing in appreciation, "oh, that's good—mysterious, yet hopeful—I like it. Consider it done."

"I really did win the roommate lottery, didn't I?" I asked, giggling at her enthusiastic response and hoping Trevor felt as hopeful as I did.

"You better believe it, sugar plum. Now, call your dad. We've got plans to make."

***

I pulled into a spot at Eatery A and cursed my luck.

Of course my father was already in Des Moines today.

Of course his lunch meeting cancelled last minute.

Of course he'd want to meet me a half hour after I called.

Darcy was thrilled when the lunch date was set so quickly. She had so many plans already made for us this summer, but I was still nervous to have this conversation. I was always nervous when I talked to my parents and this would be the first time he saw me since my big makeover.

I stepped inside and hovered in the entryway for a moment. I loved the dark wood, exposed piping and modern flair of the restaurant. It was always filled with an odd combination of hipsters and business people, and they had the best wood fire pizzas. I knew my mother would never let my dad have pizza otherwise, so I was also his excuse to eat more than the salad his assistant was on orders to bring him. I was totally fine with that.

I found my father in the open seating area and was relieved to see his blue eyes clear and bright, although I didn't miss the look of shock as he took in my black, cropped hair and color-less wardrobe. He surprised me by standing as I approached and pulling me into a quick hug.

"Hi, honey, it's been a long time since I've seen you with dark hair. I like it," he said with a relaxed smile that surprisingly looked genuine.

"You do?" I forgot to even greet him properly, my shock overtaking my manners.

He tilted his head and shrugged as we both took our seats. "You always liked your hair like that, so I guess I assumed when you were ready, you'd do it again."

Thankfully, the waiter arrived and took our drink order to save me from fumbling through a response. I never thought my father paid attention to little things like my hair, or that he'd not only be okay with it, but anticipating its return.

"I was surprised to hear from you today, but glad I was already in town. What did you need to talk about?" he asked as he took a sip of his Diet Coke.

I took a slow breath and reminded myself I was talking to my lucid father, the one who met with clients and acted normal. This could be a reasonable conversation.

"We're almost done with this semester, it ends next week actually, and I'd like to spend the summer with my roommate, Darcy, and her mom. They live north of Des Moines." The words came out rapid fire and my eyes jumped over his shoulder as I struggled to maintain contact.

"I see," he mused. "I'm curious, what does your roommate and her mom have that we don't at home?"

"Space," I blurted out before I could stop myself. My face flushed red and I stammered to backpedal my way out of it as my father put one hand up.

"Charlie," he interrupted, "honey, it's okay. I get it."

"You do?" I gripped my Cherry Coke with both hands and flicked my eyes back and forth from the bubbles rising through the liquid up to his.

"You forget I've been around a while, and I did raise...two girls." A pained look flashed across his eyes. "Everybody deserves some room to breathe, and right now, this is your time."

"You're not mad?" Shame crept in. I'd done a lot of little things for myself lately, but this wasn't little. This was big and it was selfish and it felt so wrong and so right all at once.

He reached out and wrapped his warm hand around my cold one, pulling my palm from the glass into his. "Honey, look at me," he requested.

I felt tears burn the back of my eyes, utterly unprepared for what he could possibly say next.

"You are a child who is almost a woman," he started, squeezing my hand. "You have seen sides of life no one should at your age and look at you, look at who you've become, despite it all — despite your mother and me."

"No, Dad, you—"

"Charlie, I know what we did to you and I know it was wrong," he said, surprising me with how dad-like he sounded. "Dr. Thompson and I have talked a lot about what our family has been through and I wanted to reach out to you before now, but he told me to wait until you were ready. I think you asking for this time means you are. It means you're ready to become the real Charlotte Lydia Logan, free from the burdens of your parents or your sister. That's what I want for you."

I couldn't speak. I couldn't believe what he was saying to me. These were the things my family didn't say out loud.

"It's what both your mother and I want for you," he continued. "I know you think your mom is...tough to deal with, and I haven't helped much with those opinions, but I'm doing really well lately and you need to understand living with someone who is bi-polar isn't easy. I'm not the man your mother started dating in college. This didn't come on until the year after we got married and your mother has been a trooper. She knew she loved who I was and she believed I was still in there, so she stuck with me. And she knows structure helps me. She has to be unwavering, or when I'm at my worst, I'll just run right over her. That attitude transferred to you and Katie, and it shouldn't have. But you need to cut your mom a little bit of a break, sweetie. She loves you. We both do."

He held my hand and I could only stare at my dad. My very foundation was shaken. The idea that all this time my mother was actually sacrificing, that she was fighting for my father — the man she loved — was almost impossible to wrap my head around.

"But, Dad—"

"No," he interrupted again, shaking his head, "I am not your problem. Your mother and I have talked at length about this. I will relapse. I will have bad days. But she is never to call you again. This should never have been put on you. We will handle it because contrary to our previous behavior, we're the parents. She got so overwhelmed and I put the two of you through an unnecessary amount of trauma after Katie left us. I only made it harder on everyone when I didn't follow Dr. Thompson's orders and manage my illness properly. We have a lot of work to do as a family to find our way back to each other, but I think that's what your sister would want, and it's what you deserve. I also think you taking this summer is a great idea because it will give your mom and me some time to focus on each other. Of course, I need to talk to her, but I don't see a problem with it."

I sat in stunned silence as our pizzas were delivered and the waiter replaced my empty Cherry Coke.

He let me stay that way, without pushing. My dad picked up his first piece of pizza and started in, watching me but not speaking. I had so many questions, so many specifics I wanted to make him explain, but it didn't seem worth it right now. There would be time. They were my parents and we had time to sort through the mess we'd made.

It wasn't until I finally moved, pulling a piece of Margherita pizza to my plate, that he said, "Charlie, it's going to be okay."

I nodded absently as I took my first bite, trying to decide what made sense to talk about now.

"Life is all about choices," he continued. "Your choices define you as a person. They tell the world who you aspire to be and they show everyone around you what you truly believe about yourself. This choice you've made to spend the summer with your roommate, it shows me you are thinking about you and your future.

Life isn't perfect, honey, but if you surround yourself with the right people—people who love you—you can make it through anything."

As I drove home from what felt like a life-changing hour with my father, all I could think about was I needed it to be tomorrow and I couldn't wait to see Trevor.

CHAPTER

thirty-four

Trevor

"You're helpless, you know that," Sam chided as he retied the mess I'd made with my bright blue tie.

"I know," I said, groaning. "Just think, you'll have all summer to make fun of me for my inability to tie a tie or properly match my socks to my pants, or my shoes, or whatever that dumb rule is."

Sam rolled his eyes as he yanked and swatted at areas of my suit. "Stick with me, kid, and you'll look like a proper gentleman yet."

I snorted a laugh and stepped back, holding my arms out. "Can you believe we made it?" I asked. "Just a few finals left, I survived juries today, and tonight — this is the fun part, this is the big finale."

"If she comes," Sam stated.

"She'll come." I turned to mess with my freshly cut hair and flatten the inevitable cowlicks. She had to come. She'd promised and too much hinged on it. Besides, Darcy passed along her message and I could not have agreed more, I just wasn't sure if it meant the same thing to me as it did to her.

"What are you going to say?" he asked, buttoning his own crisp black shirt and tucking it into his dress pants.

"I don't actually know yet. I'll say whatever I need to, I guess." I'd only been running this speech over in my head for days, trying to choose the perfect words to make sure nothing got misinterpreted and Charlie understood every last ounce of what I felt for her.

A light knock on the door surprised us both. I pulled it open to find my mother on the other side. She wore a floor-length black dress and her normally unruly hair was in an elegant knot at the base of her neck.

"Mom, what are you doing here?" We hadn't spoken since I walked away from her at the store and while she looked good, I was still wary.

"My son is playing his first real concert, including material he's written, did you think I would miss that?" she responded with a hesitant smile.

"Um, come in," I said. "Sam, this is my mom, Belinda. Mom, this is my roommate, Sam."

They shook hands and Sam quickly excused himself. "I'll see you there, Trev. Nice to meet you, Mrs. Adler." Sam stuck his head back in the door before he shut it completely. "Break a leg, man," he said, grinning.

The door to my room closed and we faced each other, the silence uncomfortable but not one I was willing to end.

"Your father was arrested a few nights ago," she finally said.

"Oh?" was all I could come up with. I knew Detective Weber would get him eventually and I was relieved it was finally over.

"He was," she said. "And his lawyer says they want to make a deal with him to get information on the man he owed money to. If he does it, we'll have to leave Des Moines."

"After all this, you'd go with him?" I asked. "You would go start all this over again somewhere else?" I could hardly fathom it. She'd been given the perfect out and she refused to take it.

"I know you don't understand this, Trevor, but I love your father." She looked so sad, yet still fiercely defended him.

"You have a life here, Mom," I argued. "You have a job, and friends, *and me*. I'm here. You'll just walk away from it all so he can screw your life up in another town, except this time it will be where you have no one and nothing."

"He's getting help," she replied. "They're going to put him in a program when he gets out and he'll get the help he needs. He'll be himself again, I know he will." She looked at me and I realized why she was really here. She needed me to tell her it was okay. My mother stood tall in front of me and silently begged me to stop arguing and let her go.

"You have to do what makes sense for you." I could already feel the inevitable distance that would come between us. "But know I'm not lying when I say I won't have anything to do with him ever again. I love you. I want to see and talk to you, but I won't come home for Thanksgiving or Christmas, or anytime in between. You love Dad and the two of you seem to need each other, but I don't need him, not anymore."

"I understand, Trevor," she said, tears glistening in her eyes. "I respect your choices and I'm glad you respect mine. You're my son and that will never change. We will find our way through this."

I nodded, swallowing down words it made no sense to say. Instead, I held out my hand, and said, "Would you like to come listen to my first and last concert?"

"What?" she exclaimed. I took her hand and pulled my mom toward the door.

"After tonight, I may never play music in front of a crowd again," I said, a deep-seated relief making me almost giddy. "I'm quitting the program."

***

I took the stage and sat down with my acoustic guitar. I was joined by a violinist, and a fellow classmate who sat on a cajon to provide the percussion. We'd worked on this song constantly for the past few days and we were ready.

The bright lights of the stage kept me from seeing the audience as more than a blur of humanity. I couldn't pick out Charlie, but I knew she was there. The idea that she could see me but I couldn't see her made it easier to say what I was about to say. I'd spent two weeks without her and now knew what I needed to do. I needed to appeal to the side of her that felt more than it thought. I needed to sing to her so she'd finally hear me.

I adjusted the mic and introduced myself. "Hello, everyone, my name is Trevor Adler. This is a song I wrote recently and goes out to the only girl I ever loved enough, and was dumb enough, to walk away from. This is a song about how it all went wrong."

Gracefully, gracefully
I wanted to leave
Gracefully, gracefully
I wanted to leave
But it ain't easy
When your heart isn't yours anymore

Honestly, honestly
I told her before
Honestly, honestly
I told her before
But it ain't easy
If somebody else is afraid
And it ain't easy
If somebody else doesn't see

How the lies we tell, tell ourselves
Kept us both from facing it all
We've made it far, a world apart
You're playing house and I'm playing rock star.

It got cold and pale. Every nail
Sealing me into a beautiful failure
All the stones we should not have thrown
Were building up walls that kept me from saying

Gracefully, Gracefully
I never wanted to leave
Gracefully, Gracefully
I never wanted to leave

But it ain't easy
If somebody else is afraid.

It took me an extra twenty minutes to get myself away from Professor Davis once I explained I was quitting the music program. I was still smiling at his repeated use of the words "phenomenal performance" and "so much potential" as I rushed outside. He couldn't understand why I'd walk away, but I didn't have time to explain the path of my life and the fact that I needed music to be mine and mine alone.

I hit the metal bar on the door and popped it open, rushing out into the warm night. People milled around outside the auditorium. I saw my mother standing with Sam and Darcy, but as I raced down the steps, I didn't see Charlie anywhere. She was the only person who mattered right now and I had to find her.

"Hey you," I heard from behind me. I spun around to find I'd passed right by her. In two bounds, I landed a step below where Charlie stood, hardly able to process the girl in front of me.

I reached out, the ends of her jet-black hair soft between the pads of my fingers. Her eyes were lined and the combination of her hair and makeup made her look like an urban Egyptian goddess.

"You look…" I started, unable to find the words.

"Like a ghost?" she asked with a nervous laugh.

"Like I'm seeing you for the first time since I drove away," I breathed out. She was my past and my future, wrapped in this one beautiful package.

"Trev—" she started.

"No," I cut in, running my fingers from her elbow to her hand and taking it in mine, "you have to let me go first, Charlie."

She pressed her lips together and nodded, her fingers twitching in my hand.

"You said we can't do this," I started, "that we can't have this much history, be so entangled in each other's lives and still have a functioning relationship, but I think you're wrong. I think who we've been and how far we've come is part of our journey together and it makes us special. It lets us skip those steps where we have to decide what to hold back and what to be honest about. We don't have to worry our secrets will come out and the other person will run from the truth of who we are and the baggage we bring. We already know it all and it doesn't matter. None of it matters."

I reached out and grabbed her other hand, my own sweating as I prepared to say the thing she had to hear, hoping the words wouldn't fail me.

"You heard my song?" I asked. She nodded again, the crease between her brows giving away the annoyance I anticipated when I wrote the lyric. "You heard me say you were afraid, but I want you to know why I chose that phrasing. You aren't afraid of me, Charlie, or even of us. You're afraid of you. You're afraid you won't be enough, or you'll be too much, or because you don't know who you even are, that once you do, I won't want you anymore."

I watched her, my eyes scanning her face. I saw the shine of truthful tears in her eyes, the slow breath she drew into her nose and her trembling lip.

"I've asked you all year to choose me, Charlie, and I was wrong. I was so wrong," I said, apologizing. "I should have been asking you to choose *you*. There cannot be a *we* until *you* are the best, strongest, surest version of yourself. And that's more than a haircut and a change of clothes — don't get me wrong, those things are an amazing start — but I don't want to distract you from finding yourself. So, for now, I'll walk away. I'll disappear if that's what you want. But when I go, I want it to be clear that I'm leaving so I can come back.

"When you're ready, I want to be there for you. I want to support you and love you the way I have since before we were old enough to even understand what love was. You are my person. You are the person I trust, the person I love, the person I want to spend every minute of every day with. It doesn't matter who you choose to be, Charlotte Lydia Logan, I have always, and will always, love *you*."

She closed her eyes and smiled, a soft sigh of a smile that made my heart burst with the need to know what was behind it.

Finally, she spoke. "I've realized something too in the last week," she said, "something that occurred to me both in tiny increments and in an overwhelming tidal wave while you sang."

"Oh, yeah?" I failed miserably at sounding casual and struggled to keep myself from yanking her to me.

"Yeah," she responded, her smile still in place. "I realized I was right when I said I can't need you."

"Wait—"

"No," she interrupted, "it's my turn now."

I snapped my mouth closed and nodded for her to continue, my stomach rolling as I tried to reconcile her growing smile with her words.

"There's a difference between needing someone and wanting them." Her gaze warmed and relief bloomed in my chest.

"I can't need you," she said, her voice firm. "I can't give you my pain and let you take me away from what's happened. I have to face all of that myself. I have to grieve my sister's death and decide who I want to be. I have to make those choices for me, not for you or anyone else."

She paused, her eyes looking skyward before reconnecting with mine. She squeezed my hands, and said, "But that doesn't stop me from wanting you. It doesn't stop the way I think about you, the way I want you near me and the way I want to hear you sing that song again and again and again. It doesn't stop the way I want to tell you everything or how I miss you when you're gone. But, you're right. I have to choose me first. The thing is, choosing me doesn't mean I can't also choose you."

We stood there, surrounded by people on the steps of the auditorium and all I heard were her words on a loop. Goosebumps covered my skin and there was an overwhelming need I could no longer ignore.

I leaned in, closing the distance between us, stopping just millimeters from her. "So, you're saying you're choosing me, too?"

"That is what I'm saying," she confirmed, her flushed cheeks and breathy response snapping the last thread of my resolve.

"Finally," I whispered as I pulled her to me at long last.

EPILOGUE

Charlie

Five years later

"Is this ridiculous?" I asked as I shoved Trevor into the back room. "Are you sure this was the best idea, because I think it might have been a really terrible idea."

He put one hand on each of my cheeks, and said, "Charlie, breathe. You've been working on this for months now. We have sponsors. There are three-hundred people out there waiting for you who believe in this. Darcy and Sam are here. Your parents are here. We're doing this together. You're not alone."

I nodded, only a fraction of the panic receding.

Trevor dropped his hands to mine and gave them a squeeze. "There is nothing this city loves more than a reason to give back, listen to live music and drink. Tonight, the Logan Foundation has given them all three."

I blew out a long breath, nodding as I questioned my sanity yet again for starting this non-profit. I worked sixty-hour weeks, made barely anything and hardly got to see Trevor, but he never complained. If he wasn't helping me with the foundation, he was at the youth emergency services shelter where he worked.

He gave me a light kiss. "It's show time, babe, are you ready for this?"

I nodded, even though I wanted to make a run for it.

"You know where the back door is, but even in heels, I don't think you can outrun Darcy," he said, reading my mind.

I rolled my eyes. "Okay, yes, let's go. But you're coming up there with me. I'm not going on that stage alone."

"Done." He turned and led the way, winding us through the backstage of Wooly's. Just as we got to the edge of the stage, Trevor turned, and said, "You know I love you, right?"

"I do know you love me," I said as I blew out a long breath.

"And you know Katie is loving seeing you go through this on her behalf, right?" he teased.

I socked him in the shoulder and we took the stage together, laughing.

"Hello, everyone," I said, pulling the mic from the stand and grasping Trevor's hand in my free one. I was trying to get used to being a public speaker, but I wasn't quite there yet.

There were murmured hellos and a few big "Wahoo, Charlie!" shouts from my insane friends.

"We're here tonight for a really important reason," I started. "May is mental health awareness month and teen suicide is the second leading cause of death in fifteen to thirty-four year olds in Iowa. While suicide in and of itself is a horrific tragedy, when someone is bi-polar, there is an even higher likelihood of them trying to take their lives. The diagnosis of bi-polar disorder in teens is really challenging. It is often dismissed as them being typical moody teenagers, and often misdiagnosed as depression. These teens in particular are at a high risk for suicide.

"When my sister, Katie, took her life at seventeen years old, we had no idea she likely had bi-polar disorder. Even now, we can't entirely confirm it, but after extensive discussions with doctors and our family history, there is a good chance she was. And if her illness had been diagnosed sooner, it's possible she'd be here with us today.

"I started the Logan Foundation as a haven for teens, young adults and their parents. My goal is to provide counseling, resources, access to the right services and the support they need. Whether it's our crisis line, where we let kids text or call with their problems, or our resource center where we can connect families with the help they need to properly discuss and diagnose issues, the Logan Foundation is here to make sure our youth make it to adulthood. They are our future and we need to make sure they make it there."

The crowd erupted, the clapping coming from all sides. I saw my parents near the stage, both of them wiping their eyes while clapping furiously. My mom waved when she saw me looking down on them and my dad mouthed, "I'm so proud of you." We'd come a long way.

Sensing my emotion, Trevor pulled a little on our joined hands, so I handed him the mic. "Tonight, we're here to raise money for this amazing foundation," he started. "We have an awesome lineup of musicians who have donated their time, the guys at Wooly's have donated the booze and all we're asking you to do is enjoy the evening and give what you can as the servers come around with the donation buckets. Charlie and I will also be taking the stage together in a little bit to show you how we incorporate music therapy into our programs, but to really get things started, I have a special surprise."

I turned to Trevor, trying to hide my confused concern as he went off script. He grinned and took my hand, turning me toward him.

"Charlotte Lydia Logan, you astound me every day. You give tirelessly, you care so deeply and you want nothing more than to leave this world a better place than you found it."

I flushed, trying to convey my utter embarrassment with my eyes alone. Trevor only kept smiling at me as the house lights sent a bead of sweat rolling down my spine and the crowd murmured.

"I have loved you since before I knew what love felt like," he continued, oblivious. "Over the years, we have lost and found each other. We have challenged each other. We pushed each other to be more. Sometimes, we even drove each other nuts, but we stayed together."

Suddenly, Sam darted out from the wings and dropped something into Trevor's outstretched hand. He gave me his toothy grin and then was gone again. When Trev got down on one knee, the room went silent. My pulsed raced in my ears and my heart thudded in my chest.

"What are you doing," I mouthed down to him, knowing full well what he was about to do in front of all these people. We'd talked about this moment and we'd dreamed about our future, but I never expected it to happen here, tonight.

"I'm giving you the happily ever after you requested," he said with a smirk, glancing out toward the audience as they snickered.

Trevor shoved his glasses up his nose and looked up at me. "There is not a single day of this life I want to spend without you, Charlie. I want to share every exciting, mundane, totally random moment of it with you. And today, of all days, when your parents and our closest friends are all here and Katie is looking down on everything you've accomplished, I knew it was the right time. So, all I need you to tell me is if you choose me to be your partner in crime, your shoulder to cry on and your forever. Will you marry me, Charlie?"

He put down the microphone and held up the ring, a shiny silver band with a single diamond at its center. Trevor looked up at me, knowing exactly what I'd say, though his nerves still showed. I wanted to smooth away the crease of worry between his eyes, but I was momentarily frozen.

Live the life you want. I heard Katie's words as clearly as if she'd whispered them in my ear.

"Yes! Ohmygod, YES!" I almost shouted, feeling like my heart would burst if I didn't get them out.

Trevor leapt up, putting the ring on my finger before kissing me in front of three hundred potential donors. From somewhere in the back of the room, over all the whooping and hollering from the crowd, I heard Darcy yell, "Way to go, baby cakes! About damn time!"

Trevor pulled away and brought the mic back up. "Now that we've taken care of that detail, let the fun begin! Dig deep, friends, we have to save our extra money for a wedding!"

As the crowd went wild and the musicians behind us started up, I dragged Trevor off the stage and wrapped my arms around him.

"Happily ever after, huh?" I asked as I peppered his face with kisses.

He laughed and captured my cheeks between his hands before pecking a kiss to the tip of my nose. "You better believe it. Starting right this minute."

a note from the author

I wrote this book for a lot of reasons, but chief among them was the fact that in my home state teen suicide is a real problem. Too often we hear of young people taking their lives before they've truly begun. Personally, I was there when my husband lost his best friend when we were just twenty. So many moments have passed when I've wondered how our lives would be different if Brett were still here. He would be in our wedding photos. He would have been in the waiting room when my kids were born. He would have been with my husband for every Cubs game through the World Series. But he wasn't. And he won't be. And that is a devastating reality we face constantly.

If suicide is even the briefest thought in your mind, I urge you to tell someone. A friend, a parent, a counselor…anyone who can remind you that no matter how you feel, there are people you will leave behind who will be forever changed. There will be a hole in their lives that nothing can ever fill because it was the place you were meant to be. You matter. You are important. You are meant to be here with us.

If you don't want to talk to someone you know, use the National Suicide Prevention Hotline (1-800-273-8255). You are not alone and you don't have to feel alone.

about the author

Stormy Smith calls Iowa's capital home now, but was raised in a tiny town in the Southeast corner of the state. She grew to love books honestly, having a mom that read voraciously and instilled that same love in her.

When she isn't working on, or thinking about, her books, Stormy's favorite places include bar patios, live music shows, her yoga mat or anywhere she can relax with her husband, twin sons or girlfriends.

Other titles by Stormy Smith

Bound by Duty (Book one in the Bound series)
Bound by Spells (Book two in the Bound series)
Bound by Prophecy (Book three in the Bound series)
Bound Together (Book three and a half in the Bound series)

Where you can find me

If you'd like to be alerted when my next book will release, sign up for my mailing list on my website homepage, listed below. I hate spam, so you won't get any.

Website: http://www.stormysmith.com
Facebook:
http://www.facebook.com/authorstormysmith
Twitter: @stormysmith
Instagram: @stormysmith
GoodReads: http://www.goodreads.com/stormysmith
Email: authorstormysmith@gmail.com

A note about reviews

Whether you loved it, hated it or were completely ambivalent, your review will help others decide if they would like to read my book. Please consider leaving just a few words on the site you purchased from and/or GoodReads. Every review matters and I read them all.

acknowledgments

This book was equal parts therapeutic and gut-wrenching. I laughed as I remembered my own friendships in high school and the banter I shared with my best guy friend. I cried as I embraced the heartache that came with the truth both Trevor and Charlie had to face, and the reality that so many of our young adults are in a similar situation, or perhaps much worse. But with every word I knew I was digging toward the truth of how hard it is to find yourself amidst the chaos of everyone else.

This book wouldn't have happened without:

Abe, a chance encounter somehow turned into a whole life together. You've pushed me to be honest with myself about who I am since that first moment and I will never stop loving the way you leave me speechless with how well you know me. You were an inspiration in so many ways during this story.

Richard (Dick) Prall, for creating music that has spoken to my soul for years, for being the center of many a date night for Abe and I, and for being amazing enough to allow me to include *Honore* and *Gracefully* in Who She Was. I'm thankful my readers can hear Trevor's songs for real.

Alys, my marketing soul sister, I can't count how many IMs, emails and video chats it took to get this book where I wanted it to be. You did exactly what I asked and tore it apart so I could rebuild it into something better. Cheers to being in the right place at the right moment, time in the agency trenches and the color purple.

Jess, you sent me an email a long time ago telling me how you appreciated the depth of my characters in the Bound series. It came at a moment where I questioned if I would be any good at this writing thing and gave me confidence to keep writing real characters going through real situations. Your input was fabulous and your friendship as a fellow twin mom has been invaluable. Muah.

Monica, we did a lot of work to get this book where I wanted it. You rock, as always, and I will never forget that I made your black heart cry. It is the ultimate compliment.

Toni, who knew a fleeting moment in both our careers would bring us together to create such amazing work?! I cannot imagine being an author without your gorgeous covers wrapping my words. Thank you for bringing my stories to life in ways I could only dream of.

Maggie, thank you so much for jumping in with both feet to help a new twin mom launch this book in style. You are a trusted colleague in this crazy business and I couldn't have asked for anyone better to be part of this journey.

Lieutenant Mark Buzynski and Detective Jake Lancaster, thank you for showing me around the Des Moines Police Department, talking through Trevor's situation and ensuring I did your profession and the process justice.

The city of Des Moines is one I initially couldn't wait to leave but over the years has become such an ingrained part of me, I don't want to live anywhere else. She has grown, matured, evolved…a mecca of art, music, grassroots support for local businesses and some of the most compassionate, active community members I know of. Incorporating this city into Trev and Charlie's story was one of my favorite parts of writing. I stood under the Nomad sculpture downtown and watched that scene unfold before my eyes. I hope someday you can stand there, too.

And **to every agent** who read Who She Was and gave me the feedback that it wouldn't sell to a traditional publishing house, but was perfect for self-publishing, thank you for your honesty and for encouraging me to get this book out into the world.